DAYBREAK

AMERICAN MIDNIGHT - BOOK 3

DAVID KAZZIE

GRUB CLUB PUBLISHING

This book is a work of fiction. The names, characters, places, and incidents are products of the author's imagination or have been used fictitiously and are not to be construed as real. Any resemblance to persons, living or dead, actual events, locales, or organizations is purely coincidental.

ISBN-13: 978-1-7350105-3-3

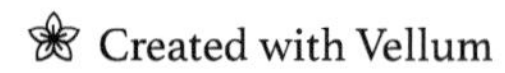

To the millions lost in the Covid-19 pandemic
Our hearts are broken

ALSO BY DAVID KAZZIE

The Jackpot (2011)

The Immune (2015)

The Living (2017)

Anomaly (2018)

The Nothing Men (2019)

Shadows (2020)

Nightfall (2020)

Daybreak (2021)

The Rising (Coming 2022)

PROLOGUE

SEVEN YEARS BEFORE THE PULSE

The girl arrived early for the rendezvous. She got off her bike and leaned it against the stone bench near the escalators descending to the trains. She checked her watch. It was 11:34 p.m., nearly thirty minutes before the scheduled meetup. A cool breeze swirled on this early spring night, making her shiver despite her jeans and sweatshirt. The Ballston-George Mason Metro station was quiet at this hour on a weeknight, mostly deserted but for a handful of drunken revelers and shift workers headed to overnight duty. She was four miles from her home.

Her father would undoubtedly say that this was no place or time for a teenaged girl to be lingering by herself. If he knew she was here right now, he would blow his stack, a display of one of his patented temper tantrums. Not that she could blame the guy. Father to four daughters, ranging in age from eight to her sixteen years. He had a lot to worry about.

But Katie Stone was doing this *for* her family.

Irony could be a bitch.

Her heart was racing, her breathing rapid and shallow. She had never been as nervous or as scared as she was right now. She didn't know what was going to happen. But she knew what she was doing was right. Tonight she had a chance to do a great thing for her family, for her parents, Gina and Rick. Especially for her three sisters, Bella, Amelia, and Sara.

It had started about three months ago.

Her mom signed up for tennis lessons with this guy Jack Thompson. He was tall and handsome. He claimed to have been a nationally ranked collegiate player. But Katie had found no record of a player by that name. She mentioned it to her mom, who was angrily dismissive.

"Oh, are you checking up on me now?" Gina had snapped, a glass of Merlot in her hand. A wineglass in her mom's hand was a common sight these days.

"Mom, I just don't trust this guy," Katie had said.

"Let me worry about that," Gina said.

But Katie could not let it go. Despite her young age, she had a pretty good set of instincts on her. Something about this so-called tennis pro had set off all kinds of alarm bells lurking inside her.

And then it had happened.

One afternoon, Katie and a friend coming off a nasty breakup had skipped their last-period English class. They headed down to the local coffeehouse for big iced mochas, something with as much chocolate and whipped cream as coffee. It was an unseasonably warm day and the outdoor patio was bustling with customers. Katie almost didn't see her.

Gina was at a corner table with Mister Tennis Pro.

Katie stopped dead and gasped. She almost called out to her mother, not really sure why, given that she was supposed to be in school. But what she was seeing was so odd, so outside the paradigm of normality, that her ability to think clearly had simply evaporated. At the last second, the last instant, Katie had choked down her outburst, ducking into the clothing boutique next door with her friend Maya. While Maya shopped, Katie spied on her mother through the plate glass window. Gina lingered at the table with Jack for another ten minutes and then they had parted ways.

Exchanging a passionate kiss before they did so.

Another gasp from Katie Stone. Tears filled her eyes and rolled down her face, splashing her arms, which were crossed in front of her chest. Her mother was having an affair. With this tennis pro. Until that moment, she had assumed her parents were happily married. She didn't know why she assumed that; maybe all kids just figured they came from normal homes until proven otherwise.

"Katie?" her friend Maya said.

Katie wasn't listening.

"Stone?"

Katie looked over at her friend, her jaw clenched tight, her eyes hard and teary.

"You okay?"

"Yeah," she said, wiping away the tears with her fingers.

"Why are you crying?" Maya asked. "I'm the one that got screwed here!"

"I know," she said. "It's just that I'm so sad for you."

Maya bought Katie's ruse.

Katie did not sleep that night. She begged off from school the next day, claiming she wasn't feeling well. Which wasn't entirely untrue. She was exhausted and sick to her stomach. She stayed in bed all day, and her parents reasonably believed she was asleep when Jack arrived at their home.

At their *home*.

Katie cracked open her bedroom door; a discussion was underway in the living room. Jack was talking. Something about an investment. He could triple their money.

She listened a bit longer before it all fell into place.

They were being conned.

Katie didn't understand the specifics of this so-called deal, but she didn't need to. The bottom line was that her parents, her dopey mother and her trusting father, were planning to turn over thirty thousand dollars to this man on a promise that he would return their money threefold in a matter of weeks. She didn't even know where they would have come up with that much cash. They weren't a wealthy family. Her mom was a substitute teacher. Her father worked as a third shift manager at a bottling facility.

"We can't lose," the man had said.

Her mother was blinded by passion, and her dad was gullible and desperate enough to fall for such a scam, especially as he considered the prospect of college for four girls in the coming decade.

"I'll text you the meetup location," he said.

"You have my number?" Gina had said.

"You bet."

He left. Later, Gina and Rick went out to the back porch for a cigarette. While they smoked, a pleasant ding on Gina's phone announced an incoming text message. The text message that stood to ruin the Thompson family for all time. Katie grabbed the phone from the kitchen counter and read the message.

Catching a late flight. Meet me at the bench at the top of the Ballston metro stop at midnight. Don't forget your investment!!

There was even a heart emoji, which made Katie want to straight-up puke.

The fact that this shady-ass message wouldn't send her parents running for the hills raised all kinds of questions about their judgment, but that was a matter for another day.

She typed a reply.

See you then.

Then she deleted the text exchange.

Her dad, who'd worked nights as long as she could remember, had left around ten o'clock. Her mom retired early, watching television in the bedroom. Katie snuck out quietly. With four girls banging around the house, it was easy to disappear into the shuffle.

She checked her watch again. It was ten minutes to midnight.

A flight to catch.

Give me the tiniest break, she thought.

It was a weird feeling. She felt like a parent protecting her children. It made her angry. She shouldn't have had to do this. Parents were supposed to be wise and careful, to be the shields and swords for their children. But not this time, not for Katie Stone. This time, Katie had to be the grownup, to stand up to this bad man who sought to destroy them.

The evening grew chillier, and a thin fog had rolled in. It lined the lower edges of the apartment complex across the way, swirled down the escalator into the Metro tunnel. Reflecting the light from the various building, the vaporous fog seemed almost alive. Katie pulled her hood over her head, keeping her eyes peeled for the man. She favored her mother in looks and build, enough to draw the man close enough to confront.

Movement in the corner of her eye.

The man appeared out of the fog, as though he was formed of it. Not a bad way to describe him. He had come from everywhere and nowhere at the same, ready to pull his vanishing act like a fog when exposed to bright sunshine.

As the man drew closer, she stood up and pulled the hood of her sweatshirt down. He took a few more steps toward her before stopping short. He was dressed in jeans and boots and a light jacket. He was handsome for an older guy, and Katie saw why her mom was into him. There was a certain aura about him. At that moment, she understood why young women could be attracted to older men.

He chuckled.

"Well, well, well," he whispered.

"This funny to you?" Katie said, louder than she intended. Just standing here within sight of this man filled her with rage. Besides understanding the appeal of older men, she was also understanding the appeal of cold-blooded murder. She could kill this man right now and not lose a second of sleep tonight.

"No," he said. "Where's your mom?"

"She's not coming."

"So I gathered."

A beat of silence as they sized one another up.

"Does she know you're here?"

Katie did not reply. Her finger stroked the barrel of the gun in her pocket. She could do it. She could just kill this man. Lord knew he deserved it.

"Yes, my mom routinely sends me as her proxy to meet with con men."

There. She'd said it. She had said the words that needed to be said. And now he knew that she knew. Her words fell out of her mouth like hot coals.

He laughed again.

"Your mom was right about you," he said. "She said you were the brains of the operation."

Her hand slid down the barrel to the grip.

Now, Katie.

It had to be now. Before she lost her nerve.

She pulled the gun from the pocket of her sweatshirt and aimed it straight at his chest. Her uncle, a cop, had once told her that police officers aimed for the center mass. No headshots, no wounding them in the leg. You always shot to kill.

His eyes widened, and the folksy smile disappeared. She couldn't be sure, but she thought she saw a flicker of fear ripple across his face.

"Why?" she asked.

"Why what?" he replied.

"Why are you doing this?"

He blinked hard twice, his gaze shifting from the barrel of the gun to Katie's eyes. The question appeared to take him by surprise. He looked at her for a long time.

It was as if he had forgotten he was being held at gunpoint.

The gun trembled in her small hand. It was a .38, which she had gotten from her friend Eric. His dad was very into guns. She told him she wanted to learn how to shoot and was going to spend the weekend at a cabin in the mountains and there was plenty of space to practice shooting. Eric had a huge crush on her, so he didn't ask too many questions.

She flexed her fingers before wrapping her index finger around the trigger guard. All she had to do was apply a few pounds of force to it, and that would be it. This man would be dead, and he would have paid the price he deserved to pay. She had not planned to shoot him, just scare him a little. But now that she was face to face with him, she couldn't help but think how good it would feel.

"You don't want to do this," the man said.

"I asked you a question."

He scoffed.

"It's what I do."

"It's what you do?" she echoed. "It's what you *do*?"

"It's not my fault your parents are the way they are."

"How are they?"

"They wanted a free lunch," he said. "They really believed that I was going to triple their money."

Katie's face burned with shame and embarrassment. Shame that she could have descended from two fools as big as Gina and Rick Stone. Her father, always on the hunt for that home run, that one investment that would make him a rich man. Rick Stone had always struck her as weak. The kind of man unhappy with his station in life even though he had four beautiful daughters who worshipped him. Well, at least three of them did. Always blaming others for his lot in life. He apparently found it difficult to believe that at forty-seven, he wasn't banging strippers on a yacht he owned.

And her mother. Jesus. A bottle of wine every night. Sometimes she nodded off right at the dinner table. Then she and her sisters would clean up and load the dishwasher while her dad grabbed a nap before work and her mom would scroll mindlessly on her phone, polishing off the last of the Merlot or Malbec or whatever cheap wine she'd picked up at the store. All of a sudden, she hated her father, she hated her mother, but most of all, she hated this man who was like a human blacklight, exposing all the weaknesses and flaws in her family.

She began to cry.

The man blurred in the veil of tears covering her eyes.

"You really want to do this?"

"Shut up," she said. "You shut up."

"Go ahead," he said. "Shoot."

She pinched away the tears with her free hand. The man remained where he was; he had made no move to disarm her, although to be honest, it wouldn't have been that hard. He was a big man, severely built. And yet, he seemed sincere in his plea for her to kill him.

She spat on the ground.

It made her feel better. That she was in control. Not her mother, not her father, and certainly not his towering waste of space.

She lowered the gun a hair. This man had ruined so much already; she wasn't going to let him ruin her too.

Even if he didn't pay for the damage he had already done.

Someday, though, he would get his comeuppance.

"Get out of here," she said, her voice trembling. "Don't ever come around my family again."

"Take care of yourself," the man said. He made no mention of Gina.

He turned and disappeared into the darkness.

Katie's legs buckled, and she crumpled to the ground.

She wept.

1

Solomon Tigner's words hung in the air.

I know how to turn the lights back on.

Jack Goodwin reared back upon hearing them, the room shifting on its axis before snapping back into place. The clinic fell silent, as though the air had been sucked out of it. Lucy Goodwin stood ramrod still, her palm pressed against her mouth. Her eyes were wide open, fixated on the mysterious stranger before them. The way she stood there like a statue reminded Jack of freeze tag, the game they had played as children.

Solomon was still incredibly weak; it would take time to recover from his journey through the cold and the ice and the snow. He had not said anything since his dramatic pronouncement. He leaned back against the headboard, sighed, and closed his eyes.

Jack had no idea what the man was talking about. There was no context for Solomon's statement, nothing to suggest that it was anything more than the ramblings of a crazy person. Lucy exhaled noisily, like she had been holding her breath and had just remembered to breathe again. Slowly, time started to move again, and Jack began to process what he had just heard.

Jack sat down in the metal folding chair next to Solomon's bed and exhaled slowly. A bomb had just gone off in all their lives, and he needed to keep his wits about him. His military training would help, as it had these last five years since the Pulse.

What a day it had been. It had started uneventfully. He rose early, went for a run, and took a quick breakfast. Then Terri had found him in the garage bearing news of a visitor asking to see him. He had been messing with the circuit board of an old laptop computer. He'd always been good at tinkering with things, and although he didn't hold out any hope that he would suddenly solve the mystery of the Pulse, the still-unexplained event that had plunged the world into permanent darkness, it made him feel better.

Terri's message had caught him off guard. Visitors were rare, good news even rarer. A chill rippled through him. A sudden concern that he somehow had endangered his sister, her unborn child, Norah, everyone here in Promise. There were many skeletons in Jack Goodwin's closet, and the world's end hadn't necessarily ground them into dust. Barely a month had elapsed since they had defeated the Haven; he was just getting used to the idea of feeling safe again. It wouldn't last forever, but he sure hoped it was going to last longer than a few weeks.

Jack wasn't sure who he'd been expecting to see when he walked into the clinic, but it definitely had not been Solomon Tigner. He hadn't seen the man in more than a decade. He had first met Solomon fifteen years earlier, and although they hadn't known each other well, the men were connected by someone Jack had known well – the other half of the most significant relationship of his life. Solomon had once worked with Molly Thornton, Jack's longtime girlfriend. Jack hadn't seen Molly herself in more than a decade.

Solomon had been the kind of person who entered your life for a short time and faded away just as quickly. Two lines intersecting briefly before continuing away from one another. Solomon had not crossed Jack's mind since the last time they had spoken so many years ago. There was no animosity between the men; there was simply nothing between the men. They had not been close.

I know how to turn the lights back on.

The words cycled through Jack's brain like a beacon. It was as if a giant blade had dropped from the heavens, cleaving their lives in two. Everything before the moment that Solomon Tigner had uttered those nine monumental words and everything that would come after. Jack Goodwin had no idea what would come after, but everything would be different now. Of this he was sure.

"Sir," Lucy was saying. "What do you mean you can turn the lights back on?"

The sound of Lucy's voice broke him out of his trance. Jack gave his head a hard shake, clearing the fog and bringing him back to center. Lucy's hand was on Solomon's shoulder; she was gently shaking him, but he wasn't responding. His chest rose and fell rhythmically.

"He's out again," Lucy said.

"Is he okay?" Jack asked.

Lucy pressed two fingers against the inside of his wrist and closed her eyes while she checked his pulse.

"His pulse is a little thready. He's still very weak."

"Will he be okay?"

"Hard to say," she said. "We'll know more in a day or so."

Jack nodded absently.

"Jack?"

"Yeah?"

"Who is this man?"

"Just someone I knew a long time ago."

Her eyes widened in a display that was part mockery, part scorn.

"Do you know what he's talking about?" she asked. "Turning the lights back on?"

Jack scratched his chin as he considered his sister's query. He didn't even know where to begin. He opened his mouth and started to respond but then closed it again just as quickly. There was so much he didn't know.

"Jack?"

"I don't know," Jack replied.

I know how to turn the lights back on.

What the hell was Solomon talking about?

The lights had gone out more than five years ago. Anything requiring a power source was long dead. Solomon had been a climate scientist. Molly had worked with him for several years. Jack stared at the unconscious figure of Solomon Tigner, wondering if he was dreaming. It just didn't seem possible that he was here, that he had made this journey to find him.

"I need to step outside for a bit," Jack said.

"Where are you going?"

"Come get me when he wakes up," Jack said, leaving his sister slackjawed at Solomon's bedside.

He went outside. It was a frigid morning. Skies that had been clear at sunrise had filled in with a heavy blanket of clouds. The air smelled raw and damp. Snow was likely before the day was out. He stuffed his hands in his jacket, bypassing his tent, and made his way toward the border of Promise. He liked walking the community's rough edges. Few people came out this way. The forest was lined with thick bramble; there was no path to speak of.

I know how to turn the lights back on.

He hoped Solomon woke up soon. Maybe the man had gone insane. For all Jack knew to the contrary, life in the post-Pulse world had driven Solomon to madness, and for reasons known only to him, he had latched onto Jack like a beacon. It couldn't have been easy for Solomon to track Jack down. But until Jack acquired more information, he simply could not dismiss Solomon's pronouncement out of hand. After all, something had sent him on this quest to find Jack.

Something.

Or someone.

Molly Thornton.

The one and only love of Jack's life. A woman he had not seen in more than a decade. A woman he still thought about every single day of his life but discussed with no one. Normally, Jack wasn't one for regret. After they had gone their separate ways, he figured that would be that. But regret still clung to him all these many years.

~

Jack hadn't been attending the Christmas party so much as he was working it. Even had the ridiculous red bartender's jacket. The soirèe was being held at the spacious home of his commanding officer, an insufferable prick named Jonas Berkeley. Ordering a subordinate to tend bar at a private party was probably against the rules, but who was gonna say anything?

Jack was twenty-eight years old. He'd been in the Army for nearly ten years by then and had quickly distinguished himself. He enlisted right out of high school, but his proficiency test scores earned him a trip away from the front lines and into Army intelligence. He excelled at languages and mathematics, and more than once he was told he should've been at West Point. But Jack had never wanted to go to college.

Initially, he'd been disappointed by the transfer out of the infantry, but he soon discovered a fondness for intelligence work. He liked working alone, he liked the frequent travel to dangerous places, relying on nothing more than his wits and brains. Then his appendix had crapped out on him, damn near killing him, and he would be stateside for the next three months, waiting to complete his recovery from the surgery and septic shock. He was currently on loan to the CIA, assessing the daily flow of intelligence threats.

He took the sidelining in stride. Some things were just out of your control. He poured the drinks for the officers and their dates; he treated himself to some high-end bourbon, as Berkeley had told him to do. It was shaping up to be an uneventful night.

And then she had appeared.

Molly had arrived on the arm of some douchebag, a

lieutenant commander he didn't know. Jack could not recall many of the details from that night, but he still remembered exactly what she was wearing. A strapless red dress, a string of pearls around her slender neck. She had shoulder-length brown hair and deep brown eyes. She was tall, about an inch shorter than his five-foot-ten frame, graced with a swimmer's body. Try as he might, trained as he was in the art of deception, he simply could not keep his eyes off of her.

And she had noticed.

An hour in, she approached the bar without her date in tow.

Jack was sweating, his face flushed. He could not believe the effect this woman was having on him. It had never happened before in his life. Jack was no stranger to women. He was good looking and he knew it. Women were drawn to him. He enjoyed the attention, and, of course, as a young man, he enjoyed the sex.

But this was different. Oh so different.

"Hi there," she had said.

"Evening."

He became hyper-aware of everything. Of his words, of his looks, whether there was a stray piece of food stuck in his teeth.

"Do you have any Woodford back there?"

He scanned the bottles.

"Yes."

"On the rocks, please," she asked pleasantly. "Don't be shy with the pour. I hate parties."

His hand trembled as he reached for the bottle and poured the amber liquid into the plastic cocktail tumbler. He added a stirrer and a small wedge of lime before handing her the drink. She took a sip, lingering at the bar a bit longer than he had expected.

"Do I know you?" she asked.

The room grew uncomfortably warm in the light of her attention on him. It felt as though every single person was watching him interact with this woman, this date of a superior officer. He kept his hands busy by returning the bottle to its slot on the bar. He grabbed a dish towel and wiped the bar dry.

"I don't think so," he replied as calmly as he could. "Why do you ask?"

A mischievous smile lit up her face.

"Because you've been looking at me like you know me."

His eyes cut downward, and an embarrassed smile ran across his face. Perhaps the Army had made a mistake in inviting him to its elite counterintelligence program. If this woman could make him, what chance did he have working undercover against professionals?

But that had been a gross underestimation of Molly Thornton's intelligence. It was the first and last time he underestimated her. She was an officer herself, running out the last year of her tour; she was assigned to U.S. Cyber Command, helping protect the nation's infrastructure against malevolent digital actors – rapidly becoming one of the country's greatest security threats. Military life was not for her, though, and once her tour was up later that summer, she was headed to Georgetown University for a Ph.D. in computer science.

"It's okay, soldier," she said. "I'd be lying if I said I didn't have my eye on you too. I'm not normally this forward but I am trying to do more things outside of my comfort zone."

By this point, Jack's knees were virtually knocking together and his stomach was fluttering. They chatted a bit longer. Jack had the good sense to let her do most of the talking; it minimized the chances he would humiliate himself in front of her.

"I want to meet you for a drink tonight," she said. "You know Phillips Tavern?"

He nodded. It was a small Irish pub near the base.

"Midnight."

Jack's mouth was dry, but he managed to nod his understanding. The rational side of him, the one concerned about his career, about the trouble a man like her date could cause him, would have hesitated at the prospect of such a rendezvous. But Jack Goodwin would be there at midnight if he had to crawl through broken glass to get there.

"What about your friend there?" Jack asked. He nodded toward the man she'd arrived with. He was making a beeline toward the bar. He was tall and classically handsome. His nameplate identified him as Finney.

"Is there a problem?" asked the lieutenant commander.

"No problem," the woman said.

"I was starting to miss you," he said, encircling her waist with his beefy left arm.

"I just couldn't decide what I wanted," she lied, "and this nice bartender was helping me."

"Women," Finney said to Jack, scoffing. "Am I right?"

He said it in a way that suggested he believed he was always right.

Jack raised his eyebrows and tilted his head in conspiratorial agreement.

"Scotch," he said. "Single malt, neat. If it's a blend, I'll have you dishonorably discharged."

Finney laughed at his own joke. As Jack fixed the man's drink, Finney leaned in for a kiss from his date. She turned her cheek just so at the last second, leaving him to plant his smooch at the corner of her lovely mouth.

Jack handed the man his drink, worked the rest of the party without incident, and at midnight, he met the woman at the tiny pub. They sat at a corner table in the back. Poorly lit. It felt like he was breaking a rule.

"I never got your name," he said.

She took a sip from her bourbon.

"Molly."

Molly.

2

The balance of the day passed in a haze. Solomon did not regain consciousness that afternoon, and so there was little to do but fall back into their routine. Jack was in charge of Promise's security, which meant maintaining their arsenal of weapons, sorting out disputes between the residents before they spun out of control, and patrols of the surrounding vicinity. He had a lot to do, and he was up early the following morning.

Lucy came to see him as he prepared to make his way to the weapons depot. He planned to spend the morning cleaning Promise's stock of handguns, a dozen in all. They had not spoken since he'd left her at Solomon's bedside.

"Any change in Solomon?" he asked after she had taken a seat on the ground

She shook her head.

"No," she said. "Still out."

"Is he gonna wake up?"

She pulled up a chair and took a seat.

"Yeah, I think so," she said. "He's been through a lot, so his body just needs some time to recover. Any idea how old he is?"

Jack scrunched up his face in thought.

"Mid-fifties maybe? He's a few years older than me, but I'm not sure."

"That's a lot to handle for a guy on the far side of middle age," she said.

"I guess," Jack said. He wanted to smack Solomon awake. They needed to question him further.

"We'll know more by tomorrow."

"Okay."

"So do you want to clue me in?" she asked. "How do you know him?"

"He worked with Molly."

A flash of recognition on Lucy's face. Jack was an intensely private person, but eventually, Lucy had found out about Molly. They only met a few times. Jack did not understand why he worked so hard to compartmentalize different aspects of his life.

"Been a long time since I heard that name."

"Yeah."

"You made a mistake letting her go."

A hot spike of anger shot through him, but he did not respond to her barb. It wasn't anything she hadn't said before. But it still annoyed him.

"Do you know where she is?"

"Somewhere in northern Virginia, I think."

"You ever try to find her?"

"No," he said. "I'm not sure my presence would be welcomed, to be honest."

"Any idea why Solomon would come looking for you?"

"No. Unless Molly sent him."

It was the only thing he could think of. Molly was the connective tissue between Jack and Solomon. Without that link, the men would have been strangers to one another. As it was, they were all but strangers. There was no rational explanation for Solomon to have tracked down Jack unless it had been at Molly's request.

"We need to notify the Council about this," Lucy said.

Jack sighed. He had suspected that this was coming.

"Who else knows right now?"

"You, me, and Terri."

Jack's eyebrows rocked upwards.

"Don't worry about her," Lucy said. "She's incredibly discreet. She knows the effect this would have on everyone."

Jack nodded approvingly.

"Can it wait a bit?" he asked. "The Council may not be so discreet."

"Jack, we picked these people to represent us and make decisions for the community. We can't keep something like this from them. I know you don't trust politicians, but this is how it has to be."

He made a clicking sound with his tongue. He hated politicians. Always had. They had a unique gift for making things worse. It wasn't that he thought the three members of the Promise Council were bad people; it was just that when someone assumed power over others, it changed them. Every time. Even here.

"You could've run, you know," Lucy said, interrupting

his thoughts. "You would almost certainly have won a spot, in spite of yourself."

He laughed.

Jack would no more have run for office than he would have sipped on a jet fuel martini. Even if you came to it with the purest of intentions, even if you managed to stay above the temptations, you still had to deal with mind-blowing idiocy. He wasn't even sure Promise *needed* a Council. The things they had to do to keep their community safe and viable were non-negotiable. Food, water, defense, sanitation, maintenance, textiles, crops, animal husbandry, trade. The list was endless. And they had to happen whether there was a Council or not. That said, it made some people feel better. That they were part of a community, bound by loyalty and a sense of family.

"If we tell them, word will get out," Jack said.

"You don't know that."

"It's too juicy to keep," he said. "You know the old saying about secrets? Two people can keep a secret if one of them is dead. Honestly, I'd be surprised if it wasn't already out."

Jack dreaded the idea of Solomon's message becoming public knowledge. It would give people hope. Hope could be lethal. Until proven otherwise, Solomon's message was simply the ramblings of a crazy man lost in a snowstorm. But that wouldn't matter to some people. All they would hear was that there was a chance to get back to the way things were. They wanted it so desperately; even after all this time, it was a hard thing to let go. And baseless hope could upset the apple cart they'd worked so hard to build.

Back to normal.

The Covid-19 pandemic had swept the globe about five years before the Pulse. Beginning in China and spreading rapidly around the world, it killed more than ten million people and took nearly eighteen months to wrestle under control. Finally, the introduction of highly effective vaccines had helped bring it to an end. The World Health Organization's declaration of the pandemic's end had been a red-letter day in human history. It was Western Civilization's last great achievement. A little more than four years after that momentous day, the lights had gone out in the world for the last time.

As the Covid pandemic had raged, normality was that shining beacon for humanity. But as the pandemic waned, it became clear the world was not going back to the way it was before the virus had run through humanity like a buzzsaw. And if there was any merit to Solomon's claim, that they could reverse the effects of the Pulse, they would be entering a new world yet again. They wouldn't be returning to the one they had left behind on that sunny May afternoon five years ago.

"How about some tea?" Lucy asked, getting up from her seat.

"Sure."

She steeped the pre-filled bag of herbs and spices in the hot water until it darkened to his liking. Over time, he'd grown to like this particular blend of tea. Okay, *like* might have been a strong word, but it was passable. Like a phantom limb, he still wished for the days he could grab a box of teabags from the grocery store.

As Lucy heated up what passed for tea these days, Jack reflected on his relationship with Molly and the part of his life that had intersected with Solomon's. Jack had not known much about their work together.

Her work involved creating models to predict the effects of climate change on the planet. She was a brilliant computer scientist, and her work was frequently cited by scientists and academics in the ongoing debate. That said, he had no clue what she or Solomon would have to do with the Pulse much less with reversing the effects of it. Then a wild thought streaked across his mind like a comet. It seemed ridiculous, but perhaps it wasn't.

Had Molly figured out how to reverse the effect of the Pulse?

She was certainly smart enough. If anyone had the brains and the grit, the sheer, steely unbending determination to do so, it was Molly Thornton. It was what he had loved most about her. The thing he wanted to be around for the rest of his life. Until he had screwed it all up.

Maybe he should have sought her out. He could have. He could have helped her. Although the idea that she would not survive the Pulse had never crossed his mind. She was strong and resourceful; she would have figured out how to stay alive. And besides, even if it came down to death or accepting help from Jack Goodwin, he wasn't sure she wouldn't have picked the former.

Lucy had just finished making the tea when the flap of his tent rustled open. It was Terri.

"He's up," she said, looking at Jack. "Asking for you again."

3

Solomon was looking about the same when they made it back to the clinic. Not great, but not any worse. He was sitting up now; he was more alert. His hands were wrapped around a mug containing a steaming liquid. It smelled like broth. The morning sun had cleared the trees in the east, shining through the window, dappling the floor in shadowy piano bars.

"Your stomach holding up?" asked Lucy.

He nodded.

"It's about the best thing I've ever tasted," he replied.

He tilted the mug back, drained it, and then looked down in it longingly.

"Good," Lucy said. "Tomorrow we can start you back on solids. Maybe even this evening."

He nodded before turning his attention to Jack.

"Guess you're wondering why I'm here."

"How did you even find me?" Jack said.

Solomon laughed out loud.

"I've been looking for you for a while," he said. "A couple of months. Started hearing stories about some to-do involving a warlord around here. A little group snuck in and burned the place down. At least that was the story I heard."

Jack cut his eyes toward Lucy.

"Was it you all?"

"More or less."

"I started asking around," Solomon said. "Met a couple of refugees from the place. The name Jack came up a few times. Working with a woman that fit your sister's description."

Jack was impressed, and his curiosity was at its zenith. Solomon had been hellbent on finding Jack. It was the kind of guy he was. When he had something in his bit, he rarely let it go until he found it. Or destroyed it, but that was another matter.

"I started following trading parties north and south of Interstate 64," he said. "Things started getting hairy in the last week. I traded away the last bit of my food for info about where you were. You know the rest."

"What are you doing here?" Jack asked.

He took a deep breath and let it out slowly.

"Molly sent me."

Jack rocked backward, as though Solomon had punched him in the face. Even though he had expected it, hearing Solomon verbalize it made it that much more real.

"Where is she?"

"They caught her."

"Who caught her?" Jack asked.

With some effort, Solomon waved his hands at Jack.

"Let me start from the beginning."

"Fine. Start."

"Okay," Solomon said. "First, a little background to catch my lovely nurse here up to speed."

He glanced at Lucy, who was leaning against the wall of the clinic, her arms crossed against her chest.

"I'm a climate scientist," he said. "I have doctorates in climatology and environmental science. At least, I *was* a climate scientist. Before the big...."

He gestured grandly around him.

"You know."

Yes, Solomon, we know, Jack thought. The guy had a bad habit of running off on tangents.

"So anyway, before the blessed event, I worked for a think tank in D.C. It was called Climate First. Our mission was to develop strategies to combat climate change. There were about twenty of us – climate scientists, computer programmers, engineers, big data analysts, that sort of thing."

"Molly worked there," Jack cut in.

"Yes," Solomon confirmed for Lucy. "Jack's beloved worked there. She built models predicting the impacts of various mitigation strategies on reversing — or at least slowing down — climate change. She was damn good at it too."

He paused for a moment, took a deep breath, closed his eyes. Jack struggled to remain patient. It was the most he'd spoken since his arrival, but he wanted to hear more. A lot more.

Solomon's eyes opened again.

"You know what the biggest mistake in the history of

science is? Perhaps the history of humanity? One of them, at least?"

Jack did not know, but he suspected he was about to find out.

"What?"

"Do you know who Dr. Wallace Broecker was?"

Jack and Lucy shook their heads. Jack's fists clenched in frustration. Another tangent taking them away from the critical narrative.

Solomon chuckled.

"Virtually no one does," he said. "He was a geochemist. A professor at Columbia University. In 1975, he published a paper titled *'Climate Change: Are We on the Brink of a Pronounced Global Warming?'* It's a brilliant piece of work. But for whatever reason, the media latched onto the term *global warming* instead of *climate change*. I don't know why. Maybe it was sexier. You know how the media was."

He paused a moment, as though waiting for acknowledgment from Lucy and Jack that they did indeed know how the media was. But the room was silent.

"Anyway, when we started seeing real evidence of man-made climate change in the last twenty years before the blackout, people kept defaulting to the term global warming. So when the temperatures didn't rise dramatically, the way some of the early models predicted, it gave certain elements of society a club to wield. And scientists are not well equipped to fight off political attacks. We just have a hard time understanding why people reject science. It's our Achilles heel."

"And things kept getting worse," Lucy said.

"Exactly."

"So what does this have to do with Molly?" Jack asked.

"I'm getting to that," Solomon said. "One night, years ago, Molly came to my apartment. It was late. Probably three in the morning."

The volume of his voice had dropped a notch; he sounded grim.

"You remember that place, Jack?"

Jack did.

While he and Molly were dating, Solomon had lived in a small apartment in the District. It was tiny but had a magnificent view of the city. They had gathered there for cocktails a few times before venturing out for dinner.

"She was drunk, panicked, scared," he continued. "I've never seen anyone like that. This was about five years before the blackout, maybe six. She smelled like she had taken a bath in gin. But she was very clear-minded. It was strange. Like even the alcohol hadn't been able to settle her down. She'd been working on some new algorithms, tracking water temperatures in the North Atlantic, figuring out what mitigation efforts we needed to focus on."

"And?"

"She said it was over. That we were past the point of no return."

"Meaning what?"

"Meaning that even the most extreme mitigation efforts would fail to prevent a three-degree rise in the global temperatures within a decade."

"And that's bad?" Jack asked. "Look, I'll be honest, I don't know much about global warming."

"Climate change."

"Sorry."

"Yes, it's very bad," Solomon said. "The melting of the ice caps would accelerate rapidly at that point. Trillions of gallons of fresh water would spill into the oceans and throw off the salinity of the oceans. Hurricanes would become more intense. Many coastal areas would be underwater. Agriculture would begin to fail."

"No different than what we'd been hearing," Lucy said.

"No," Solomon said, shaking his head. "It's different because Molly had figured out that there was no longer any way to stop it. It didn't matter anymore."

Jack tried to picture a panicked Molly Thornton. It wasn't easy. She was normally calm, difficult to rattle. She never got too high or too low about anything. He had never once seen her lose her cool. One night, she had been cooking dinner, slicing up some garlic; the knife slipped and buried itself in her thumb, down to the bone. Jack had been opening a bottle of wine at the counter behind her and didn't even notice anything had happened until she calmly asked him for a hand towel.

"I need to take a trip up to the emergency room," she said matter-of-factly, sighing with some annoyance. As if this gruesome kitchen injury was nothing more than a slight inconvenience, even as blood soaked through two towels on the way to the hospital. She had not shed a tear, her voice had not shaken. Twenty stitches later and her biggest concern was that she had ruined dinner. She had been making penne *alla* vodka, her favorite.

The idea that something had rattled her so deeply was unnerving indeed.

"I'm still not following what that has to do with turning the lights back on," Jack said.

"I'm getting to that."

Before continuing his story, however, he held the empty bowl up for Lucy.

"Could I have a little more, please?" he asked. "I'm famished."

Lucy took the bowl from him.

"Not another word until I get back," she said.

Lucy left.

"Go on," Jack said. "I'll bring her up to speed."

"No," Solomon said. "Not until Lucy gets back."

Jack wanted to throttle the man. The years had not changed him; He was as stubborn as ever. Once he had made up his mind, he did not change it. It was weird. Solomon's mere presence in Promise had opened some long-closed doors in Jack's mind. Emotions that he had not felt in years rushed back like the cold waters of a rushing river. Even if he did not remember many of the details of those years gone by. He remembered how he had felt around Solomon. Because of Molly. Sometimes in life, you didn't remember the person, you remembered the way that person made you feel, a thing that had happened with that person. Things that could overshadow the person himself. That's how it was with Solomon.

"Fine," Jack said.

"Good," Solomon said quietly, looking down at the blanket covering his legs. His hands danced in his lap like clumsy spiders.

Soon Lucy returned with a second bowl of soup and a piece of hard flatbread on a tray. She set the tray on

Solomon's lap and returned to the second seat in the room. Solomon blew the steam off from a spoonful of soup and took a sip.

"This is so good."

"Solomon," Lucy said.

"Right," he said. "Bit of the absent-minded professor at work here, Ms. Goodwin."

She smiled but her patience was running thin.

"The next morning, we called for a meeting of the think tank. All hands. Molly presented her findings. The weird thing was that they didn't seem surprised." Solomon's attention drifted again as he poked around his past.

"No, they weren't surprised at all," Solomon said. "They had come to the same conclusion. There was nothing we could do to stop the coming catastrophe. There was nothing anyone could do to stop it."

He took another sip of his soup while Jack contemplated the man's story so far. He was still struggling with the image of Molly rattled. It was hard to believe. She was the most grounded person he had ever known.

"The think tank was pretty much dead after that," he continued. "We still had grant money to use, so people still had jobs for another year, but it wasn't the same. That's when the weirdness started."

"What kind of weirdness?" asked Lucy.

"The computer science team started working on some new project. It was all very hush-hush. Half the time, I didn't even know where they were."

"What were you doing during this time?" Jack asked.

Solomon chuckled at that.

"That's the funny thing," he said. "I was literally doing

nothing. One day, they came in and told me my salary was guaranteed for another year. I had started looking for a new job, but then the pandemic hit, and that put the brakes on that. To be honest, I kind of flaked out a little bit. I was recently divorced, living alone, so I kind of became a hermit."

"I have a question," Lucy asked.

"Shoot."

"Didn't the pandemic slow down climate change?"

Solomon chuckled.

"For about a month, yes," he said. "There was a significant drop in carbon emissions, and we saw the slightest hint of stabilization in the polar ice. But then we pretty much went back to the way things were. And the climate change train kept chugging."

That had been a particularly difficult pill to swallow. With the pandemic behind them, the world had enjoyed a few years of relative peace and prosperity. Not a single nation had been spared its terrible cut, and with the benefit of their shared pain, the world had moved forward together. And then the Pulse had hit. Rubbing salt in the wound.

"Anyway, the team locked itself away for weeks on end. But Molly went even beyond that. She disappeared totally. No one knew where she was. Then she showed up on my doorstep. I hadn't seen her in months. She had this small device with her. It was about the size of a flash drive with a series of numbers constantly scrolling on its little screen.

"She handed me the device," he said, his face going blank as he drew on his memory banks, "and told me to press the button on the side of the device. I started to make a joke, but she did not look to be in a joking mood, so I kept quiet and pressed the button."

He chuckled.

"My apartment went dark. Everything. Lights, phone, clock on the wall. Just like that. Dead. I didn't know what to do or think. She took the device back from me and fiddled with it. An instant later, the lights all came back on. It lasted maybe ten seconds. It was a prototype, not powerful enough to sustain a blackout for very long, but it showed the team what was possible. Within a couple of years, they had built the Machine."

"The what?"

"The Machine. The device generating the Pulse, as you call it."

"A machine caused this?" Lucy asked.

"A machine *is* causing this," he said. "That's what no one understands. Everyone thinks it was an electromagnetic pulse that caused the blackout, but that's not entirely correct. The team built a machine that could generate a persistent pulse operating at various frequencies to permanently interrupt the world's power grid. It kills all alternating and direct currents. Electricity generated in any form, mind you. Solar, wind, hydroelectric, nuclear. Every form."

The slightest hint of suspicion had taken root in Jack's mind, and he was anxious to see where Solomon's story was headed.

"I have a question," Jack said.

"Shoot," Solomon said, sighing.

"Was Molly part of this computer science team?"

"She was."

"Why didn't you or her go to the police?"

"No, Jack, you're not listening. Molly wasn't trying to stop them from building the Machine. Molly *helped* them build the Machine.

Jack's legs buckled.

"Jack."

"No," he said, feeling lightheaded.

"Molly helped cause the blackout."

4

The room was silent. Jack's breath held tight. His heart was pounding so hard that he was certain Lucy and Solomon could hear it thumping against his ribcage. Solomon was looking down at his hands like a small boy who'd confessed to breaking a family heirloom.

"You're lying," Jack said. It was all he could manage.

Solomon's head popped up, his eyes wide with surprise. It seemed that being called a liar was not on his to-do list for the day.

"Jack, I'm not lying."

"You bastard," Jack said. His voice was dripping with rage. "Where is she?"

"Jack, you have to listen to me."

Jack smacked the bowl from Solomon's hands; it bounced onto the edge of the bed and clattered to the floor.

"Jack, calm down," Lucy snapped. "Let the man speak."

Jack was shaking with anger. Molly was probably dead, and this man was dragging her name through the mud, recklessly accusing her of perhaps the greatest crime in human history. Maybe Solomon was insane. Yes. He had lost his mind these past five years and had come here with this fantastical tale of conspiracy and genocide.

"Do you hear him?" he yelled. "Do you hear him, Lucy? He's accusing her of causing the apocalypse."

"I hear him," his sister said. "But it's clear he's got more to say."

"Well, he needs to get to it quickly," he said, turning his attention back to Solomon. "Or I'll feed that soup bowl to him."

Solomon swallowed hard, clearly intimidated by the bigger man.

"Look, I'm sorry, Jack, but it's true. She did help build the Machine. But you need to let me finish."

"Fine," Jack said, scoffing. "But make it quick."

"I have a question," Lucy said, interjecting. "Was she right? Was it too late to stop the worst-case scenario?"

Solomon sighed and pushed his dinner tray a bit farther down his lap.

"There are very few absolutes in science," he said. "A lot of it is eliminating what you learn is wrong, based on trial and error. You make a hypothesis, you test it, and you record the results. Whether it matches your preconceived notion or not. At some point, you've eliminated enough wrong answers and you're left with the right one."

"That's a fancy way of not answering my question," Lucy said.

A wan smile darkened his face.

"Yes, I think she was right."

"Were you on board with their solution?"

"No," he said. "It was real apocalyptic shit. But they were so obsessed with stopping a climate catastrophe. They really believed that the Pulse was the lesser of two evils. That there was no other solution."

"What did you think?" Lucy asked.

"I thought we'd be trading one cataclysm for another."

"Who was in charge of all this?"

"A woman named Iris Erickson."

"Who's she?"

"She was the head of the think tank," Solomon said. "My boss, actually. Another climate scientist. She was a real fanatic. A real doomsayer. She hated people."

"Charming," Lucy said.

"Why didn't you go to the police?" Jack asked.

"Honestly? In the beginning, I didn't think it would work. Do you understand the magnitude of what they were attempting? Constructing a single device that would wipe out all of the world's technology? It was lunacy. Absolute lunacy. So I just let them play out their fantasy, figuring they would eventually move on."

"And yet, here we are," Jack said.

Solomon pressed a thumb to a corner of each eye.

"Here we are," he said, echoing Jack's words.

The trio sat in silence for a bit. Jack was having a hard time processing what he was hearing. If Solomon was telling the truth, two people he had known, one of whom he had loved deeply, had been instrumental in bringing about the fall of man. It was hard to believe.

And Solomon did not sound like he was lying.

"As we got closer to the day of the attack," he went on,

his voice barely a whisper, "I started to panic. I didn't understand the technology they were using. They had started making concrete plans to activate the Machine. Even if it didn't work like they intended, I was worried they would cause a big explosion and kill a bunch of people."

"Then Molly came to see me again," he said. "Three weeks before it happened. She said the Machine was going to work. And she had changed her mind. She wanted out."

"What do you mean, 'she wanted out?'"

"Exactly what I said. Like she suddenly realized what she was doing. It was right after that first simulation. It was still theoretical, of course, it would be theoretical until the day they actually did it. I mean, you really can't run a real-world experiment on a doomsday device."

Jack chuckled. It was funny in a gallows humor kind of way.

"But something about that simulation seemed to knock her back into reality."

Jack couldn't decide if this made him feel better or worse. Did her last-minute change of heart absolve Lucy of her terrible sin? At what point in the life cycle of this Machine, of this terrible weapon, was it too late to say, *nope, I'm out*!

"Did you try talking them out of it?"

"We did," he said. "But they wouldn't listen. I even went to the FBI. But they had someone on the inside. Don't ask me how."

"And?"

"They tried to kill me."

Silence.

"They blew up my house," he said. "If I were a cat, I'd have used up eight of my lives that night. I couldn't sleep that night. I wasn't sleeping at all back then. It was a nice night, so I decided to go for a walk. Four a.m. and I'm shuffling around the block in my bathrobe. I was about a hundred yards clear of the house when it went up like a Roman candle."

Silence fell across the room.

"Then we ran. Two weeks before the Pulse, I faked my own death. Made it look like a suicide. I'm not sure what Molly did. We agreed on a rally point."

"Why didn't you just turn it off?" Jack asked. "Or destroy it?"

"Yeah, if only," Solomon said gravely.

"I take it we can't just turn it off," Lucy said.

"I asked Molly the same question."

"What did she say?"

"No," he replied. "You can't just turn it off. It's a quantum machine."

"What does that mean?"

"I have no idea."

Jack's head was spinning by this point; it felt like he was aboard a ship in rough seas. Tossed and flipped and unable to get his feet under him. There was so much data blasting his senses he didn't know where to begin.

"Then what happened?"

"We met at this cabin in the Blue Ridge Mountains," he said. "It belonged to her family."

Jack was familiar with it. He and Molly had spent several weekends there. It had been in her family for generations; she inherited the place following the death of her parents in a small plane crash when she was twenty-three. Totally isolated, accessible via the narrowest of roads that could barely be described as a road. He had loved going there. Away from the world, just the two of them. Some of his happiest memories had been sourced inside that cabin. He recalled one morning, chopping firewood; taking a break to stretch his back, he looked up and spotted a black bear at the edge of the trees lining the property. She was a massive specimen, but she made no move toward him. He made no attempt to run, as he was a good piece from the house and she would have chased him down with little effort if the mood struck her. They sized each other up for a bit before she melted back into the trees.

"We made a plan to meet there if the Pulse worked," he said. "Then we would regroup."

Jack held up his hands like a traffic cop. Solomon's shoulders sagged and he let out a slow, ragged breath. He looked exhausted. Telling his tale had taken quite a bit out of him. Jack glanced over at Lucy, who was watching Solomon carefully. Her arms were crossed high on her chest and she scraped at her lower lip with a thumbnail, as she often did when deep in thought.

"Okay, let's slow down for a second," Jack said. He had zeroed back in on the first words Solomon had said to him.

"Okay."

"You said you know how to turn the lights back on."

"Yes."

"How?"

He smiled wanly.

"Molly," he said. "Molly can do it."

He yawned.

"Do you think we can pick this up later?"

A belt of frustration tightened around Jack's chest. They needed to know what Solomon knew, and they needed to know it now. He glanced back at Lucy.

"Solomon," Jack said, sighing.

"I know," he said. "I've got a lot more to tell you, but I'm feeling run down."

"Are you not feeling well?" she asked him.

"Just extremely tired. Some chills."

She got up from her chair and lay a hand against his forehead.

"No fever," she said. "How's your stomach?"

"Fine."

Solomon sighed. Jack had to admit the man did look worn out. As it was, his eyes looked heavy, and he appeared to be drifting off.

"What powers this Machine?" Lucy asked.

"Enriched uranium," he said sleepily

"Where did you get enriched uranium?"

"I'm not sure where they got it from," he said. "There was still a lot floating around after the collapse of the Soviet Union."

"That was more than thirty years ago."

"Uranium lasts quite a bit longer than thirty years."

"True."

"So you created some kind of beam, powered by a nuclear reactor, and this beam neutralizes all electrical or battery power."

"Look, I'm a climate scientist, not a nuclear physicist, so I don't know all the specifics, but that's the gist of it."

Anger bubbled inside Jack like lava in a long-dormant volcano. For five years, the world had been winding down, breaking down, coming apart at the seams. Flung into a new Stone Age that virtually no one had been prepared for.

"You've got to be kidding me," Lucy said, exasperated.

"I most certainly am not," Solomon replied softly.

He was drifting off again; Jack wanted to keep questioning him.

He leaned in and lightly patted Solomon on the face.

"Wake up, buddy," he said. "We're not done yet."

Solomon grunted softly.

"I think he's out again," Lucy said.

"Dammit."

5

Jack could not sleep. It was late, still full dark, the absolute peak of night. A light rain stippled the shell of his tent. It was comforting, the sound of rain. It reminded him of his youth, of rainy winter nights when his mother would build a fire for him and Lucy. She would make them hot chocolate and they would play board games and pretend that it was normal to wait in fear for their father to return home, stinking of cheap whiskey, and hope that he would pass out before taking a belt to one or more of the three. This was when Jack was small, back before he got too big to smack around, big enough to protect his mother and sister from their drunken father.

He'd been seventeen the last time Donald Goodwin had tried to put a hand to any of them. Perhaps the senior Goodwin simply hadn't noticed that his only son was now a full two inches taller than him, heavier by fifty pounds, and built like a freight train. Perhaps he could have been excused in failing to notice that, drunk as he was when he got home, the family sedan parked half on the driveway, half on the front yard.

A laceration above his father's eyebrow, still bleeding down into his eye, matting his hair against his forehead, told Jack this had been a special night for Don Goodwin. He was surly from the moment he entered, breathing raggedly like a riled-up bull. He started barking at them, incoherently as he often did; he flipped the Monopoly board upside down, scattering the pieces and the dice and the Community Chest and Chance cards.

When Linda Goodwin had snapped at him, Jack's father stepped around the card table, his fists clenched, and that was when Jack stood up in between his mother and this father-shaped demon that rained down hell on them on Friday nights. He placed a hand on his father's chest, hoping to calm him down. It did not work, and his father reared back with one of his sweaty paws. But he was drunk and old and slow, and Jack was sober and young and fast and in the blink of an eye, he had Don Goodwin's arm pinned behind his back, almost to the point his shoulder was coming loose from its joint. He bucked and thrashed, but Jack was too big and too strong. He slammed his father's head down on the card table that until a few minutes ago had held their Monopoly game.

"You ever gonna touch us again?" Jack hissed.

His father bucked some more, unleashing a torrent of profanity that Jack had never heard from his father. So he applied more pressure to the armbar, driving his elbow into the base of Don Goodwin's neck. Then the man had gone slack, the pain becoming more than he could handle, whimpering and crying like the pathetic piece of shit that he was.

"No," he squeaked out.

Jack's heart broke at that moment, knowing how weak and useless this man was.

"Say it," Jack said. "I'll never touch you all again."

"I'll never touch you again."

Don slept on the floor that night and moved out the next day. The pair divorced not long after. He never paid a dime of child support or alimony as ordered by the court, but he never bothered Jack or his mother and sister again. They spoke only rarely after that. When Jack was in the Army, he'd gotten a call from his mother that Don Goodwin had died. He had been found in his apartment in an advanced state of decomposition. No one had been looking for him. No one had missed him. Jack occasionally had nightmares about that.

Jack lit a lantern and set a pot of water to boil. As the water heated up, he pulled the hood of his sweatshirt over his head. It was a cold night, one of the coldest this season. But he barely noticed. Solomon's revelations about Molly, about the Pulse, were still rattling about his head. That she had been an architect of their destruction was difficult to wrap his head around.

Despite his objections, Lucy had notified the Council of Solomon's revelations. She had insisted that his story was too important to hold back. A credible lead on reversing the effects of the Pulse, no matter how remote, was critical intelligence and should have been held close to the vest. He had hoped the Council members would remain discreet and keep it to themselves, but it was too juicy a tidbit, and by dinner, virtually everyone had known that a woman Jack had once known was perhaps responsible for their damnation and their possible salvation.

Sweet, determined, brilliant Molly.

He dunked in a pouch that passed for tea these days and waited for the water to steep. Five minutes later, the tea was ready. He wished he had some sugar or even real tea, but this would have to do. Hot was hot. The first sip scorched his tongue and the back of his throat, but he instantly felt warmer.

There was so much information he didn't even know where to begin. Molly, the Pulse, the Machine. And it was impossible to chew on one of those issues without overlapping one of the others. A bizarre Venn diagram.

Most people had long suspected that the Pulse had been an attack. There was nothing natural about it. But in the chaos that followed, there had never been any way to prove that, let alone find out who had been responsible. So to have it confirmed now, after all these years, was still a revelation.

Not only that, but now there was a face to it.

Solomon, in his own way, had been part of it.

And Molly.

Jack was still having a hard time envisioning how she could have come so untethered to participate in such a diabolical scheme. Sure, the air was cleaner now, but hundreds of millions of people were dead as a result. Kind of defeated the point of having the clean air in the first place. Millions more died each year as resources grew increasingly scarce. Which meant that Molly had believed that ushering in a technological apocalypse was the only way to save humanity from itself. It mattered little whether she had been right.

What mattered was that she *believed* she was right. Because it had driven her actions. It had brought about consequences that she decided had been worth the price she had paid for them.

It must have destroyed her.

Molly was a kind and gentle soul. But she could also be transactional when she needed to be. And it must have required some dark calculus to arrive at such a decision. Climate change had been hard to visualize. Sure, one could see the viral videos of polar bears struggling to find purchase or the increase in the frequency of hurricanes targeting the U.S. mainland. But it was a bit ephemeral, like trying to grab a puff of smoke. It was there and it wasn't all at the same time. It just seemed hard to believe that Molly had been so certain that this was the only alternative. That the option of last resort was the only option left.

His mind kept working as he sipped his tea. The heat had dissipated a bit and now it was just hot and not volcanic. It was doing a good job of keeping him toasty and alert. Although to be honest, it was unlikely he would have been able to sleep even without the caffeinated assist of the terrible tea.

Not that he didn't deserve some punishment for breaking her heart. To this day, he still didn't know why he had ended things with her. The bulk of their relationship had transpired while she working on her Ph.D. and he was assigned to counterintelligence at Fort Belvoir. It had been his first and only long-term relationship. He'd had several short flings over the years, but those usually lasted as long as it took him to get out the door. With Molly, it had been different. Around her, he never felt like he was supposed to be somewhere else or that he wanted to be somewhere else.

Maybe it had been the job itself. He was farmed out to undercover work overseas, duty stations that took him out of the country weeks or months at a time. And although she worried about him desperately, the time apart never seemed to bother her. She was immersed in her work, which she loved, and she was possessed of preternatural focus that allowed her to progress quickly on her dissertation.

But when he was home, he was happy, an emotion he was unfamiliar with, which made it an uncomfortable happiness. It was like a transplanted organ his body was rejecting. Happiness was not a default state for Jack Goodwin.

After they'd gone their separate ways, he re-upped for another four years, thinking the work would keep him on the straight and narrow and deal with the massive shock of his separation from Molly. But the work had not been enough and he had slept with his superior officer, who had been married to another superior officer, and that had been enough to get them both dishonorably discharged.

And that was when Jack Goodwin, decorated war hero, had embarked on his life of crime.

Molly had never known this version of him. A wave of guilt washed over him as he drained his tea. Molly's role in building the Machine had been unforgivable; that much was clear. But Jack was pretty far down the list of people who had the right to sit in judgment of anyone. Least of all someone doing the wrong thing for what they believed was the right reason.

Katie Stone.

The name lit up in his mind like it was on a garish, buzzing marquee.

It was the last con he'd ever run.

Shortly before his Emma, his niece, had died.

He could still see the gun pointed at his face outside the D.C. metro station so long ago. Behind it, the fierce, determined face of the daughter of the couple he'd nearly conned out of their life savings. Shame flooded through him like a reactor core melting down. He slept with Katie's mother; then he had convinced the couple to invest thirty thousand dollars. Katie's parents were going to give him thirty grand in exchange for a promise that their money would return to them threefold in a matter of weeks. A little-known tax rebate for an investment in alternate energies. A total scam. It was everything they had. And Katie had sniffed it out, protecting her family from financial ruin. He wondered if they ever learned that their teenaged daughter had saved them.

He'd left her there crying, making his way into the darkness, even remembering the fog swirling around them during their showdown. He had walked home, weeping as he did so. He went up to his third-floor apartment and drained a bottle of average bourbon. Right from the bottle. He smoked a pack of cigarettes. Then he threw up all over the kitchen floor and passed out on the sofa.

Katie Stone.

He had seen her once since that rendezvous at the Metro station. About a year ago, at the Market. He was not surprised to see her, to discover that she had survived the Pulse. He kept his distance from her, not wanting her to spot him. Because she would recognize him instantly; his face was undoubtedly burned on her brain. For a moment, he considered approaching her and apologizing. But he decided against it. It would have sounded so stupid.

Why did people ever apologize? It was a pointless act. What possible good would it do now? The damage had been done. From the sound of it, he had ruined this woman's life. Fortunately for Jack, the apocalypse had come along as an intervening act and blown whatever was left of this woman's life straight to hell.

The thin walls of the tent closed in around him; he wasn't normally claustrophobic, but sitting here, working through the various detonations in his life, it felt as small as it ever had. It was as if this place had become his entire world. In a way, it had been. Promise was his whole world; he had given himself over to it entirely. He had nearly died for it several times. But was this it? Was this how and where he would spend his whole life?

Molly.

There had been a void in his life all these years. He tried to pretend it wasn't there, but it always was, almost out of view but not quite. In the periphery. The sense that something had been missing from his life. He told himself it was something he couldn't put his finger on it, but that wasn't entirely true. He just didn't want to put his finger on it. It would be an admission that there was something he had wanted, something to fill that void.

But knowing you wanted something brought its own set of challenges and threats. Failing to achieve that goal would be the ultimate tragedy. Better to keep that thing in his head, in his mind, where it remained perfect and unspoiled. He never wanted his love for Molly to feel spoilage, to be touched by the tedium of life, first chewing away at its edges before annihilating it.

He put on his heavy parka and slipped outside into the night. It was extremely cold, the air dry and hard, filling his lungs with a frigid burn. At least it wasn't snowing. Snow was such an unrelenting pain in the ass. He wondered how many people were still living in the northern climes; winters in the upper plains and the northeast would be unbearable. Life was hard enough. There was no need to add degrees of difficulty.

A flood of stars pricked tiny pinholes in the black sky overhead. The walk helped. Out here in the big open, surrounded by sky and trees, breathing in the cold, clean air, his problems didn't seem as big or as intimidating. At the northern edge of Promise, the land came to a point before a large stretch of pines. The cold air was sharp with the smell of a Christmas tree lot. In a flash, he was transported back to his childhood, the Playstation video game console he'd gotten when he was ten years old. It was the greatest Christmas gift he'd ever gotten. His mother had worked extra shifts to squirrel away extra cash to buy the console. Nothing had ever come close. It reminded him of a time when his life was pure and easy.

Before his parents had split for good, one summer his mother had packed him and Lucy up and moved them to the farmhouse in Goochland County. They had left in that narrow space between their dismissal from Vacation Bible School and his father's return from the garage he owned. She had let them bring one item each. Of course, he had carefully packed the game console and his three game discs into his backpack. He held it close in the back seat of his mother's 1989 Toyota Tercel, stinking of fast food and cigarettes, as she drove them to their new life, the car silent as a tomb. Lucy did not say a word during the drive, indifferent to the sudden move. He didn't know if he would ever again see the only home he had ever known. They had come back a month later, his father ripe with promises that things would be different.

The memory faded as he made his way back toward camp, its hold over him directly proportional to his distance from the tree line. The connection between memory and the olfactory sense was bizarrely powerful. Even the smell of the pine had evinced other smells from his childhood. His mother's perfume, the particular spice of his father's cheap whiskey.

It was extremely quiet as he neared the center of the village. His favorite time of night, when the world slept and kept itself out of trouble. A sleeping baby was an angel. Same with their world. His return trip would carry him past the clinic; perhaps Lucy would be up. He could keep her company. As he neared the trailer, a flash of movement in the clinic window caught his eye. He froze, his instincts on alert. The full moon shone through the window on the far side of the building. Another shimmer of movement. A flutter of suspicion and concern rippled through him. Lucy was on duty tonight. He was getting to the age where he needed reading glasses, but his distance vision was as sharp as ever.

The clinic was technically open twenty-four hours a day, as injury and illness knew no timetable. Lucy had several people on night duty. The nursing staff rotated overnight shifts to monitor the patients or do intake. If needed, they could wake Terri or Lucy up to come to the clinic. It wasn't a perfect system, but it worked well enough, and it gave Lucy and Terri most of their nights to sleep.

The clinic was usually quiet at this hour, but occasionally, patients needed care, the shimmer of lantern light visible throughout the camp. Most nights, though, the trailer was dark and quiet. Rest was an extremely important part of care. Jack drew closer to the trailer, approaching the window on the side where Solomon was convalescing.

When he was about a hundred yards short, the door of the trailer opened slowly, as though whoever was behind it was anxious to remain stealthy. The figure emerged from the trailer and continued moving north, back toward the cottages. It was a man, but in the dark, Jack couldn't tell who it was. Average height, average build.

Then Jack noticed something odd. It was completely dark inside the trailer. If a patient was just leaving, then Lucy would likely still be awake, using a candle to light her way. Suspicion tickled Jack's gut. Then the individual stopped just on the far side of a large oak tree near the center of Promise's midway. He glanced around furtively and then broke into a jog, looking back as he did so.

That, too, Jack found suspicious. From this distance, Jack could not identify the person. He was reasonably sure it was a man, but even that wasn't entirely certain. Jack accelerated into a jog without realizing it. Even as he processed the oddity of this late-night clinic traffic, his legs were starting to pump underneath him. He broke into a run, cutting his eyes to the south, in the direction the man had gone. The man had disappeared from view, toward the direction of the barracks.

He paused once more. The night was silent. Nothing moved. The tickle in Jack's gut had become more pronounced. At first glance, he shouldn't have been suspicious; however, he had spent years being trained to be suspicious. It was a weapon in his toolbox. They had drilled it in him in the Army. Always trust your gut. It was the greatest early-warning system they had ever known.

He recalled an experiment the psych guys had run during his training. Each trainee, blindfolded, would enter a mock-up of a small house they used for practice raids, not knowing whether a second individual had been placed in the house. Left alone in the living room, they had to decide within sixty seconds whether they were alone in the house, based on nothing more than their gut instinct. Seventy-four percent of the time, the trainee correctly guessed whether they were alone in the house.

Trust your gut, his commanding officer had said.

And that's what was happening now. He could head back to his tent, assume that someone had woken up feeling sick and had come to the clinic for a little medicine. Because it happened. Maybe someone had cut their hand. They lived a rural existence, and accidents were common. And maybe he had just missed Lucy extinguishing her light before heading back to sleep on her cot.

But his gut wouldn't let him do that.

He was already on a warlike footing. He curled off the path, coming in through the woods. He wanted to approach it from the back. This course took him through a thin line of trees before it opened up on the glade in which the clinic sat. The back door was closed. The trailer appeared undisturbed. It was pitch black. There was no evidence of any activity inside.

He stepped up to the window. Even at six-foot-three, pushing up on his toes, Jack could just barely peek inside. Nothing. The interior of the trailer was black. It seemed unlikely that if Lucy had been tending to Solomon that calm had fallen so quickly. Unlikely that the overnight person had woken up. Then he heard a soft moan. He primed his ears, listening for it to repeat. A moment later, another moan, louder this time.

He continued west to the corner of the trailer and peeked around the side. Nothing. He moved ahead toward the front of the trailer, keeping his back pressed against the corrugated metal exterior wall. It was hard and cold, even against the heavy jacket he was wearing. Now he had a clear view back to the midway and south toward the residences.

A pit formed in his stomach. If only he had come up a minute earlier. Something bad had happened, of this he was increasingly certain, and it had turned on a mere matter of seconds. Better if he'd been asleep in his tent and had never even had the chance. But this was worse, maddening. The way things turned on dumb luck, a few seconds here and there making a difference between this universe and that parallel one.

The door to the trailer was slightly ajar; the last person through it had not latched it shut. His heart pounding, he gently pulled the door open and listened for anything out of place. Nothing. He climbed the single step leading to the front door, using the door to shield himself as he waited for his eyes to adjust to the inky blackness. The door wasn't heavy and opened easily with a toe. As head of security, he didn't want to contaminate the scene with additional fingerprints. He didn't have a ton of forensic equipment at their disposal in a post-Pulse world, but he could dust for prints. He'd gotten pretty good at fingerprint analysis with practice.

When his vision adjusted, he slipped inside to the main patient bay. The triage area was rectangular, wider than it was long. He tipped his head up and sniffed the air. The aroma of rank, desperate sweat and body odor mixed with the antiseptic smell of Lucy's infection control procedures. Although there were no private rooms, a series of curtains provided some privacy. Two of the beds, the ones closest to the door, were empty. In the corner bed lay Natalia, who was recovering from a nasty stomach bug.

Three beds in the fore, three more at the back. Only two were currently occupied. Solomon and Natalia. Both appeared to be sleeping. But as he drew closer to Solomon's bed, he could tell something was out of place. Solomon's blanket was askew, half of it hanging off the bed.

A figure lay prone on the floor in between Solomon and the door.

"Help me," came a harsh whisper.

Oh no.

Lucy.

6

Jack rushed to Lucy's side, sliding down onto his knees next to her. A pool of blood had puddled underneath her. She was on her back, her left hand grasping her shoulder. Her arm and sleeve were bright with blood, which was seeping through her fingers.

"Luce!" he cried out. "You with me?"

She let out a sharp breath through gritted teeth.

"Knife," she said. "I'm fine. Go check on Solomon."

"What?"

She took another deep breath and let it out slowly.

"I heard a scream," she said. "I saw someone by his bed. When I called out, he turned and charged at me."

"You sure you're okay?"

"Yeah."

But Jack wasn't so sure. Even in the dim light of the trailer, her face looked extremely pale.

"Let me see it," he said.

Her hand was stained red; blood continued to seep

through her fingers. She lifted them away from the wound; blood spilled from the gash. Jack was worried the knife had hit an artery. He guided her hand back to the wound, pressing it firmly to slow down the bleeding.

"Seriously," she said. "Go check on Solomon."

Jack glanced back over his shoulder. Nothing stirred but for Lucy's shallow breathing. No such sounds emanated from Solomon's bed. He took another tentative step toward Solomon, his head on a swivel. But Jack was alone. Whatever this was, it had already happened.

Then he reached Solomon's bedside. He was on his back, slightly out of place. His head was hanging over the side of the bed. His throat had been slashed. His left arm dangled below it. Jack closed his eyes and sighed. He placed a hand on Solomon's chest, but it was still. His eyes were open, fixed sightlessly on the ceiling. Moonlight streaming through the east-facing window illuminated smears of blood at his nostrils and the corners of his mouth. His pillow lay limply by his head; it bore streaks of blood.

Solomon was dead.

He returned to Lucy's side. The bleeding had slowed, but it had not stopped.

"Tell me what to do," he said. "How do I fix this?"

"We have to stop the bleeding."

"How?"

"We need a tourniquet."

"Isn't that dangerous?"

"Not as dangerous as me bleeding out on the floor."

Good point.

He slid his arms under her legs and back and lifted her onto the bed. Then he stacked a pile of pillows at her feet; with a pained grunt, she lifted her legs onto the pile. He checked her wound again. It was still bleeding heavily.

"How are we doing, Luce?"

"Damn, this hurts," she grunted.

He stood up and looked around the room. He grabbed a sheet from the closest bed and pulled it to the floor. Then he tore a long strip off to wrap around Lucy's wound. The blood flow slowed.

"Who did this?" he asked, keeping an eye on her grievous wound.

"I don't know," she said. "I didn't get a look at his face."

"I'm gonna get Terri in here. Keep that pressure on there."

He bolted from the clinic, making a beeline for Terri's cottage. He burst through the door, not worrying about waking anyone up. There was a killer on the loose and his sister was possibly bleeding to death. Terri's unit was in the corner, near the back. Fortunately, Jack knew the layout of these cottages by heart. He banged on the wall to her unit.

"Terri!"

She was a light sleeper and quickly came to.

"What is it?" she asked, sliding out of bed, reaching for a jacket. She'd been around long enough to know that trouble was brewing, and her body reacted almost automatically.

"Get to the clinic," he said. "Lucy's been stabbed. Solomon's dead. That's all I know right now."

As Terri got herself together, Jack raced back through the cottage and out the door, sprinting back toward the clinic, working up a plan of attack. The killer had disappeared into the darkness. Jack studied the ground around the clinic. To Jack's fortune, moonlight carved a silvery path for him to follow, illuminating the faintest of footprints in the soft ground.

He ran hard for fifty yards, hoping the footprints would carry him to his quarry, but they quickly faded into nothingness. The trail went cold at a T intersection leading toward a series of residence cottages. He paused, breathing hard. He kicked at the dirt before turning back for the clinic. Although Lucy was currently unable to identify her attacker, details of the attack might come back to her in the coming hours.

Terri was already at the clinic, tending to Lucy when Jack returned. She was busy working to stitch the deep laceration closed.

"How is she?" he asked.

"The bleeding is slowing down," she said. "Not as much as I would like, but I don't think it hit an artery. Probably got some nerve and tissue damage in there too. It'll take me a while to get it stitched up."

He took Lucy's good hand and squeezed it.

"What the hell happened?" Terri asked.

"I was out for a walk," Jack said. "When I was up on the north end, I saw someone come out of the trailer. I came inside and found her on the floor."

"Jesus," Terri said, her voice barely a whisper.

Jack ran his fingers through his hair as he tried to process the situation.

"We need to find out who did this. And why."

7

Thirty-six hours later, Jack still did not know who was behind the attack on Solomon and Lucy. He had not slept and yet he felt wide awake, alert. This wouldn't last, of course, and soon he would need to fill these crevices of fatigue with genuine sleep. But for now, he was content to check on Lucy and sit with her as she ate her breakfast.

When she finished eating, Terri tended to her wounds. As a trained medical professional, she was the best and worst kind of patient. The good news was that she could direct Terri on how to suture and dress her wound. The bad news was that she did. Terri had sewn up multiple residents of Promise over the years and was quite proficient at it. But she kept quiet as Lucy kept telling her how close to knit the stitches, where to pull, where to tug.

The thought of losing Lucy was too much to bear. She was all he had left. He tried to avoid going down that dark road about what might have been, but he could not help it. Jack was a pessimistic person. He had always prepared for the worst, and the world had not disappointed him. Forget hoping for the best. His thoughts were already focused on what might go wrong with Lucy's recovery. Infection, septic shock, miscarriage, death. If she made it through this, all the better. But he wasn't going to count on it.

Terri was changing her dressings, keeping the wound clean. Now that the risk of lethal blood loss had subsided, infection was the biggest concern. A wound that large and deep would be a prime target for dangerous bacteria.

Antibiotics had largely disappeared from the landscape in the last couple of years. Lucy and Terri had worked hard to develop a suitable alternative. Over time, they had developed a regimen that included echinacea, coconut oil, and lavender. Lucy had found that coconut oil had been most effective; a trip to the library had revealed that the oil's lauric acid contained antibiotic properties. They packed wounds with the oil, and it worked more often than it didn't. Not always, as nothing would be as good as some of the old penicillin and its progeny, but that was difficult to manufacture at scale.

Lucy was still in a lot of pain. The knife had sliced through several ligaments, making it virtually impossible for her to lift her arm over her head. Time would tell whether the ligament was only partially bisected and might eventually heal. If not, she would have radically reduced motility going forward. She was, of course, worried about the pregnancy. She had lost a decent amount of blood in the attack, and there was no way to know how that would affect the fetus.

While Terri worked, Jack glanced across the room

toward Solomon's empty bed, stripped of the blood-soaked mattress and sheets. They had moved Solomon's body from the clinic and buried it unceremoniously in the woods. Jack wasn't crazy about disturbing the crime scene, but the risk of contagion was too great. Even in the cold, flies had begun massing near the body. The smell of disinfectant was sharp, which was not unusual. But the place felt different. It felt like a crime scene.

Promise was buzzing with gossip and rumor in the wake of Solomon's murder. Word of the nighttime attack had spread quickly at breakfast, bringing out the looky-loos. A small crowd had formed about fifty feet clear of the clinic building, but they had complied with Jack's request to stay away from the clinic. The residents of Promise may not have cared much about Solomon himself, but they did care very much that a brutal murder had occurred while they slept a few yards away.

It was not a reflection on Solomon. Jack understood that at a rational level. Even if it distressed him, he couldn't begrudge them for considering their own well-being first. They all had a lot on their plates. And yet, this was his life, his past, part of the story of Jack. He felt guilty thinking that. All of them had their stories that predated the Pulse. Lost loves, lost family, lost friends, lost lives. He was no different than anyone else.

Although few were mourning the passing of Solomon, a man no one, save Lucy and Jack, had even known, an undercurrent of anxiety was rippling through the populace. Jack did not know which prospect was worse – that the killer was local or that an intruder had slipped into Promise to kill Solomon. And if an outsider had killed Solomon, that meant he'd been followed.

At this point, Jack wasn't sure what to think. He doubted that Solomon's murder had been random. It stretched the limits of credulity that someone – local or otherwise – had killed him just for kicks on the very day he disclosed his dark secret. It was possible, of course, the way it was possible that a meteor might crash through the atmosphere sometime today and put them all out of their misery, but it wasn't within the realm of reasonable probability.

So his working assumption was that someone had targeted Solomon. Someone had killed him for what he knew. With respect to turning the power back on, Jack only knew what Solomon had seen fit to share with him. Anything he hadn't disclosed he had taken to his grave.

But why?

Why would someone kill Solomon?

That's what he would need to find out.

He did not have much experience in criminal investigation. He did take the introductory course that all military police officers went through as part of his training. Some of the lessons lingered in his mind, two decades later. One lesson stood out in sharp relief: to preserve the scene as carefully as possible. Perpetrators always left tantalizing clues behind. Locard's exchange principle provided that a criminal always brought something with him to a crime scene and, conversely, always left with something.

Yellow crime scene tape he had scavenged from a nearby Sheriff's office hung limply around Solomon's bed, leaving the scene as undisturbed as possible. Without cameras to record the scene, he carefully logged every item in the clinic in a notebook. He also dusted for fingerprints, using an old amateur kit he'd found at a surplus store a couple of years earlier. That was more for show. Identifying a suspect through prints would be impractical guesswork. That said, it might spook the killer, elicit some kind of response, or more hopefully, a mistake that revealed his identity.

Jack's chief deputy was a man named Bode; the name suited him perfectly. Perpetually tan, even in winter, long tangled brown hair that hung to his shoulders. A stereotypical beach bum. But he wasn't that at all. People assumed it, but he didn't even like the beach. He was a quiet, unassuming man. He liked going on supply runs; he had a knack for finding caches of medicines, canned goods, even weapons. He was out and about looking for witnesses.

It was mid-morning. The sun had risen but heavy cloud cover left the morning ensconced in gloom. It was dank, a heavy, damp cold that sat on you and did not look like the skies would clear soon. If anything, snow was in the offing. The air had that cold, sharp smell of moisture ahead. It was his favorite weather for sleeping. Deep cold, clear, calm night, the sky black but for the diamond dust of billions of stars scattered across the heavens. He slept in layers, thermal underwear and flannel pajamas and long sleeves and sweatshirts under heavy comforters he'd sourced over the years.

Solomon was dead. It was difficult to believe. Dropped from the heavens and then taken away just as quickly. He recalled a night out with Molly and Solomon. She had just completed her dissertation defense. A night to celebrate. Solomon was still married to his then-wife Georgane at the time; Molly had told him they were having problems, but that night, it was like old times. They were laughing and touching each other's arms, still the happy couple. They had split not long after.

They had drinks and dinner at the Palm, a well-known steakhouse. It was one of those nights where the food was delicious, the drinks just strong enough, the company easy and fun. He and Molly were in the heady early days of their relationship. When everything was clicking and they spent as much time undressed as they did clothed. They took frequent trips when they had time. One weekend, they had flown to Rome just because they could.

It was hard to square that memory with the present, the end of the story that had been Solomon Tigner. Trekking through the cold and the snow in their post-apocalyptic world, desperate to find Jack and deliver a final message to Jack only to be murdered in his hospital bed. He was such a bright guy, able to talk about his work in a way that was approachable for the layman. He loved science and wanted everyone around him to love it too.

But mostly Jack thought about Molly.

Ever since he'd first seen Solomon sitting in that bed in the clinic, Molly was not far from his mind. Solomon's reappearance had fired up that part of Jack's brain, an old film reel stuffed deep in his subconscious, suddenly given a new run in his mind. From the first time he'd met Molly, like he'd been waiting his whole life for her, everything pointing toward that night tending bar so he could be there when she'd arrived.

He often looked back on the party. There was nothing special about that night. If anything, it was a poor use of his time and his skills. If he'd put up any fuss, the CO probably would've backed off, as he wouldn't want a complaint filed. Not that Jack would've filed a complaint. Military men dealt with a lot of shit from the day they signed on the dotted line, turning their lives over to the U.S. military. And he hadn't even been Lt. Commander Finney's first choice. He'd hired a real bartender, but the guy had called out sick at the last second, leaving him scrambling for help.

At the other end of that continuum, the Point B to the party's Point A, had been Solomon's violent and bloody end here in their little clinic.

And the identity of the killer remained elusive. For the time being, he had no suspects. Jack himself might fall under suspicion; after all, he was the only person who had known Solomon. Only God knew what long-dormant motivations might have been percolating in the depths of his mind.

Solomon was dead. Gone. And gone with him was whatever knowledge he had yet to share about Molly and the Pulse. He could only hope that there wasn't more he had carried to the grave.

It was weird. Solomon had been out of sight, out of mind for more than a decade; then he had burst into their lives like a meteor striking the earth and then just like that, he was gone again, this time for good. It had all happened so quickly, he hadn't had time to consider whether he was even sad. Before his surprise appearance in the snow three days ago, Solomon's life and his death would have meant nothing to him. Solomon hadn't just been dead to Jack. He'd been nothing to Jack.

But now. Now. Now he was special, not because of who he was, but because of the information in his skull.

A mind that had given up its last secret. And yet he did feel sadness. Sadness that another link to his past had been broken. A link to Molly.

"How's it looking?" he asked Terri as she finished up her work.

"Not bad, all things considered," she replied. "She's lucky. It could've been a lot worse. We'll have to keep a close eye on it, make sure there's no infection. I've got it pretty cleaned out. Lucy talked me through that part, but don't tell her that."

"Thanks for everything," he said.

"No thanks necessary," replied Terri. "She's like a sister to me."

Jack hugged her. It caught Terri off guard, but she returned the embrace.

"I'm gonna get some fresh air and a bite to eat."

Jack nodded.

"How are you feeling?" he asked his sister after Terri had left.

She smiled, but it looked forced.

"I have felt better," she said.

She had refused painkillers, not wanting to risk harm to the pregnancy. Terri told her that controlling the pain would reduce stress on the baby, but Lucy would have none of it. So it would be a rough couple of days as the pain peaked before subsiding. Jack admired his sister's resolve.

"Back to interrogate the prime witness?" she teased.

"I hate to put you through this," he said.

Eventually, his sister would pay an emotional price for enduring the attack. This would be different from the generalized trauma they'd all experienced since the

Pulse. No, this had been savage butchery directed at her specifically. She was lucky to be alive; the downside was that she would relive the attack for months if not years to come.

"Any other details coming back to you?"

"I wish they had," she said.

"Do you mind walking me through it again?"

"Sure," she said. "I was asleep and heard a scream. I thought maybe Solomon was having a nightmare or maybe it was some internal injury we hadn't picked up yet. I got out of bed and stepped into the clinic. I was still half asleep, so I didn't process what I was seeing right away."

She paused for a moment as she relived the horror of what came next.

"The moon was shining in through there," she said, pointing toward the western window, "and I saw the silhouette of a man standing over Solomon's bed. His arm came down in a stabbing motion two or three times. I must have gasped because he got startled and cried out."

She held a fist to her mouth, tapping her lips slowly. Tears welled up in her eyes.

"He came right at me," she said. "I didn't know what to do, so I just held my ground. I didn't want to turn my back on him. He just came in slashing at me."

She closed her eyes again as the memory unspooled in her mind.

Then her eyes flashed open wide.

"I think I scratched him before the knife got me."

Jack's body buzzed with excitement. He took a breath, not wanting to rush her and cloud her recall of the moment.

"Where?"

She scoffed with disgust.

"Wish I'd cut his damn jugular," she said. "But I got him around his neck or jawline."

"Did you draw blood?"

She studied her fingernails. Her hands still bore some bloodstains; most of it was her own.

"Maybe," she said. "I can't be sure. I definitely got nails in the skin. Two of them broke off."

She showed him her right hand as though he might not have believed her. Sure enough, the nails on the index and middle fingers had been torn away. This was good news. If the killer was still in Promise, he might be sporting the scars of his encounter with Lucy. He would need to start assessments of the men in Promise immediately. With every passing minute, any scratch marks Lucy had left would be healing.

There was no time to lose.

8

They kept a handwritten census in the clinic. Terri had been responsible for maintaining it these last few years. She was good at it, thorough, and it was about as complete a list as one could hope for. There were one hundred and ninety-eight people currently living in Promise. One hundred and ten men, eighty-seven women, and one who identified as non-binary. Of these, forty-seven were under the age of eighteen. Most of the kids lived with their parents, but a few, like Norah, had been orphaned in the disaster.

Jack spent the evening developing a plan. Almost everyone ate dinner together in the cafeteria. That would probably be the way to go. Wait until everyone was in their seats and then announce a very brief interruption of their meal. The way Jack saw it, only one person would have any objection.

Jack quietly recruited a handful of volunteers to check the others for scratch marks, after ensuring they were not sporting the aftereffects of a run-in with Lucy's nails. He divided the list evenly, with each person taking about thirty names. He felt they could safely eliminate the younger kids from the list. Anyone over the age of thirteen, though, would need to be examined.

Dinner was at least an hour away. Jack wanted to explore the clinic a bit more in the dead time between now and then, look for any clues the killer may have left behind. When he returned to the clinic that afternoon, Lucy was asleep. Terri had been working on cleaning the copious amounts of blood from the scene. Solomon's bed had been stripped, the sheets burned. This was a safety precaution. Blood-soaked sheets could attract bears to Promise. Predators had flourished in the post-Pulse years and attacks were common.

"How goes it, Terri?"

"Just doing the Lord's work here," she replied a bit sardonically.

He felt awkward.

"I'm just teasing," she said. "By the way, I never got a chance to say I'm sorry about your friend."

"Yeah, thanks," Jack replied. "He was an interesting guy."

"I'm just glad Lucy's okay."

"Me, too."

"She does a lot for this community."

Jack nodded in agreement.

"That she does."

"Any idea who did this yet?"

"Working on it," he said. "That's why I'm here, actually. Solomon had a backpack with him when he arrived, right?"

"Yeah," she said. She nodded toward the storage

room. "It's in there. I don't think anyone's touched it since he showed up."

Lucy had inventoried Solomon's belongings when he arrived. A backpack, an unloaded pistol, a heavy winter coat, a scarf, a pair of winter gloves, and a hat. No one had inventoried the contents of the backpack. Perhaps there was more to learn inside.

"I'm gonna check it out," he said.

The office was small but cozy. In the corner was a well-worn cot where Lucy and Terri had spent countless nights on shift. In the other corner, closest to the door, was a file cabinet. Here Lucy kept medical records on each of Promise's residents. Only Lucy and Terri had access to the cabinet's locked drawers.

The sun shone through the office window, filling the small room with warm golden light. Although it was quite chilly out today, it was remarkably comfortable inside the room. Jack sat on the cot and set the backpack next to him. It was old and beaten down. The straps were frayed and the zippers were broken on several of the pockets. It had been the man's faithful companion these past five years, now left behind like a dog that has outlived its owner.

He had brought a pad of paper and a pencil and itemized each find as he worked.

He unzipped the largest pocket. Inside was an empty water canteen and a plastic baggie with a strip of dried beef and a small piece of hard flatbread. Two paperback novels and a pair of binoculars. A first-aid kit. Jack opened the small plastic box, but there was little of value. A few bandages and a couple of unmarked pills. He moved on to the second pocket, where he found his first surprise.

It was an old photograph of Solomon and Molly, one that made him gasp. They were on a beach together, the ocean behind them blue and glassy. Long shadows behind them stretched down to the water's edge. In that classic selfie pose, Solomon's arm extended toward the camera before disappearing from view. Molly's arm was wrapped around Solomon's head and she was kissing him on the cheek.

They had been together.

Reflexively, Jack turned it over, searching for a date inscription. July. About ten months before the Pulse. This was not a subject they had broached before Solomon's death. Jack felt extremely uncomfortable, although he did not know why. He and Molly had gone their separate ways years earlier. He had no more right to the ins and outs of her private life than those of a stranger on the bus.

He set the picture aside and continued his examination of the backpack. Even though his sole motivation was to understand why someone had killed its owner, this exercise suddenly felt invasive and voyeuristic. He found a few more sundry items in this pocket, including a pack of chewing gum and a box of waterproof matches.

He moved to the third and final pocket. It contained a single item, secured in a small plastic baggie rolled up tightly and bound with a rubber band. He removed the rubber band, letting the baggie unfurl. Inside was a flash drive. He held the small device, about the size of a cigarette lighter, between his fingers.

A strange token for Solomon to carry across the dark wastelands of their world. Was it related to his claim about turning the lights back on? Or was it something more mundane, a relic, a memento from a world gone by?

Jack repacked the backpack, double-checking his written inventory as he did so.

Then he slid the flash drive into the pocket of his jeans.

JACK WAITED until dinner was in full swing. The dining hall was large, able to hold four hundred people, so even with a full house, it seemed a bit empty. It was one of the happier places in Promise. Mealtime brought them together as a community, cutting across the sociopolitical debates that always seemed close to fracturing the group.

Potato soup was on the menu tonight. Heavy on the soup, light on the potatoes. The next two months would be the tightest on the calendar as the fruits of the summer and fall harvests ran dry. The food supply was tightly guarded. This year would be particularly tough, as the Haven had taken much of their summer harvest as tribute. Donations from other communities had helped, given to Promise as thanks for their efforts in defeating the Haven.

Even before Solomon's arrival, Jack had already been thinking about the future that awaited them. They could not afford to let another strongman like Simon Conway rise to power. The time was coming to consider stronger bonds between the various communities. Promise's primary trading partner, the all-female community led by Sister Julienne, was particularly interested in such an idea.

But that was for another time. Tonight, Jack was focused on finding Solomon's killer. He scanned the crowd, studying the faces that had become so familiar to him over the years. Strange to think that a killer was likely among them. Perhaps someone he was friends with, had raised a glass with.

He stood up and tapped a spoon against his glass. The tinkling echoed in the large space and immediately cut through the muted chitchat in the dining hall. He tapped the glass until the conversation died away. When he had everyone's attention, he cleared his throat and set his spoon down in his bowl. His hand-selected group of inspectors had the exits covered in case someone decided to run. They had conducted a stealthy roll call. All but nine residents were present. Jack would check them later that evening.

"Sorry to bother everyone during their dinner," he said, his voice echoing. "I know the evening meal is a high point of the day and a chance to get away from the hard work that's part of living in Promise."

The crowd was silent but for a few sniffles and clearing of throats. He looked out across their faces, dirty, gaunt, tired, pale. There were a few who didn't pull their weight, but these were mostly hardworking people who did their best to keep the community afloat. Once upon a time, they had been teachers and lawyers and stay-at-home moms and engineers and mechanics. Now post-apocalyptic warriors. They had given so much to get them this far; often he wondered how much they had left in the tank. Everything was difficult all the time.

"There's been an important development in the investigation," he said. "And I'm asking for your help tonight."

The room fell completely silent.

"These four gentlemen are going to come around the room and examine each of you," Jack said, remaining deliberately vague. "This will not be invasive."

Now to lay the trap.

"Lucy scratched the killer on the arm as he fled," Jack said. "She drew blood."

A ripple of murmuring washed across the room. The killer might be right here in the room with them!

"If you'll each pull up the sleeve of your right arm," he said. "We'll be done in just a few minutes."

The four inspectors spread out to the corners of the occupied tables and began working their way in. No one raised a fuss; each resident dutifully rolled up a sleeve, proudly showing evidence of their innocence, unaware that the inspectors were actually eyeing each of their necks.

Ten minutes later, the inspections were complete. Jack accompanied the four men to the corner of the cafeteria, keeping an eye on the crowd, which sat in stunned silence.

"Anything?" Jack whispered.

Three of the men shook their heads. Paul Poytress glanced back at the crowd before leaning in close to Jack.

"Danny Bowen's wearing a turtleneck," Paul said. "Can't say I've ever seen him wearing one. Don't swear me to that though. It just looked weird on him."

"Anyone else with their necks covered?"

He waited for the men to reply. One at a time, they shook their heads.

Jack scratched the stubble on his chin as he considered the findings of this very *ad hoc* committee. Accusing a man of murder was a hell of a thing. He considered the evidence they had before them. First, Solomon's murder had almost certainly not been random. Second, they did not know for certain that the killer was from Promise. But it seemed doubtful that the killer was *not* local. Too many unlikely things would have to be true. That the killer had tracked Solomon all the way to Promise without striking before he got here. He could have killed him anywhere. That he would have spent enough time here to locate the medical clinic without his presence being noted. Promise just wasn't that big. That he would have been here long enough to learn the community's patterns.

Now then.

Danny Bowen.

Jack didn't care for Danny. He was a loudmouth, a jackass, the kind of guy who liked to hear himself talk, who thought he knew better than everyone else. He worked just hard enough to stay out of trouble. He was pretty handy, able to fix just about anything when he put his mind to it. His previous claim to infamy had come months ago. He'd been on guard duty when a captive from the Haven had escaped, killing another guard, and precipitating their deadly conflict with the Haven. People had never quite forgiven him for his lapse.

"We're gonna stay quiet for now," Jack said. "Let's keep an eye on Danny, see how he acts for the rest of the meal."

The others nodded.

9

Jack returned to his seat at the table to finish his dinner. As he ate, he watched Danny from the corner of his eye, careful not to make eye contact. Danny kept his focus on his food and did not engage in any chit-chat with his seat neighbors. He ate quickly, finishing before anyone else. He got up to return his tray, a bit of urgency in his step.

He looked over his shoulder, briefly, seeking out Jack, making eye contact, and then bolted out the door.

Jack gestured to his cohorts, directing them to fall in line as he followed Danny outside. The sudden burst of activity resonated with the crowd and the dining hall fell silent.

"Jack, your tray," a meek voice called out behind him.

He ignored it, accelerating to a jog as Danny exited the dining hall. When Jack made it outside, Danny was halfway across the grounds, back toward the residences.

"Danny!" Jack called out.

Danny stopped, his shoulders heaving up and down

from the small bit of exertion. He turned around slowly, clockwise toward Jack. He fumbled with something in his pocket as he rotated. Jack bolted toward him, suddenly realizing that Danny was reaching for a gun.

"Gun!"

The others scattered for cover while Jack charged at Danny, thinking he could reach Danny before the man fired. He closed the distance between them quickly. Jack's speed startled Danny, and he lost his grip on his weapon. The gun bounded away from him, landing with a thud on the ground. Jack picked up his pace, desperate to close the gap between them before Danny could recover the weapon.

Ten yards.

Danny dove toward the ground, his gaze fixed on a black lump sitting atop the remains of the previous week's snowfall.

Five yards.

Danny reached for the gun.

Jack dove, laid out in full, his arms outstretched like a receiver desperate to corral a ball just beyond his reach, his fingers searching, searching for the gun.

Their bodies collided.

Danny had a better grip on the weapon, but Jack was stronger. That said, the longer it took him to get the gun from him, the better the chance that Danny would squeeze off a shot. And at this range, he wasn't likely to miss. Behind them, a commotion had erupted as folks began pouring out of the dining hall, aware that something was afoot.

Jack swung a leg over Danny's back and snaked his arm under Danny's, preventing him from getting up on his knees, getting the leverage he sought. Then he used his size advantage to drive Danny back toward the ground. Danny struggled to get purchase on the weapon. Jack slammed his forearm into the back of Danny's head, eliciting a grunt of pain. He threw a second forearm shiver and then a third. But then Danny got high on Jack's chest; it gave him just enough wriggle room to break the restraint.

Danny scampered to his feet and broke into a run. Jack accelerated as well. Danny was heavyset and did not exercise much, if at all; however, he was now a cornered animal, and cornered animals could react in dangerous ways. Danny cut past the cottages, toward the southern bank of the lake. Jack pushed himself to his absolute limit, as far as his body would allow.

He disappeared into the alleys between two residence cabins, moving as stealthily as an elephant. His desperate flight had him gasping for air leaving an auditory trail for Jack to follow. He cut east briefly before turning north again. He crashed against a woodpile, stumbling but keeping his feet underneath him. He cleared the alley, breaking free of its shadows. Ahead lay a large grassy glade leading to the water's edge.

A moment later, his quarry came into view.

When he was about twenty yards shy of his target, he stepped on a large branch along the path; it snapped underfoot. In the silence of the night, it sounded like a gunshot and alerted the man to his presence. Then Danny cut sharply to his left and bolted around the lake's western bank, seeking cover in a line of trees flanking that side.

Jack followed suit, cutting behind a row of pines and

moving northwest. He had to slow down here. The thicker brush and exposed roots of the trees were harder to navigate, but he continued eating into the gap between them. Danny pushed deeper into the trees, giving up all pretense of stealth now. His ragged breathing was audible in the night air. The sounds of a desperate man.

The terrain rose slightly here, running parallel to the trail that the man was now on. Jack had the high ground. He did a few quick calculations before veering toward the embankment and crashing down toward Danny. He was just feet away now and no longer needed to conceal his presence. He lowered his shoulder and drove hard into the man's left flank. Jack's momentum kept them moving off the trail and down another embankment.

Danny swung out wildly as they careened down the hill. His runaway fist collided solidly with Jack's jaw, dazing him a bit and causing him to loosen his grip around the man's midsection. But he recovered quickly, delivering a sharp elbow to Danny's gut. Danny grunted and exhaled sharply, making a bizarre sound like a wounded animal. Jack slipped his arm around the man's neck and pulled him close, cutting off his windpipe. Jack was the larger man and now had the upper hand. Danny flailed a bit, his hands slapping at Jack's face behind him, but the battle was over.

"Settle down," Jack hissed. "Or I'll kill you."

Danny understood the battle was over. His arms dropped to his side and his flailings eased. The others had caught up and surrounded Jack and his prisoner.

"No funny business, okay?" Jack said.

Danny nodded. Jack held the man's arm in an armbar

as they rose off the ground together, covered in mud and dead leaves.

"Danny, it's over."

Another grunt from the man, but this one was more of surrender.

"Are we gonna be calm?" Jack asked.

He glanced up. A large crowd had formed, making a semicircle around them, two and three deep. A few people carried lanterns or candles, throwing rippling light over the scene.

"Yeah," Danny replied. "Yeah."

"Stand up," Jack said.

Jack eased his weight off the man and pushed himself to his feet. Danny followed gingerly, stood before the group, massaging the back of his head. Jack was breathing heavily, his heart racing. Sweat poured into his eyes despite the nighttime chill.

"Someone hand me a light," he said, reaching his hand out to the crowd.

With a lantern in hand, he turned his attention back to Danny.

"Pull down your turtleneck."

Danny cut his eyes to the ground. He clicked his tongue against his cheek.

"Now."

He reached tentatively for the fabric. Then he pulled it down and away from his neck.

Three deep scratches were carved into the side of his neck. Blood had dried around the edges of the lacerations. Jack was vibrating with rage; it took all his willpower not to snap this man's neck. What he had done to Solomon was bad enough, but he had nearly taken out his sister and her unborn child to boot. His own flesh and blood. His family. No further investigation was necessary. They had found their man.

Bode stepped forward from the crowd, sensing Jack needed some backup.

"Let's go, Danny," Bode said. He fell in beside the killer, gently took his elbow and escorted him off the stage.

He still couldn't believe Danny had killed Solomon.

Danny Bowen.

Why in the hell had he done it?

This question rattled around his head like a loose rock in his shoe as the crowd dissipated. People retreated to the fire pits for a bit of fellowship. They didn't linger. The days were long and now that the mystery of the attack had been solved, they could get back to their normal lives. People worked too hard to get too wrapped up in things that didn't affect them directly. Besides, someone would share the dirt before too long. Eventually, they would all know. Nothing remained secret.

DANNY SPENT the night in Promise's holding cell. Jack himself did not sleep a wink. He stayed up, working by candlelight, scribbling out dozens of questions he wanted to ask Danny on a legal pad. Jack and Bode arrived to question him the next morning.

He was lying on his cot when they arrived. He sat up with a contented sigh as Bode unlocked the cell and the two men entered, each carrying a folding chair that they kept in the corridor outside the cell.

Danny had come to Promise in its early days. He had helped with the construction of their irrigation and sanitation systems. He may not have been the most educated man in Promise, but he had been an extremely valuable asset to the community. And this was such a waste. Crime was uncommon in Promise. Petty theft and drunken brawls were usually the order of the day. There had been one sexual assault a year earlier; the perpetrator, a middle-aged man named Steve, had slipped away from Promise in the middle of the night as Jack had come to arrest him. That one still stung him. The victim, a young woman in her early twenties, had struggled with the decision to come forward, and when she did, someone had tipped him off, sparking his decision to run.

"Morning, Danny," Bode said.

"Hey, Bode," Danny said.

There was no fight in Danny's voice, no defiance. According to the overnight guard, Danny had slept all night, snoring loudly. Perhaps he was relieved they'd caught him. Perhaps he was happy with what he had done and was willing to pay the price for it, whatever that price turned out to be.

Jack and Bode took their seats. They had agreed that Bode would take the lead in the questioning. He was calmer; after all, Lucy wasn't his sister.

"I killed Solomon."

"Yeah, we figured," Bode replied.

"I don't regret what I did."

Jack and Bode exchanged a glance.

"So why don't we start there," Jack said, unable to help himself.

Danny turned and stared directly at Jack.

"Is Lucy okay?" he asked.

A spike of rage pierced Jack. He took a deep breath and let it out slowly.

"No thanks to you."

"I'm sorry about that," he said. "She surprised me and I panicked."

"A few inches the other way and she takes that knife in the throat," Bode said.

Danny let out a shaky sigh.

"Please tell her I am sorry."

"Danny, can we focus?" Bode asked gently.

Jack appreciated Bode's redirection. He was not inclined to give Danny the forgiveness he was seeking for his terrible crime. However, he wanted the man to cooperate; perhaps agreeing to this request would grease the skids.

"Jack, please?"

Jack found the man's sincerity disquieting. As though Lucy's forgiveness was more important than anything else.

Jack nodded.

"I will tell her you said you were sorry."

A thin smile crossed Danny's face.

"But you have to tell us everything."

"Okay."

He cleared his throat. Then he clasped his hands together and set them against his chin.

"I don't want the power to come back on."

Jack's theory was confirmed. This had not been a random killing.

"Why not?"

"Because the world is better this way."

"What way?"

"Quiet. Raw. Pure. As it was meant to be."

This was not an uncommon belief. Apocalypse junkies. The ones who had found more satisfaction in their broken world. They cloaked it in an undying love for the natural world, but as the saying went, some folks just liked to see the world burn.

"I belong to a group called the Shepherds."

The name was unfamiliar to Jack. He glanced over at Bode, who shrugged.

"We are committed to protecting the world in its natural state."

It was weird to hear Danny talk like this. He was a blue-collar guy all the way. Often talked about his blue-collar life before the Pulse. Worked as a handyman, played beer league softball, spent his evenings in a bar, pounding beers and shooting pool before stumbling home and starting the whole thing over the next day. This version of Danny sounded like some latter-day revolutionary.

"That's why you killed Solomon?"

"I am sorry, but we had no choice."

"Did you know who he was?"

"We had a name and physical description," he said.

Danny stifled a chuckle.

"When I heard about this mysterious visitor, I couldn't believe it. Of all the places he could've ended up, it had to be here."

Jack took a moment to process what Danny was saying. Not only had he confessed to killing Solomon, but it was part of some larger plan. Danny was just a cog in a machine.

"What do you know about Solomon's partner?"

"The woman."

The hair on Jack's neck stood up.

"Yes," Jack replied, his jaw quivering with rage.

"They caught her."

"Is she alive?"

"I believe so."

"Where is she?"

"In D.C."

"Where exactly?"

"I don't know."

"Tell us more about the Shepherds," Jack said. "How'd you get wrapped up with them?"

"It was about a year ago, eighteen months," Danny said. "I was at the Market. I got to talking to these guys. I guess they were recruiting. Feeling me out, that kind of thing. After I told them I thought things were better now, they took me in."

"So what the hell are you still doing here?" Jack asked. "Why didn't you go live with your brothers-in-arms? No one's forcing you to be here."

"I haven't qualified yet."

Jack wanted to beat the man's head in, but instead, he closed his eyes and took a deep breath.

"I still don't understand how Solomon and the woman fit into all this," Bode said.

"All I know is this," Danny said. "They'd been looking for them for a long time. A couple weeks ago, the Shepherds got some good intel on their whereabouts. The woman got caught. Solomon made it here. That's all I know."

"Danny, why on Earth would you not want the power

to come back on?" Bode asked. "Do you like living like this?"

"I'm not going back, man."

"Back where?"

And then he had told Jack and Bode his story. At the time of the Pulse, Danny Bowen was three years into a twenty-year stint at Red Onion State Prison for voluntary manslaughter. As he told it, he had been laid off from his job during the Covid-19 pandemic; he had turned to the bottle for solace. One evening, after another fruitless day of job searching, he had stopped off at a bar for a nightcap, something to take the edge off his shitty day. He drank three rum and cokes, very heavy on the rum. On his way out the door, he stumbled across three men harassing a young woman in the alley behind the bar. Danny stepped in, and that was when things had gone to hell. One of the men had taken a swing at Danny. He ducked, returning his own jab. The man took the punch flush on the jaw. The punch itself had done little damage, but he'd lost his balance and fell straight back to the pavement. His head hit the ground with a sickening crunch. The man's skull had fractured, and he had suffered a massive brain bleed. He died the next morning in the hospital.

The man had been the son of a high-powered lawyer, a recent graduate of Vanderbilt, handsome, his whole life ahead of him. The girl from the alley refused to testify, leading to speculation the boy's family had paid her off, and the dead man's two friends told police that Danny had initiated the confrontation. Danny could not afford a lawyer and had to make do with a public defender. The prosecution was looking for a maximum sentence of twenty-five years and Danny, too afraid to take his chances in front of a jury, agreed to a plea deal in which he would serve seven years.

Prison did not agree with Danny Bowen. He contracted hepatitis sharing homemade needles. He survived several severe beatings at the hands of violent inmates. He considered suicide. But then on that magical May afternoon, the entire prison had gone dark. The electronic lock system had failed, leaving the doors as secure as a baby's Halloween candy.

While the prison devolved into a melee of fights, assaults on the guards, and looting, Danny had slowly made his way to the exit. First from D-Block, where he'd been taking a nap. He napped a lot in the afternoons, as he did not sleep much at night. Down through the common area, through central processing and then through the heavy doors into the visitors' lounge. No one paid him any mind.

He walked right out that door like a man who'd finished his sentence. All he needed was a couple of guards to shake his hand. He was free. He didn't know what was behind the utter chaos within and beyond the walls of the prison, but he didn't care. Hours on the run became days. Days turned into weeks and months. No one came looking for him. Then he had found Promise. And thanks to the Pulse, he would never again have to live in a world enclosed by bars and walls.

And he was never going back.

"That's your motive for killing Solomon," Jack said when he was done. "For joining up with these Shepherds."

"You don't know what it was like," Danny said, his

voice quivering. "I can't do it. I can't ever be in a cell again."

Jack's jaw clenched as a wave of rage washed over him. Was Danny delusional? Even if they got the power back on, did he think the Virginia State Police was going to show up at the gates of Promise looking for him?

Which means he had killed Solomon for nothing.

"You're a real moron," said Jack. "I mean, a real dumbass. No one was going to come looking for you."

"How do you know?" he blubbered. Tears were streaming down his round cheeks. Dirty stubble thatched his face. The type of guy that perpetually looked like he needed a shower.

"I mean, how can you know?"

THE COUNCIL STRUGGLED with what to do with Danny before settling on a punishment. Danny had admitted his guilt, his motive, and there was strong circumstantial evidence corroborating his confession. They gave him a choice.

Life in house arrest. He would spend his days working sanitation for Promise, its worst work detail, and he would spend his nights in a detention cell. Or he could hang from the gallows.

The Council and Jack waited while he chewed on his options. Part of him felt bad for the man. The Pulse had indeed been his salvation, freeing him of a literal prison. While everyone else had mourned the loss of everything they had known, Danny had been happy to bid farewell to that old life. Jack could only imagine Danny's first days of freedom. Walking around with a dopey smile on his face as civilization crumbled around him. The smile only a free man could smile.

"What's it gonna be, Danny?" asked Carol, a member of the Council.

He sat in his chair, looking down at his hands. His big hands looked like two giant spiders. He looked up, tears streaming down his face.

"I don't want to die," he said. This didn't surprise Jack.

Few people went willingly to their death. He wondered if Danny would feel the same way a year from now. It was fine with Jack, even if it was a little unfair. It wasn't fair that Danny had thrived in a world like this one while so many others had suffered. The ones who had done things the right way, gotten jobs, raised families, contributed to the community, they had been left adrift when the lights had gone out.

And that was why it was only a small part of Jack that felt bad for him. He'd gotten his taste of freedom. Five years he had lived a free man, having paid the barest of debts for his crime. Perhaps this was karma. The universe setting things right. Because he did owe a debt to society. One that could never be fully repaid.

Whether he chose life or death, he would pay his debt. It was the dead of winter, and life in the cell would be anything but pleasant.

"You ruined my life!" Danny yelled.

It wasn't clear who Danny was screaming at, so Jack didn't say anything. The three Council members sat silently, glancing at one another uncomfortably.

"I'm talking to you, Goodwin!"

Jack's brow furrowed in confusion.

"What the hell are you talking about?"

"The Haven."

Now Jack was thoroughly confused. The Haven had been a violent community about thirty miles away from Promise, run by a sadistic bastard named Simon Conway. For six months earlier that year, the Haven had occupied Promise, forcing it to contribute half of its production to the larger community. Six residents of Promise had died at the hands of the Haven. Jack had attempted infiltrating the place to attack it from within. The effort had failed, and only his niece Norah's secret relationship with Simon's son had precipitated his escape. If it hadn't been for the kid, who had died helping Jack, he'd likely be dead.

"What does the Haven have to do with anything?"

He laughed hysterically, throwing his head back. It was so dramatic that Jack could not tell if the man was serious or faking. The man's hysterics died down like an unexpected thunderstorm that passes through quickly.

"They promised me."

Jack glanced at the Council members. They looked equally befuddled. He looked back at Danny, certain he was about to hear something he wouldn't like.

"What? What did they promise you?"

"You think I wanted to work here the rest of my life, spreading fertilizer, cleaning out shit?"

"Well, I am sorry that the maid service hasn't come by, my liege," Jack said. "You ungrateful prick. Why would the Haven offer you anything?"

A miserable little smile slashed across Danny's face. The smile of a troublemaking schoolboy who knew he shouldn't be smiling but could not help himself.

"Who do you think let Eddie go?"

Jack's stomach flipped. He scrunched up his face in frustration and rage. They had long suspected that someone inside Promise had betrayed the community. Early on, Jack and Lucy had captured a man from the Haven, well before they understood the threat the Haven posed to Promise. But he had escaped and returned home, revealing the location of Promise to his people.

"You?"

It was rhetorical. Of course it was Danny. Danny had sold them out. Danny had killed Ernesto and let their prisoner go. The prisoner, Jack had never even known his name, returned to the Haven, carrying with him the precious knowledge of their community's hidden location. He took with him critical intelligence about Promise but also about the Haven, intel that could have saved the lives of dozens of innocents. Several weeks later, the Haven had arrived on their doorstep, unleashing hell. And it had all been because of Danny.

"You piece of shit," Jack said gutturally.

Danny did not react. He didn't seem to care. His life was basically over, and he knew it, so he might as well squeeze the sponge for all it was worth. If they had just known, if they had found the Haven before it was too late, they could have short-circuited unfathomable bloodshed. They could have saved so many lives. Including that of Tim Whitaker, the father of his sister's unborn child.

"I thought you were waiting to go live with the Shepherds."

"I'd much rather have waited it out at the Haven than in this dump."

Jack stepped toward the man, delivering a right cross

to his face. Jack's heavy punch connected solidly with Danny's jaw, all fist and bone crashing together. Danny had not been expecting it, and the blow knocked him off-center and to the ground.

As Danny lay on his back, rubbing his damaged jaw, he laughed.

Jack stormed out of the room.

10

Lucy was discharged from inpatient care two days later. Her wounds were healing well, and there was no sign of infection. Her arm was in a sling, where it would remain for at least six weeks if not longer. There was a good chance she wouldn't regain full use of the arm, but given how close she'd come to death, it was a small price to pay. The primary concern was for her unborn child. She was not far enough along to feel the baby kick, so there were no reassuring flutters in her stomach to put her mind at ease. But there were no signs of bleeding or abdominal issues that might signal a threat to the pregnancy. All they could do was wait and see.

Jack went to see Lucy that afternoon. They had interviewed Danny twice more since their initial encounter, but there was precious little information to be gleaned. Initially, Danny's slavish devotion to the Shepherds had surprised Jack, but as he thought more about it, he began to understand it. After all, Jack Goodwin was guilty of many things that he could easily have served time for, and he had considered how the Pulse had all but foreclosed any possibility of a life behind bars.

Even if he had done it for Emma.

Emma.

Lucy's daughter had been diagnosed with an aggressive form of leukemia after he had left the military. Jack was living in northern Virginia at the time and had just gone to work for a syndicate after he had snared the daughter of a local crime lord with a con very similar to the one he'd run on Katie Stone's parents. He worked hard for his new employer but made frequent trips to Richmond to be with his sister as she tended to Emma.

Lucy's phone call breaking the news of the diagnosis was still burned on his brain. He simply adored that kid, and the idea of losing her nearly broke him. He could not imagine what the effect had been on his sister. He took a week off from work (his boss, a cold-blooded killer, had been remarkably understanding – *nothing more important than family*, the man had said) and drove down to be with Lucy and his niece as they navigated the horrifying world of pediatric oncology.

A month later, the first bills arrived. Lucy had pretty good insurance at the hospital, but the out-of-pocket costs of Emma's care were astronomical. Every month, a new bill from a new provider magically appeared at her door. Doctors, treatments, drugs, facilities, equipment, diagnostics. It added up quickly. One night, after tucking Emma into bed after a particularly difficult round of chemo, he'd found his sister sitting at the kitchen table, hunched over a stack of bills.

As if watching your child die wasn't bad enough, the parents of young cancer patients had to deal with the staggering financial burden. Lucy would be fighting a war on two fronts. Keeping up with the bills and nursing her daughter back to health. And of course, she would do anything for Emma.

Jack invited Lucy and Emma to come live with him in Alexandria, but she declined. Her job and Emma's doctors were in Richmond. They could not leave. Besides, Jack lived in a small two-bedroom apartment in Old Town. Not a place the three of them would be comfortable. No, she was staying in Richmond. But she would need his help.

"These all came in the last three days," she said without looking up.

She looked thin. She hadn't eaten in days. They were only a couple of months into Emma's treatment, and already it had taken a terrible toll on his sister. He traveled to Richmond twice a week to help out. If that wasn't enough, he would move here. He wondered if his boss would go for it. He could convince him there were new markets to exploit here. There were just as many marks here as there were in Old Town Alexandria.

She held up one of the bills.

"Six hundred dollars," she said, reading from the document. "Diagnostic testing."

She scoffed.

"I'm a damn nurse and I don't even know what this is for."

He sat down across from her.

"We don't need to do this now," he said.

"I don't know when else to do it," she had said, her voice cracking. "These bills are going to keep coming and coming."

She looked like she was on the verge of a nervous breakdown.

"When was the last time you got a good night's sleep?"

She laughed.

"Let's see," she said. "Three months ago?"

He smiled.

He gently plucked the document out of her hand and set it back on the stack of bills that seemed to grow exponentially each week. He took her by the elbow and guided her down the hall to her room. He pointed at the bed.

"Get some sleep," he ordered.

"I've got so much to do," she said.

He laughed. Her eyes were bloodshot with fatigue.

"You can barely stand up," he said. "Sleep."

The fight went right out of her. She staggered toward the bed and crawled under the covers. He watched her from the door for a few moments. She was asleep in seconds. He turned out the lights and closed the door behind him. Downstairs, he collected the bills and tucked them back into the plain manila folder she kept everything in. He locked up behind him as he left, taking the stack of bills with him. That was the last time Lucy had to worry about the astronomical costs of her daughter's care.

She asked him about it only once. He told her that early in his military career, he'd made some shrewd investments that had paid off handsomely. He'd been single, childless, didn't spend much money, so he was free to plow his extra money into various business ventures. He wasn't sure she believed him, but she did not ask again. There was just some awareness that the bills were paid each month. Sometimes, Lucy's out-of-pocket costs reached five figures a month. But Jack proved himself to be a good earner for the crew. Even after his captain's cut, he was clearing fifty, sixty, sometimes seventy grand a month.

Without a face to accompany her brother's transgressions, it was easy to put it aside. Not that it was difficult for Lucy to put his contributions aside. The emotional cost of tending to Emma took everything out of her. She didn't have the mental bandwidth to spend a lot of time thinking about how exactly her brother paid for his niece's medical costs. Which was probably for the best.

He remembered his final con.

"Luckily for my idiotic parents," Katie Stone had said that night. "I saw your last text message to my mom. That's why she didn't show up."

Jack clicked his tongue and scoffed at himself. It had felt like she was talking about someone else. Some slimy greaseball who preyed on innocent women. The kind of guy he'd take a baseball bat to these days. There were so many predators out there. He had to protect the people of Promise from them. The way he and Lucy had protected Promise from the Haven not three months ago. He wanted to tell Katie Stone where the money had gone. That it had gone to save a little girl named Emma. Would it have mattered? *Should* it have mattered?

But he had no regrets.

He would do it again.

After Emma had died and the last bill had come in, he had left that life behind for good. The last bill. He still remembered it. Like a tsunami of grief, the damn things kept coming for nearly a year after she had died. It felt particularly cruel of the billing companies to place Emma's name in the envelope's address window.

Emma Goodwin

c/o Lucy Goodwin

You might be dead, but you lived on in billing computers. Yes, indeed. The last bill was for the home health nurse, the one who'd been there at the very end when Emma had taken her last breath.

No regrets.

He had been glad to do this thing for his sister. Others might have questioned his means, but there was no other way. He'd sold his condo and moved to the farm, but there was little profit. He had not served the full twenty years in the military, so his pension was a pittance. Lucy was young and had little in the way of savings. In short, there was no other source of income.

Knowing Lucy could be there for Emma without the crushing financial burden had more than justified the means by which he had relieved that burden. Did he feel bad for Katie Stone? Of course he did. He was no hero. It wasn't black and white. But did Mr. and Mrs. Stone have to watch their daughter die? No. They made their choices. He didn't force Gina Stone into an affair. He didn't force them to buy into his utterly ridiculous "investment opportunity."

Lucy wasn't showing yet, but it wouldn't be long. She was early in her second trimester. He was worried about her, but he did his level best to conceal his concern. There had been a handful of births in Promise in the past half-decade. Half a dozen or so. One mother had died during childbirth; the baby had not survived either.

Admittedly a small sample size, so it was difficult to read the tea leaves.

"Something in that bag for me?" she asked.

The pregnancy had left her ravenous almost all the time. The yeasty scent of fresh bread from his bag filled the room. He had made it that morning. He handed her a piece and sat on the foot of the bed. She was a sucker for good bread.

"How's that shoulder?" he asked.

"Better," she said. "I don't have to choke down a scream every time I move it now."

His stomach flipped at this. The injury would haunt her for a long time to come, if not for the rest of her life. In a way, this was his fault. Decisions he had made long ago were now coming home to roost. Maybe the Pulse was his fault. Perhaps if he had made different choices, the Pulse would never have happened at all. Maybe if he had stayed with Molly, maybe she would never have worked on the Machine. And if she had never worked on it, maybe it would never have come into existence in the first place.

"Sorry," he said, tearing off a small chunk of the bread. "Sorry for everything."

He took a bite and chewed it slowly. It was good bread. Crispy on the outside, but soft and warm in the middle. It had just come out of the oven; steam curled from the bread's interior.

"You make this?" she asked.

He nodded. Baking had proven to be quite the stress reliever.

"You're getting better."

He raised his eyebrows at that.

"That supposed to be a compliment?"

"Sure," she said.

A smile briefly cut across his face before disappearing just as quickly. Lucy opened her mouth to say something and then closed it again.

"You don't need to say anything," he said. "You did nothing wrong."

"But I knew," she replied. "Deep down, I knew what you were doing.

"You had enough on your plate," Jack said. "I just didn't want you to have to worry about where the money would've come from."

"I would've figured it out," she said. "Not that it would've mattered. I mean, if I couldn't pay the bill, I just wouldn't pay it. I could've declared bankruptcy."

Jack was shaking his head.

"I didn't want you to have that weighing down on you and Emma after it was over."

He chuckled.

"Weird to say it like that," Jack went on. "It never crossed my mind that she wouldn't make it. I just assumed that it would all work out. It never occurred to me..."

His heart climbed into his throat and he stopped talking. He did not want to tear up in front of Lucy. He had cried for his niece many times, alone, in the dark, wishing he'd been able to protect the things he had loved the best in this world. He had been trained to keep the country safe, but he could not protect a little girl from rogue cells killing her from the inside.

They sat in silence for a few moments, as they often did when talking about Emma. His sister had made it clear that it was always okay to talk about her because talking about her kept her alive, kept her with them, but that didn't mean it was always easy. Sometimes it was hard, damn hard to talk about that kid.

He remembered this thing Emma had done when she ate canned spaghetti, the kind with the chopped-up hot dogs. He wasn't much of a cook back in those days and so whenever he looked after her for Lucy, he made them for her lunch. She would eat the noodles first and then stack up the hot dog slices to the side. Then she would count them; there were always between eighteen and twenty-three slices of hot dog in a can.

Weird how a memory like that would just sneak up on him.

Eighteen to twenty-three hot dog slices.

After she died, he saw those two numbers everywhere.

On highway signs. Flight numbers. License plates. He was fully aware that those numbers had always been there in the same frequency, and that they just stood out now because of his personal connection to them. Still, he liked to think of them as little messages from his late niece. Grown-ass man looking for signs in hot dog slices.

"I'm going to step down as head of security," he said.

"Is that so?"

"I need to look for Molly," he said.

That wasn't the whole story, however. His connection to Solomon had bred distrust from the others. He could feel it.

"I want Bode to take over."

She did not reply.

"The situation with Solomon has everyone unnerved," he said. "This is the best thing for everyone."

It would have been easy to do nothing. It would have been easy to say that Jack had never done anything to hurt Promise. That he had done nothing but help the people of Promise. But that would have been a lie. He had hurt people just like the ones in Promise. He had hurt a lot of people; that it had been in furtherance of some greater call, like paying for Emma's medical care made little difference. Even if they didn't know about his old life.

Emma would not have liked it.

That hit him right there as he sat with the mother of that extraordinary child. She would have been very disappointed in her uncle. And not just in the way of an eight-year-old who knew that lying and cheating and stealing were wrong. But because it would have shattered her view of him.

"Bode will do a great job."

"I know," she said. "I just don't want you to leave."

"We need to find out what Solomon was talking about," he said. "I need to go look for Molly."

"Yeah, I figured you'd be saying something like that," Lucy said.

"I found something," Jack said. "In Solomon's things. I don't know if it's related to his story and just didn't get around to telling us."

"What?"

He pulled the baggie containing the flash drive from his pocket and handed it to her. Lucy reached out for it with her good arm. She held the device gently between her thumb and forefinger.

"Why would he be carrying this?" Jack asked.

"Yeah, that's weird," Lucy said.

He watched her as she studied the device, her mind naturally imagining a world that once was and that might be again. Actionable intelligence about reversing the effects of the Pulse. It was what they'd all dreamed of.

Sometimes, he literally dreamed about it. Sitting alone in a corner of his favorite steakhouse, Buckhead's, sipping on a bourbon on real ice, eating a perfectly cooked ribeye. Jack Goodwin wasn't one for vice or fine dining, but there was something transcendent about a good steakhouse experience.

And that wasn't all he dreamed about. He dreamed of driving a car, of ordering plane tickets, of downloading a new book he wanted to read right away. He dreamed of things he had never done when he did have power, but now things that seemed so exotic, so foreign, like a taboo sex act. Deep down, his subconscious was grasping for a world that no longer existed.

But if Solomon had been telling the truth, perhaps it was a world still out there, just out of their reach. Behind a locked door. A door that could be opened with the key. They just hadn't known the key existed, let alone where it was.

It occupied his every waking thought now, much like it did everyone else. Days after his stunning revelation, it was still all anyone could talk about. Before long, word of it would slip outside their community, into open waters, and that presented its own threat. Promise could become a target. Dark forces could converge here on nothing more than conjecture and rumor.

But conjecture and rumor, falsehoods and lies, could

do very real damage. Who knew what lengths someone might go to for the holy grail, information that could lead to the return of their technological existence. A world that could be controlled and manipulated by and for the few at the expense of the many.

He'd already decided, he finally understood. He'd decided the minute that Solomon had started telling his story, telling him that Molly was wrapped up in this in some way. Doors he had never completely closed, perhaps because he never had wanted to close them in the first place. It wasn't a specific plan, more the idea of a plan.

"I think Solomon coming here changed everything," he said. "Promise will change. Clearly, Solomon knew something. Otherwise, they wouldn't have gone to all this trouble to get rid of him. It'll remind everyone that what we're doing here isn't real."

"Isn't real?" she replied sharply. "It doesn't get more real than this."

"We're not cut out for this kind of life," he said. "We're meant for more than this. If we keep going like this, all this will be gone. Everything out there will be gone. This world is falling apart, Luce. Can't you feel it? First it was Simon. Eventually, people are gonna stop believing in any kind of future. I don't want that."

Lucy opened her mouth to speak; then she closed it again without saying anything.

"Time is an arrow," he whispered.

"What?" Lucy said.

"Time is an arrow," he said. "It moves in one direction. We had moved forward as a society, as a civilization. A world with power. With technology. For better or worse, that was the path we charted, and the path we were walking. To pull us off that path has been disastrous."

"You're not normally this gloomy," she said. "And that is saying something."

"I can make this better," he said. "I can make everything out there better."

"Would it really be possible?" she asked, a tincture of hope lacing her voice. "I guess I just got used to the idea that this was it. Sometimes I'll be doing something, and I'll think how much easier it would be with electricity. Like an ultrasound."

Her hand passed protectively across her belly. She zeroed in on a spot over his shoulder.

"I wish I could come with you."

"I know," he said.

There was no one he trusted more than Lucy. She would have been an ideal companion on this quest. But it was not to be this time.

"Do you think he was telling the truth?" Lucy asked.

"I don't know," Jack replied. "But I'm going to find out. One way or another. I have to get to the bottom of this. For you, for me, for Norah, for all of us."

"But Jack—"

"I've made up my mind," he said. "I'm leaving in the morning."

11

Jack felt better than he had in a long time.

It was his fifth day on the road. Evening was drawing near, and he had made it some ninety miles northeast of Promise, just a few miles shy of the Virginia-D.C. border. As had been his routine, he was up at dawn, on the move after a quick breakfast of peanut butter and jerky. He was careful to keep a balance of fat, protein, and carbohydrates to keep his body performing. Fifteen to eighteen miles a day on foot, even just walking them, took a toll on his forty-six-year-old body.

He was on Route 1; ironically, this was the inverse of the route his sister Lucy had taken after she had escaped Washington, D.C., in the days immediately following the Pulse. As the weak sun touched the horizon, the Arland D. Williams Memorial Bridge came into view. The dead traffic had progressively gotten thicker the farther north he had ranged. He checked as many vehicles as he could for supplies, but they had all been long since stripped.

The automobile graveyard sat silently, glinting in the noonday sun on this cold winter day. Some still had their doors hanging open. Flat tires as far as the eye could see. He could just picture it. The Pulse had hit at lunchtime, a busy time for the Beltway, which meant the vehicles probably were not moving along very quickly anyway. Their drivers busy, rushed, annoyed, what the hell was going on, suddenly their phones dark, the satellite radio falling silent. It would have been a Catch-22 for these drivers. They couldn't go anywhere, but they couldn't leave. Couldn't well leave your car in the middle of the interstate.

Even if every single vehicle on this highway simply rolled over and died, they would come back in a minute or two or ten. That's what they would have told themselves. Just a solar flare or freak electrical incident. But, of course, none of them had, and eventually, every single person had abandoned their vehicle. Every one of them had to accept that something truly terrible had happened. Leaving the car would have been an acknowledgment of that. An understanding that one was pushing off into uncharted waters, and there was no roadmap, no playbook for such a crisis.

The George Washington Parkway was the final exit ahead of the bridge. As he drew closer to the river, his speed slowed and he became increasingly alert. The river crossings over the Potomac were likely to be guarded by various factions, as they would be of strategic importance. He decided to rest for a few hours while deciding how to get across the river. He curled off the freeway and followed the spur to the bottom of the exit ramp. He crossed under 395 and took refuge in a large grove of trees on the west side of the interstate. The husks of two vehicles, one a sedan, the other a large SUV, lay entangled at the foot of the treeline. Jack studied the scene for a moment, a bit confused, before looking skyward. Then he saw what had happened. The vehicles had crashed through the guardrails and fallen sixty feet to their destinies. The fire-ravaged skeletons of the vehicle's occupants remained entombed in the burned-out remains.

He continued into the safety of the trees; a small open glade about thirty yards in looked like a good place to pitch his tent for the evening. When his campsite was ready, he set up a perimeter, running cable from tree to tree until it encircled his tent. The cable was lined with small bells that would alert him to another's presence. It wasn't a perfect security system, but it was better than nothing. He also set three snares; they would produce dinner soon enough.

There was life nearby, of this he was certain. The smell of cookfires, the murmurs of conversation. The social, economic, and political dynamics would be different in urban areas than he was used to in the agrarian Promise. It had been a long time since Jack had been in an urban area. Maidens had been the closest town to Promise; it had been picked clean in the days and weeks after the Pulse. Back when the smart cookies had quickly deduced that this was no ordinary blackout. And that deduction had been no guarantee that they would survive the dark days ahead; it had merely qualified them for the opportunity. Tens of millions had died in the opening weeks. Cities were far more dangerous; it was a supply/demand thing. Too many people. Not enough resources.

By sunset, Jack had built a small fire and seen to a pair of rabbits he had captured. He was tired but alert. He would need to be. The more people there were around, the greater the odds one of them might try to kill him. As he dined, the silence broken by stitches of laughter or bouts of coughing, the foul smell of homemade cigarettes on the wind, he was reminded by how far from home he was.

Jack's departure from Promise had been subdued.

Norah had not taken his planned journey well.

He went to see her on his last afternoon in Promise. She'd been working in the clinic, tending to a little girl named Bella. The woodstove they had retrofitted into the trailer chugged along mightily, filling the room with warmth. The girl's mother, a hard woman named Nancy, lingered in the corner silently.

"Hey, kid," he said.

"Hey," she said, glancing over her shoulder before turning her attention back to the kid. Norah had recently started working in the clinic; she had her eyes on joining Lucy and Terri as a third medical provider. She was wrapping a bandage around the girl's left hand. The girl had sliced her hand open on a broken piece of glass.

He was going to miss her terribly when he left. She was one of the loveliest people he had ever known. Possessed of a kind and generous spirit you rarely saw in someone as young as she was. She'd had to grow up quickly in this post-Pulse world. She'd already experienced her share of grief, losing the boy she loved. A boy who had died saving Jack, who had died saving Promise, who had died for her.

"Sorry about your friend," she said.

"Yeah. Thanks."

Norah fell silent again. He reminded himself that he was talking to a seventeen-year-old kid still learning how to navigate the very adult waters she was constantly finding herself in.

"I'm gonna be leaving Promise for a while."

"Yeah," Norah said. "Lucy told me. I want to come with you."

He was shaking his head before she finished speaking.

"You can't," he said. "It's not gonna be safe. And I need you here to look after Lucy."

"Terri can take care of her," Norah said. "And you'll need backup. I can be the eyes in the back of your head."

"No," he replied. He would not budge on this. Promise needed Norah.

She finished up with the girl and sent her and her mother on their way. Then it was just her and Jack alone. Her arms were crossed at her midsection and her gaze was fixed at a spot over Jack's head. She seemed unsure how to disengage from a conversation she found uncomfortable. She fumbled with her hands, picking at a piece of dry skin on her thumb. When she looked up, it was only for a moment. Then she would look back down again. For her. Jack was doing this for her.

The door to the clinic clattered open, breaking the awkward silence that had fallen between them.

"I have to get back to work," she had said.

He grabbed her and hugged her tightly. She did not pull away, but she did not return the embrace. It would have to do.

His final day in Promise flew by in a flash. After

bidding Norah farewell, he set to finishing the preparations for his journey. He'd been away from Promise for a few nights in the past, but this was the first time he was leaving with no specific timetable for a return. He did not know if he would be gone a few days, a few weeks, or forever. There was just no way to know. The world wasn't getting any safer or more hospitable.

By nightfall, he was exhausted. The dinner rush was underway. The murmur of small groups of people making their way to the cafeteria caught his attention, and it filled him with sadness. He decided against joining them for dinner. There had been a lot of rumors about Jack Goodwin flying around; it felt right to stay out of the way. Already he felt like an outsider. Like he was watching an old movie of days gone by.

Lucy had seen him off the next day, shortly after dawn on a clear, cold winter morning. She tried talking him out of leaving but only briefly and with little conviction. Once Jack had made up his mind, that was it, a trait with which Lucy was profoundly familiar.

Better that way.

Jack had been an important cog in the machine that was Promise but he was not indispensable. None of them were. They couldn't be, by design of the world they inhabited. The world was too dangerous. The threat of death was always close by. If you couldn't be replaced, you needed to find and train a replacement post haste. Otherwise, you were inviting ruin.

Just deciding to make this trip had dislodged the splinter in his mind. Thoughts of Molly, of Katie, of his life on the wrong side of the law, had swirled together to clog his thinking like gunk blocking a drain. But taking action, grabbing the thread that Solomon had laid at his feet and following it to its conclusion, whatever that conclusion was, filled him with new purpose.

It was different purpose than the one behind the recent battle with the Haven. That had been elemental, a battle for survival. This was something else. An opportunity to improve everyone's life. A chance to bring light back to their dark world. Not just preserving a fairly sad status quo. He would finish the job Solomon had come to recruit him for or he would die trying.

And the prospect of seeing Molly again was never far from his mind. Admitting you had a problem was the first step, after all. Strange how another person could become part of your DNA, part of your essence.

Molly.

But their paths had crossed and she had changed his life in ways he did not expect.

As he cleared the Promise gates, he had turned and looked back on his home the last five years. Rarely had he lived in a single place that long, and he cared about it and the people in it very deeply. Forming connections was not like him; but for his year with Molly, he had been on his own for most of his adult life.

His travel away from Promise had taken him along Route 235, a two-lane road lined with thick pines on either side. The air was fragrant with the scent of pine. It reminded him of Christmas tree lots from his childhood when his mother would haggle with the lot operator for the dinkiest tree on the lot because that was all they could afford, and even then just barely.

He saw no one that first day on the road. The skies threatened snow, and no one wanted to be caught away from home during a bad storm. Experienced in navigation, Jack wasn't too worried about that. A commanding officer had once called him a human compass. During his training, they had dropped his platoon deep in the middle of the Maine woods with nothing but their shorts and t-shirts (embedded with tracking devices for the platoon leaders to find the ones who got lost) and orders to make their way to a bar in Portland. Jack made it in less than three days. The other six soldiers became desperately lost; one had nearly died of exposure.

He spent his first night in an abandoned farmhouse about fifteen miles north of Promise. It had not seen human habitation in some time. He did take the time to scavenge the main residence for supplies but came up empty. His dinner consisted of a squirrel he trapped in one of his snares. Squirrel meat was tough and stringy but he liked the taste. Not many agreed with him, but no one turned it down. Meat was meat.

Just like this tasty rabbit he had enjoyed tonight in the shadow of the bridge. He threw the fragile bones and skin of the rabbit into the fire, his appetite sated for now. It was a cold night, but there was a light wind blowing. Although a bit counterintuitive, a slight breeze was not unwelcome; if it held, it would prevent the air temperature from crashing overnight.

There was a small creek about fifty yards from his campsite. It ran cold and clear; that didn't mean he could just lower his head to whatever stream or brook he came across. Most waterways were contaminated. But accompanying him on his journey was a portable water filter he'd learned to build in the Army.

The filter was housed in an empty two-liter soda

bottle. It contained equivalent quantities of gravel, charcoal, and sand, the three sediments filling up about half the bottle. There were three holes in the bottom; The gravel prevented the sand and charcoal from escaping. Together, the three substances did a remarkable job of filtering out contaminants. Before leaving Promise, he tested his contraption, pouring untreated river water through it and catching the runoff in a kettle. Then he boiled it for two minutes and set it off to cool. When it had cooled off sufficiently, he drank the water to ensure it worked.

He drank four pints of water, enough to get him through the next day or so. As he shivered from the chill of the water, he wondered about folks in the American Southwest, places like Phoenix or Albuquerque that had relied on water being imported over long distances. There would have been no way for people to live there without technology. It rained less than ten inches a year in many parts of the southwest. Those places would be ghost towns by now.

Although he was likely safe on food and water, he would have other problems. He could scavenge, and he'd become a passable hunter. He'd built his share of snares and captured small game that folks in Promise enjoyed. Rabbit was quite popular and remained plentiful. No matter how many they captured, there were always more. He recalled how hesitant they'd been at first, all of them getting used to this new world. Their brains were still imprinted with the memory of buying a three-pound package of frozen chicken breasts or perfectly cut ribeye steaks.

He also packed a nine-millimeter pistol. Fortunately

(or unfortunately, depending on your vantage point), firearms continued to work. The only exceptions were the newer weapons containing smart technology. Many of those contained advanced circuitry that was now as dead as everything else. And even these would be rendered useless before too long. Ammunition grew scarcer by the day.

Because in the end, there were bad people out there. Maybe they hadn't been born bad. Maybe they'd been good people who paid their taxes on time and volunteered at the food bank but who had turned in the aftermath of the cataclysm. People whose souls had rotted in the heat of the disaster. People like Simon, the now-deceased ruler of the Haven.

He considered taking a horse but dismissed the idea just as quickly. Promise had only five horses in its stable; he couldn't justify depriving the community of one. Put another way, they needed them a lot more than he did. Besides, he wouldn't have to worry about keeping a horse fed. That was a much bigger deal than people realized. And the idea of letting a horse starve or abandoning it to its own devices was a notion he could not brook.

If only Solomon were still alive.

There was no way to know if there was more story to tell. He'd gone through hell just to get to Promise. He may have carried additional intelligence to his grave. He paused, thinking about what Molly would have done to maximize the chances that her message would reach Jack successfully. She trusted Solomon, but there was a limit to that. She trusted only Jack completely.

But there had been no guarantee that Solomon would successfully deliver the message to him. If time had been short, and it sounded like she'd had to decide on the fly, she would have built in at least one redundancy.

His eyes grew heavy. He needed a good night's sleep, but the idea of sleeping in the tent made him wary. There was more human activity around him than he was comfortable with.

After a final check of his security perimeter and extinguishing his campfire, he ascended an ancient oak tree deeper into the forest. A pair of thick braided branches, twice as thick as his torso, and complete with a weed-choked divot made for an excellent nest. The tree's thick trunk blocked some of the wind. Even better, he was virtually invisible from the ground.

He was asleep within minutes.

12

Jack was on the move early the next morning, rested and ready to go. He was a bit stiff, befitting his middle age, but otherwise, he felt good. With any luck, he would be across the river by lunchtime and another step closer to finding Molly.

The question was how to get across the river.

The Potomac, and the bridge swooping across it, lay a half-mile to the north. Jack slipped into the cover of the trees and made his way toward the water's edge. It was a sunny morning, but shadowy in the gloom of the thick woods. The trees thinned out as he neared the bank. He paused at a support beam and looked east and west along the riverbank. The water lapped gently at the shore. A chilly wind blew in from the water, icing his cheeks.

In the distance, to the east on the far side of the woods, stood a row of small homes, mostly ranch and compact Cape Cods. He reached for his binoculars and scanned the landscape. He shifted the glass to the riverbank, studying the piers poking out into the river. Most were barren, but there appeared to be a small motorboat about a mile away moored to the pier. It would be self-propelled now, but if it was seaworthy, it might get him across the river.

To the west, abandoned commercial and residential districts rolled away like quilts. There was some activity, but not much. The smoke of campfires curled away into the bright morning sky. Jack was not familiar with the settlement dynamics that had arisen here in the years since the Pulse. The D.C. metropolitan area, including northern Virginia and southern Maryland, had once boasted one of the highest population densities in the country; that meant the battle for resources here would have been fierce in the weeks and months following the Pulse. Lucy had been here when it happened; she had seen firsthand how quickly things had spun out of control.

He ducked back into the trees, trekking east now, the river on his left. In the distance, the city shimmered in the morning sun. He had not been to D.C. since the Pulse; it made sense that the bridges were now occupied territory. Their guardians would likely charge a pretty penny for access to and exit from the city, assuming they allowed it at all.

Urban areas provided the starkest reminders of the cataclysm that had befallen them. Back in Promise, it was easy to forget that the Pulse had set the world back three centuries. People farmed and took care of the animals and made their clothes. Just living that homesteading lifestyle! But here, near the former capital, his memories of the disaster came rushing back.

On the day of the Pulse, Jack had been in downtown

Richmond, taking a meeting with a man he should not have been meeting with. But money was getting tight; the cost to buy his freedom from his syndicate captain, combined with the money he had funneled to Emma's care, had taken its toll. He had no regrets at all and would do both again in a heartbeat, but scruples and principles did not pay the bills. The man had a suggestion for a job, a big payday, to do it right took four men, that whole rigamarole. Jack didn't want to take the meeting but he had taken it anyway, and if you take the meeting, then maybe you *did* want to take the meeting after all.

It made him question who he was. For all his talk that he'd only gotten into this game to help Lucy and Emma, with all those bills and debts paid off forever, here he was again, looking to buy his way back into the game. For what? For the thrill of the chase? What was he missing at his core that kept bringing him back to places that other people easily avoided? People who got up in the morning and went to their jobs and paid their bills on time.

It was an old Vietnamese restaurant; it had been there on 6th Street for as long as Jack could remember. It sat in a basement unit, just below a shoe repair place. Six tables, a tiny kitchen, reeking of ginger and meat and cigarette smoke. The owner, Duy, was a diminutive Vietnamese immigrant who made the kind of pho you found in the back alleys of Saigon. Jack ate there frequently, as did a number of the folks populating Richmond's underworld. Duy was friendly and cared deeply about his customers. If he knew that his best customers weren't exactly Boy Scouts, he did not let on.

A cigarette was clamped between Jack's fingers when the man slipped into the chair across from him. Duy did not object to smokers in his restaurant. It got him written up from time to time, but he didn't care. Jack sipped from a glass of Kim Son, a rice wine that was popular in Vietnam.

"Glad you decided to meet me," the man said. His name was Larry.

"Well, let's hear it," Jack said anxiously.

Jack had this urge to rush through the meeting, as though that might make the plan a bit more palatable and less illegal. Ridiculous. The meeting itself was a crime. Conspiracy was something he'd learned about early in his days on the wrong side of the law. It was how the cops and prosecutors could get you even before you'd pulled a job. Just the agreement to commit the crime was enough, and you could always get someone inside to flip, largely because that mark usually had charges pending.

Larry was getting revved up about the potential job. It involved the cash gate from an upcoming three-day concert at the local raceway. Larry had a man on the inside, the guy who would be taking custody of approximately two hundred thousand dollars in cash. All Jack and his crew had to do was "hijack" the truck. As Jack sat there, wondering what the hell he was doing with his life, the world changed forever.

It had happened without warning.

One second they were talking about pulling the job like they had so many times before, and the next, they were sitting in the dark with their thumbs up their rears.

"What the hell is going on here, Duy?" Larry had asked calmly and coldly as they sat in the dark.

"Not sure," Duy replied.

Jack's hand drifted to the handgun in the small of his

back. He didn't know what was going on, but he didn't want to be caught off guard.

"Nobody fucking move a muscle!" Larry yelled out.

Then: "Why isn't my phone working?"

Jack had drawn his weapon by then; his phone was in his free hand, but the screen was strangely dark.

"Stay calm, Larry," Jack said. "It's just a blackout."

He didn't know why their phones weren't working, but he wanted Larry to stay calm. The guy was twitchy and just about anything could set him off.

"The hell kind of blackout shuts down our phones?" he hissed in the dark.

Jack did not know.

"Duy, turn the fucking lights on!" Larry yelled.

"I didn't do this!" Duy barked back. "I light some candles!"

His voice was high and tight. The fright in his voice was evident.

Jack remained seated, the gun resting on the table in his right hand, his left hand covering it. His dead phone lay face-up on the table. Jack was a quick draw; he just needed to stay calm and think about his next move. The place was quiet but for the heavy breathing of the nervous customers and the clatter of Duy digging through his supplies.

"Hurry the fuck up, Duy," Larry ordered.

Muted, anxious chatter filled the room. Jack tried to recall who'd been in the room when the power had gone out. Two thugs from a local crew at a table in the corner. One table had a single occupant. A woman Jack didn't recognize, but she was in the life. You could just tell. Three tables had been empty.

A few moments later, the room brightened with a bloom of orange light as Duy busily lit a handful of candles. A bead of sweat traced a line down Jack's back. Silhouettes of people he wouldn't trust to look after their own mothers moved shiftily in the dark.

"Larry, we're gonna pick this up another time."

"Don't you fucking move," Larry hissed.

Larry's chair screeched against the flooring as he pushed away from the table. The outline of the man's gun was plainly visible in the shimmery, flickering light. Jack rotated his aching shoulder, earning him a delicious pop. He took a deep breath and let it out slowly. The temperature felt like it had jumped ten degrees. The sharp aroma of panic sweat filled the room.

Jack edged his way out of the booth, keeping his gun up, not pointed at anyone in particular but ready in the event he needed it. Duy had disappeared into the kitchen. A wise move, given that all his customers now had guns drawn. Jack was about fifteen feet from the door.

"Listen up, everyone," Jack called out. "We're all gonna stay calm and walk out of here one at a time, okay?"

No reply.

"Okay?" he said again.

A murmur of *okays* and *yeahs* followed.

"Duy," said Jack. "We're all gonna come back and pay our tab, okay? Right everyone?"

A second flurry of agreement.

"Now then," he said, nodding toward a figure near the entrance. "You there. By the door. You first. Just back out and go.

This evacuation proceeded smoothly for the first two

diners. Jack motioned for a third person to leave when it all went bad. Later, Jack would conclude that someone had inadvertently knocked a water glass off the table; unfortunately, the sound of the glass shattering in the overheated environment was mistaken for a gunshot. That led everyone else still in the restaurant to instantly open fire. The sound of multiple guns firing was deafening in the small restaurant. Jack knew better than to engage in such close quarters battle and instantly dove for the floor, taking cover at the foot of the booth. The firefight wouldn't last very long; that much was certain.

Jack had been right.

The guns fell silent in seconds. Left behind was the gun battle's residue. The moans of pain, the gasping for air of the wounded. He waited for a few minutes, keeping himself frozen to the ground. He looked back toward the kitchen; Duy was curled up against the door. Their eyes met. His face was rigid with fear. Jack waved him away, directing him to flee through the restaurant's back entrance. Duy complied. He slithered through the door to the kitchen on his hands and knees. Jack never saw him again.

After another stretch of time, maybe thirty minutes, maybe an hour, Jack moved clear of his hiding spot toward the kitchen. He pushed through the swinging door, crawled down the narrow aisle between the ovens and prep counters, toward the back door opening up on 7th Street.

He climbed to his feet, scratched and bruised but otherwise unharmed. A quick look around this little corner of the city confirmed that the day had gone to hell for just about everyone else.

What a day that had been, Jack recalled as he made his way east toward the pier in his sights.

As he rounded a curve, an access road paralleling the river caught his eye; it ran close to the water's edge, servicing what looked to be a small marina. A handful of small boats were bobbing in the water. Hard to tell from here if they were still seaworthy. Without internal combustion engines, even small vessels would be rendered useless. Canoes and kayaks would be the only option for hitting the open water.

There!

Near the pier, jammed into the tall grasses, lay a small canoe. It looked to be in relatively good shape, but he'd need a closer inspection to confirm that assessment. If he followed the line of the access road, he could approach it from the west, and perhaps stay out of the line of sight of the custodians of the bridge.

Farther to the east lay a small neighborhood. It was almost too small to even be called a neighborhood; half a dozen Cape Cods wedged around a small cul de sac. The homes were from the post-war era, nearly eighty years old. They had that look of homes whose original owners had refused to sell this prime riverfront property as the city developed around them.

He scooted down on his bottom, confident that he was out of view of the watch, braking himself at the bottom. The access road ran straight before starting a shallow descent to the water. He stayed in the shadows cast by the highway above. His heart was pounding but in a good way. He felt alive. He was in his element. This was who he was. A life lived in the shadows.

The road began to descend; the canoe was about a

hundred yards distant now. The closer he got, the more optimistic he became. It was in good shape. A single oar lay across the bench. Anticipation tickled the back of his neck. As long as he kept the canoe under the bridge superstructure, he could avoid detection by the bridge guards.

As he started down the embankment, a sound caught his ears. The sound of whimpering. At first, he thought it was a wounded animal. Not an uncommon sound. Animal traps were everywhere, as small game constituted a large part of many survivors' diets. But then the sound grew in intensity and clarity. It was a human voice.

"Help me!"

Jack froze.

He waited for a moment.

He must have imagined it. No one was out here calling for help. He continued down the embankment.

"Help! Please, please help me!"

He froze again.

Shit.

Everything about this smelled wrong. You didn't come across people yelling for help and then ride in to save the day. It wasn't how the world worked. He made his way farther down the embankment, just a few steps away from the canoe now. He grabbed the edge and began dragging it down the embankment when the voice called out again. Above him, the guards on the bridge continued to chatter away, smoking their shitty-smelling cigarettes.

Just get in the canoe and go, Jack. Just get in and go. There were people in every village, town, and city all over right now in dire need of help, and no one was coming to rescue them.

But he stood rooted in the soft terrain, his boots shifting underneath him. The river lapped at the banks. A sharp wind blew in from the city, chilling him. Even though the sun was shining, this was shaping up to be the coldest day on the road yet.

He set the canoe back down; he wasn't going to be getting in it just yet. He was going to do something stupid because if he didn't, it would haunt him. Was it because of his memories of Katie Stone currently streaming in his mind? If it wasn't for her, would he be having this crisis of conscience?

He liked to think so.

But that was a lie.

He was a lie. He was a fraud. But he didn't want to be. He could take ten minutes to go check this out and then he could be back on his way. He wasn't out of his element here. Few had the skills he did. Anyone who challenged Jack did so at their peril.

He sighed. Then he retreated up the embankment toward the access road. It split off to the east, away from the bridge, running parallel to the river. He chanced a glance back at the guards on the bridge. They were still distracted by their cigarettes and their gossip.

He walked east, his ears primed for the distress call. It seemed to be coming from one of the small homes in the out-of-place *cul de sac*. They were old, decrepit, falling apart without steady maintenance these last few years. His gun was out now, his eyes sweeping the area for the slightest hint of trouble. The clock in his head was running. He would give this fifteen minutes. That was it. If he couldn't find out what was happening, he was gone. That canoe had his name on it.

"Help me!"

The voice was closer now. A prepubescent boy, if he had to guess, but it might have been a teenaged girl. Hard to tell. He continued along the riverbank for a few more yards before crossing over to the sidewalk on the southern side of the street. It had buckled and cracked; weeds and small bushes had sprouted in its many fault lines.

The voice called again:

"Help!"

He had zeroed in on the house at the corner of the next intersection. The brick siding was cracked in places, lined with fissures. The front door was missing.

The desperate voice ramped up in volume.

"Help!"

Jack stood at the threshold. He put the odds of someone actually being in trouble at one in three. More likely worse than that. It was almost certainly a con. But he could not be certain, and if he didn't confirm that, it would haunt him. It would haunt him the way Katie Stone haunted him. There was but so much room inside you that could be haunted. Too many ghosts could destroy you.

He pushed the door open and stepped inside.

13

Jack didn't know where he would lay his head tonight, but his soul would be restless if he didn't see this through.

The house was musty and cold. It burned his nostrils. Sunlight streamed in through the front windows facing the river. It brightened the corridor, gave the house a sense of warmth it didn't deserve. He set out on a loop of the house, starting in an old sitting room. It had two dilapidated couches. Dust from their guts floated in the sunbeams piercing the windowpanes. An old built-in bookcase was stuffed to the gills, sporting the cracked, striated spines of well-read books.

Around the corner, he came upon a small galley kitchen. At the far end was a small pantry door. A dead end. He checked the larder, which was, of course, empty. No surprise. But it was still a good habit to have. You never knew when you might find a can of beef stew. Canned goods, undamaged, could last for years. But not today.

He doubled back through the kitchen, back to the sitting room. There was a small dining room on the far side of the threshold. The remains of a dining tabletop sat on the floor. At some point, termites had had their way with the legs.

Confident the downstairs was secure, he turned his attention to the narrow flight of stairs climbing into the darkness. Yeah, this was a good idea. Might be a human abattoir upstairs for all he knew. The occupants? Maybe out getting their knives sharpened. Who knew anymore. The world was a weird place these days. It wasn't all like Promise. They'd gotten lucky.

"Help!"

He drew closer to the steps. The steps were a bit rotted but had a little bit of life left in them. Staying close to the wall, a hand on the railing, he took the steps one at a time. The wood was soft and paper-thin, each step bowing under his weight. Halfway up, a step did buckle. His leg gave out under him, and he hooked his arm around the railing to keep his leg from sinking into the maw of the ruined staircase.

He pulled his leg free and pushed up to firmer ground. Another step and then another and he was near the top. It was much darker at the top landing, where the sunlight did not reach. His heart was pounding. He heard a sharp crack. The lower half of the steps collapsed, leaving a dark gap between the lowest step and the ground.

Well, he was committed now. He scampered to the top quickly, unsure if the remaining staircase would hold. He made it to the landing safely. Behind him, the steps held. He gauged the distance to the ground. If he needed to, he could make the jump. He didn't fancy the idea, but it was doable. The second floor was small and cramped. A bathroom directly ahead. A bedroom on either side of the landing.

He paused again, listening for signs of life. He had a good ear for this sort of thing, honed during his time in the military. The air was full of dust and the smell of something he could not identify. There was no activity he could discern. He waited a full five minutes, but there was no sound in the house. A stitch of laughter in the distance carried on the breeze. Probably the guards on the bridge.

He stepped carefully toward the room on the eastern side of the house, but then a sound caught his ear. Not the laughter from the bridge. This was coming from inside the house, behind him. He held his weapon close to his chest, backing up against the hallway wall. He curled around the corner of the second bedroom.

"Is someone there?"

The voice was strained and weak. He took a step toward the room, staying out of the line of sight. He chanced a quick glance around the corner, unsure what to expect. A flash of movement on the far side of the bedroom. He stepped into the room, his gun at the ready. A boy of maybe thirteen was on the ground; his left leg was pinned under an armoire that had tipped over. His face was gaunt and pale, his eyes sunken. Jack checked the room once more before moving in to help. They made eye contact; Jack could see the pleading in the boy's eyes.

Jack sized up the large piece of furniture pinning the boy down.

"Help me," the boy said.

"It's gonna be okay," Jack said.

The boy nodded.

"Can you move your fingers?"

"Yeah," he said. He waggled them for Jack.

"What happened?"

"I was looking for some food," he said. His voice was raspy, barely a whisper. "I climbed on it and it fell on me."

Jack ran his hands along the edge of the armoire. It was a lovely piece. Hand-carved. Even exposed to the elements, it had survived. He didn't know why he became fixated on the furniture. It was just a thing. He took a deep breath and let it out slowly.

"What's your name?"

"Brett," he said through clenched teeth.

"Okay, Brett," he said. "We're gonna get this thing off you."

He nodded.

Jack reared back and took another look at the armoire. It had cracked in the middle but had not broken all the way through. Brett's leg was pinned at the upper thigh. Hopefully, the injuries weren't too severe. Jack didn't love the idea of moving him, but if he didn't free him, the kid would freeze to death. Jack was simply playing the only card either of them had.

He crouched down near the center of the object and wedged his hands under the lip of the wood, wrapping his fingers around an edge. Driving his legs into it, careful not to strain his back because he was on the final approach to fifty, after all, he lifted the armoire a few inches clear of the boy's thighs.

"Ehhhh," the boy moaned.

"Brett," he said. "I need you to move."

"My leg hurts like hell."

Sweat broke out on Jack's forehead as he struggled to maintain the lift. His muscles were burning. A few more seconds, a minute at the most, and his thighs and quads would give out, and the armoire would come crashing back down on top of Brett.

"Crawl, man!" Jack pleaded. "Drag yourself clear!"

"I'll try," he said in a whisper.

The kid curled onto his side, propping himself up on his right elbow. With a mighty tug, he began to pull himself clear of his prison. One swoop of the elbow, then another, and then another. Jack closed his eyes. His muscles were screaming. Despite the cold, his body burned with exertion. Sweat was pouring into his eyes, making them sting and burn. But he held on.

"I'm clear," Brett called out.

Jack let go; the armoire crashed to the ground.

THE BOY'S injuries were bad, but they did not appear to be life-threatening. Jack guessed he'd fractured his thighbone. Internal bleeding was a possibility, but there wasn't anything Jack could do about that. So he decided not to worry about it. He'd just hope for the best. The boy would either make it or he wouldn't.

After taking a few minutes to recover from the strain of lifting the armoire, Jack conducted a rudimentary assessment of the boy's condition. Brett was exhausted. Jack helped sort him into a sitting position.

"Brett, what are you doing here?"

"I like to explore," he said.

"It's not a great idea, bud," he said. "It isn't safe."

Brett looked down at his lap, looking very much like a teenaged boy who'd gotten busted. Jack felt bad for him; growing up in this world couldn't be easy. Brett was dealing with things Jack could only have imagined at that age.

"You got any family nearby?" he asked.

"Yeah."

"Okay, we're gonna rest for a bit and then we'll get you home."

After covering Brett with a crumbling bedspread, Jack went in search of fuel for the large fireplace on the far end of the sitting room. It took him a while to clear it out of the cobwebs and dust and ensure the flue was open. Matches and lighters were relics of the past, so he had to do this old school. He collected branches from the small backyard and some old papers scattered through the house. He also gathered kindling – some ratty old clothes from a closet, dead grass, old papers scattered through the house. He ensured everything he used was as dry as possible. He set to work, kneeling at the opening of the hearth. It was a lovely old fireplace, lined with brick but crumbling from years of inattention and exposure.

With his pocketknife, Jack carved out a divot in the plank of wood and then inserted the end of a stick he had sharpened. It wasn't easy work; it never was. Even wood that looked dry could harbor moisture, and the slightest bit of dampness could prove fatal for a fire.

But this was not his first rodeo, and over the years, he had become adept at finding dry wood. It was a gift, an important one in this world of theirs. He set the stick between his palms and began rubbing his hands together as fast as he could. His forearms began to ache. Eventually, a wisp of smoke bloomed at the base of the small divot. He doubled his efforts, sweat pouring into his eyes despite the heat. He was careful to keep the perspiration from dripping onto the wood and extinguishing his nascent flame. He kept one knee on the plank to keep it steady.

Rub, rub, rub, then: an ember burst to life. The tiny orange glow, signifying the birth of fire, life-sustaining fire. He offered a gentle breath to feed it oxygen; just a puff of air. Too much would extinguish and he would have to start over. The nub of fire bloomed, catching the surrounding kindling and doubling in size. He exhaled. A successful fire in the wilderness was never a guarantee. He always recalled his first time having to build his own, his early days in Army survival school.

He'd been twenty-two years old, dropped in the Maine woods in the middle of January with nothing but his wits to keep him alive and a GPS tracker so they could find his body if he didn't make it to the rally point. The cold sucked dry your ability to think clearly; no matter how many times they told you, you didn't understand it until your brain felt like taffy.

The irony was that he had successfully built his fire, but in the ultimate rookie mistake, he had built it at the foot of a large pine because he wanted to lean up against something. Of course, as he slept, a stiff breeze had blown a cord of snow from the heavy branches right down on his fire, snuffing out the blaze. The temperature dropped into the teens that night, and although he had made it to the rally point by noon the next day, one of his fingers had sustained severe frostbite. That was why he now sported nine and one-half fingers. The nub of his left pinkie reminded him how wild and dangerous the outdoors could be, the attention to detail it demanded.

Once the fire was rippling, he used some old books and crumbling chairs as fuel, feeding it until the room filled with a blazing warmth. The temperature had dropped into the twenties. It was a clear and black night. No moon.

The boy slept, but bad dreams punctuated his slumber, and he cried out several times.

"You did this!" he howled. "You did this!"

Jack, who had been dozing, started awake.

"You did this!" he said again.

Brett had pushed himself up in a partial push-up. In the glow of the fire, Jack could see the whites of the kid's eyes. He looked manic.

"You did this!"

Strangely, the incoherent ramblings of this half-conscious boy filled Jack with a flood of deep shame and regret. As though this was his fault. All of it. From the boy's broken leg to their dark, dead world, to the millions out there suffering and starving to the tens of millions more who had died in the last five years.

It was all his fault.

Jack scoffed, embarrassed. What a stupid thing to think. He was out here doing the best he could, giving this poor guy comfort in what was likely the last few hours of his life. This wasn't his fault. And yet he couldn't help but blame himself. For this. For all of it.

The boy woke up. His face was clear and he appeared cognizant of his surroundings.

"Water."

Jack held a cup to his lips and offered him a few sips. He drank it greedily until he couldn't keep up and it dribbled out of his mouth. Jack pulled the cup away. Then Brett lay his head back down.

"How are you feeling?" Jack asked.

"Hurts like shit. What was I saying earlier? I was talking in my sleep, wasn't I?"

You did this.

"I'm not sure," Jack said, his eyes cutting to the floor. "I may have been snoozing."

You did this.

Maybe he *had* done this. Maybe decisions he had made long ago had set the world on this path. When you signed up for the military, you signed over everything. But he had loved it. And then they had made him leave for his ill-advised affair with his commanding officer's wife.

They had sent him back into the civilian world, a place he had never inhabited before with a set of skills that were of no good to anyone. Was it any wonder he had drifted to operating on the wrong side of the law? That's what he had been trained to do. That's all he had known how to do. To operate in deception and shadows.

The boy had fallen asleep again.

Listen to yourself, you schmuck. Your whole life, you demanded that people take responsibility for their actions, and here you are blaming the military for the course your life had taken.

The ultimate hypocrite.

He recalled the steps he had taken to cover his tracks, the way he had lied to Lucy about how he was spending his post-military life. He had told her he was going into security consulting, the way so many ex-military and ex-intelligence types had done.

He even filed the paperwork to make it an official company. Cobalt Consulting. Lucy didn't need to know that it was an offshore company, veiled from careful oversight by the federal government. He ran the proceeds from his early cons through these companies before bringing the money back to the U.S.

And she had known all along.

A gut feeling.

A hunch. She had called him on it based on her hunch. From the time he had known her, she had operated on instinct. She rarely dismissed her gut and understood from the very beginning that Jack was up to no good.

That had been a terrible night. Their first, worst, and last argument.

Then it was over.

Brett stirred awake. He pushed himself up on an elbow, looked Jack squarely in the eye, and then fell back asleep. Jack tossed and turned a bit, unable to settle his nerves enough to fall asleep. He went outside, checked his snare, and found two rabbits had fallen prey to his handiwork. He roasted them over a fire.

It didn't have to be this way. People suffering for no reason. Assume for the moment that Solomon had been telling the truth. That there was a way to reverse the effects of the Pulse. Could they work their way back to a pre-Pulse world? Did they have the wherewithal to put down their weapons, to thaw the mistrust, to do away with the conflict that had dominated these last five years?

Could they go back to a world where kids like Brett just went to school and broke a few rules and played sports and hung out with their friends and did all the things that teenagers were supposed to do?

This was no way to live. This was no way to die.

Night wound toward morning. Jack slept, his slumber punctuated by terrible dreams. In one, he was at a vicious dogfight. Two frightened dogs forced into battle by shapeless figures around him; when he tried to call out his objection, the words would not come. In another, a terrible storm bore down on him, but his body refused to comply as he tried to flee the tempest. His legs would churn and churn and carry him nowhere.

He would wake and check on Brett, who seemed to be no worse but also no better. His face was shiny and his pulse was rapid and weak. Then he would sleep again, and then the dreams would fire up again, as though touching a flame to still-burning embers.

In the morning, the sun broke through the eastern-facing windows, filling the drawing room with bright white light. He woke slowly, the burst of light rousing him from his deepest sleep of the night; his eyes were gummy and his body was slow to respond to his commands. The worst way to feel after a long restless night.

Brett was awake and alert.

14

"Good morning," Jack said, stifling a yawn.

He was fiddling with the fire. It was dying, kicking off only a little bit of heat. No matter. They wouldn't be long for this temporary way station.

"Hey," Brett said, glancing around confusedly. "Thanks for staying with me."

"Don't mention it."

Yeah, don't mention it. Don't mention it because it was a dumbass thing to do when you get down to it. Each added side trip, every lark and frolic, increases the odds that something goes wrong. And then where would he be?

"You from around here?" Brett asked.

"No."

"Where you headed?"

"Looking for someone in the city."

The boy chuckled, grimacing as he did so.

"Wow, you really aren't from around here, are you?"

Jack did not reply.

"Look," Brett said, "all the access points into the city are guarded."

"Can you help me get across?"

He nodded.

"I'll try," he said. "The group I'm with? We control two of the bridges from Virginia."

"The one nearby?"

"Yeah, that would be nice, huh?"

The kid had some snark in him. Jack wasn't one for snark, to be honest, but if Brett had the energy to sass him, then he probably had enough to help Jack get across a bridge. He would take it.

"What say we put a splint on that leg and get out of here?"

"Yeah, let's."

It took an hour, but Jack fashioned a makeshift splint from a pair of two-by-fours, which he secured to Brett's leg with a pair of leather belts from the bedroom closet. The bonus find was a pair of crutches in the back of that same closet. The crutches' padded tops had disintegrated. Jack jerry-rigged replacement pads with a pair of old T-shirts.

After securing his pack, Jack gently guided Brett back to the stairwell. There, Jack was reminded of the partial stairway collapse from the day before. He descended what remained carefully before reaching the stairwell's new terminus. Eyeballing it, he concluded it was about a ten-foot drop to the ground.

"Well, shit," said Brett.

"Relax," he said. "I'll figure something out."

He left Brett at the landing and picked his way through the upstairs rooms, looking for a solution. His eyes fell on the very armoire that had nearly ended Brett's life. He sized it up for a bit as a plan took shape in his mind. It wouldn't be pretty, but he thought it would work. He dragged the armoire back to the landing and shoved it into the gap created by the stair collapse. He repeated the task with a dresser and a television stand from the second bedroom. Eventually, he had backfilled the gap well enough to create artificial terrain to traverse. He retrieved the mattresses from the two bedrooms and laid them out across the impromptu landfill. The second mattress reached nearly to the ground.

"We're gonna climb down," he said.

Brett nodded.

The path was rickety and unstable; the mattresses barely hanging together. Carefully, they edged their way off the lowest step onto the mattress, bracing themselves with the walls. Jack lifted himself off the top one and began sliding it out from under him and Brett. It was slow, tedious work. The tower was not particularly stable and rocked precipitously. Each movement was agony for Brett.

Trouble struck when they were a few feet from the bottom. It would have been an easy drop for men with functioning legs, but that was not the case here. The second mattress' center of gravity shifted, toppling over. Jack gathered his feet underneath him as he slid off. Brett screamed in agony as he rolled off. Jack braced the boy's body, and the pair hit the cold ground. Jack absorbed much of the impact.

The foyer was silent but their ragged breathing, punctuated by the occasional grunt of pain from Brett. It hadn't been pretty, but they were down. Jack helped Brett to his feet and slung his left arm around his shoulders. Slowly, step by step, they made their way to the front door.

Back outside, a dank chill had taken hold. Low clouds blanketed the city. Thick fog swirled through the streets. In sharp contrast to the previous day's sunshine, rain was likely before today was out. The good news was that it was likely too warm for snow. Cold rain wasn't fun by any means, but it was a hell of a lot better than snow.

They continued west. The bridge receded into the distance. Just behind him lay the canoe Jack spotted the day before.

"We can take this canoe," Jack said. "I'll lift you in and out of it."

Brett was shaking his head.

"We won't make it," he said. "This part of the city is crawling with Shepherds."

Jack's eyes went wide. Danny's group.

"Shepherds?"

"Yeah. Buncha psychos."

"So how far is it?" Jack asked. "To your bridge?"

"Four miles. Maybe five."

Jack responded with a short whistle. Five miles through unfamiliar territory would be difficult under any circumstances. Escorting this injured kid would make it that much harder. A part of Jack that he didn't want to admit still resided inside him considered leaving the boy. Jack had saved his life, and he was out of danger. He'd make it home before dark, assuming he was telling the truth about his provenance. He still had no evidence the boy was telling the truth. For all Jack knew to the contrary, Brett might simply be delivering him to his doom.

They passed by the bridge closest to them. He paused, pressing his binoculars to his face, wondering if he could make do on his own. The checkpoint was about a hundred yards distant. Two people stood guard. They were engaged with a small group traveling by horse-drawn wagon seeking passage across the bridge. A middle-aged African-American man, a white woman, and two teenaged kids. Hard to say if this family unit had existed before the Pulse or if these people had found each other in the aftermath.

Rescuing Brett had already cost him the better part of two days; he needed to get into the city, sooner than later; there was no reason to think he couldn't make the crossing here. Theirs was a transactional world. People were always trying to make a buck. That was one thing he had learned from his days as a con man. Very few criminals meant their victims harm. They just wanted a shortcut to prosperity. Violence was costly and, of course, dangerous. It may not have been fair that these folks controlled the bridge, but control it they did. At least for today. Tomorrow, another group would come along and there would be violence, probably. If he had something he could offer the custodians of the bridge, he could be on his way in a matter of minutes.

He continued his surveillance of the situation unfolding at the bridge. The woman handed over two cloth sacks to the guards. As the first sentinel secured the loot in their wagon, the second guard waved the party through. The woman reclaimed her spot next to her companion. The guards reassumed their posts in old camping chairs on the shoulder. A small firepit, its flames bright and inviting on this gray morning, kept them warm.

"Those folks will be dead soon," the boy said.

A chill ran through Jack. The way the kid had said it, so matter of factly.

"Why do you say that?"

"It's what they do," Jack said. "They believe everyone is a burden on the planet."

This sounded like the mantra Solomon had shared but even more dangerously radicalized. What the hell was wrong with people?

Jack watched until the group had safely cleared the bridge, a journey of about a quarter of an hour. Eventually, the party receded into the fog swirling around the bridge. He hoisted his pack onto his shoulders and they kept moving.

It took much of the day, tracing the cut of the river west and then slightly northwest, but eventually, he and Brett neared a bridge that his group controlled. Jack had no idea if the kid was luring him to his doom, but if he was, he was certainly committed to his mission. He had made steady progress on a bum leg, never once complaining. They broke every half hour or so to rest; but five minutes later, they were back on the move. Jack was impressed. Then again, it took this kind of intestinal fortitude to make it in the world today. No one had it easy, those fair or foul, young or old.

Brett drew up short, precipitating a sudden stop by Jack. The boy pointed his crutch toward the horizon. The George Washington Parkway curled northwest before making a westward turn near its interchange with the Francis Scott Key Bridge. It was nearing dark.

The boy sighed, and it sounded very much like one of relief. Not twelve hours ago, the boy's goose had likely been cooked. If it hadn't been for Jack, he would have died in that bedroom. He certainly owed Jack. As the boy swung his crutch out to continue their trek, Jack reached out and grabbed him by the elbow.

He started to remind Brett of the debt he owed, but Brett read Jack's mind.

"Man, don't you worry," Brett said, looking squarely at Jack. There were tears in his eyes. "You saved my ass. I won't forget that. My people won't either."

Jack raised his eyebrows and released the boy's elbow. His sincerity appeared genuine. Well, he would know one way or another very soon.

They continued up the ramp, now moving much more slowly than they'd moved earlier. The ramp was steep, and the boy's energy reserves had flagged. Ten minutes later, they merged onto the bridge, the guard station just ahead. Jack did not attempt to conceal their approach. Either Brett would get him across or he wouldn't. The more open he was, the less likely a threat he would appear to be. He dispensed with any notion of simply opening fire on them. There was no way to know how big a force he was dealing with. If they were smart, they would be on constant lookout. The bridge was a valuable commodity and it behooved its caretakers to watch over it carefully.

A few moments later, coming around a dead minivan, he drew the attention of one of the guards. A woman, Jack could now tell, as he got closer to the bridge. She signaled to her partner, who looked up from the book he'd been reading. It was a shit detail, that was for certain. Cold, heat, rain, sun, and just sitting here dealing with travelers who may or may not pose you a lethal threat.

Boredom bred carelessness and carelessness could get you killed. There were rarely second chances in this world. The woman picked up her weapon and tucked the stock under her arm. She wore jeans and a heavy black leather jacket. A black scarf encircled her neck, and a gaiter was pulled up over the lower half of her face. Only her eyes remained visible.

"Kristen!" the boy called out. "It's me! Brett!"

"Brett?"

"Yeah!"

"My God!"

She seemed overjoyed at the boy's return, but her weapon remained up.

"Who's your friend?"

"He's cool," Brett said. "He saved me."

Kristen held her position for a moment, seemingly unsure whether she was being set up. Jack respected her caution. He held his hands up to show that he was unarmed.

"Brett, come on toward me," she said. Then she pointed at Jack.

"You wait there."

Jack nodded.

Brett glanced over at Jack.

"I'll get you across," he said. "Don't worry."

Brett hitched his crutches under him and swung toward Jack and back to his people. Kristen embraced him, as did her partner. They were happy to see him; clearly, he'd been feared dead. He had been pretty far from home. An animated discussion followed the hug. Kristen scolded him for getting himself into so much trouble.

Kristen jogged toward Jack, keeping her weapon up.

"Keep them where I can see them," she said. "You got it?"

"Yeah," he called out.

"Keep moving forward. Stop there," she said, pointing to a large red X spray-painted on the asphalt about twenty yards north of Jack's position. He passed under old highway signs, the familiar green of interstate travel fading in the years of inattention. In the distance, the sound of automatic gunfire peppered the morning. The gunplay did not seem to faze the guards one way or another.

Jack made his way to the X and paused. The woman slung her rifle over her shoulder and slowly made her way out to meet him. Behind her, her colleague had his weapon up, providing the woman with cover.

"Put your bag down on the ground next to you," she said. "Do it slow."

Jack complied, setting his pack down.

"Hands on your head now," she said. "Turn around and back up towards me until I tell you to stop."

He laced his hands together and set them atop his head. Then he rotated a hundred and eighty degrees and began walking backward slowly, gingerly, one step at a time.

"I don't want any trouble," he said meekly.

"Just keep quiet," she said.

"Yes, ma'am."

He continued another dozen steps before she directed him to halt. He froze where he stood, keeping his head down subserviently. The woman approached him slowly, tensing up as she did so.

"I'm gonna search you now," she said. "Got any weapons?"

"In my waistband."

"Cooperative," she said. "Benji, we got a cooperative one here."

"I like that," called out her partner.

She lifted his shirttail and removed his weapon. She handed it over to Benji, who had drawn closer to the pair as she searched him. This didn't concern him too much. Weapons were a dime a dozen; he could probably assemble an arsenal before sunset if he needed to. What he needed now, though, was to work with honey instead of vinegar. What he needed was safe passage across the bridge.

"Keep those hands on your head and turn around," she said.

He did so. He was met by a diminutive woman with fierce blue eyes.

"What do you want?"

"I need to get into the city."

"Follow me."

15

Jack sat blindfolded in a metal folding chair.

He'd been here for at least an hour, but that was a guess; deprived of one of your senses, it was easy to lose track of time. He was just inside the city, not far from the bridge. About two hundred steps by Jack's count, give or take.

The bridge was about a quarter of a mile long, descending to the northern banks of the Potomac. The breeze had died down as he cleared the bridge, providing welcome relief from the early January chill. The smell of fires burning was robust. People burning whatever they could to stay warm.

The identity of Brett's group remained a mystery. If the kid was to be believed, then they were no friends of the Shepherds. But that didn't mean much for Jack. The enemy of your enemy wasn't necessarily your friend, after all. He did not resist or raise any stink, choosing instead to learn what he could. Brett's people didn't have to be the good guys to be useful. To his credit, Brett had encouraged Kristen to let Jack go, but she wasn't willing to do that. A decision above their pay grades, it seemed.

So his rescue of Brett had, to date, earned him little but a trip inside this nondescript building. The room was cold and musty; the sounds echoed, suggesting the space was quite cavernous. Someone, perhaps several someones, was here watching over him.

He became aware of the sounds of another person nearby. The soft hiss of respiration. The gurgle of an empty stomach. The person drew closer to him, he could feel their presence near him. A chair was dragged across the hard concrete floor. The sound made the hairs on his arm stand up. One of his pet peeves.

They did not make him wait long.

Rough hands removed his blindfold. He was on the floor of a warehouse. A warehouse or storage facility. The windows were high off the floor; the dim light of the day bathed the interior in shadows. Sitting before him was a woman about his age. Ramrod straight brown hair hung down to her shoulders. Her voice was thick, gravelly.

"Sorry for not being more hospitable," she said. "We have to be really careful these days."

He took a moment to take in his surroundings.

"Thank you for bringing Brett home," she said.

"Don't mention it."

"He's my nephew," she said. "Not the brightest bulb in the drawer. Likes to range outside of our territory. Even after I've told him a thousand times. Anyway. I digress. What's your name?"

"Jack."

"I'm Trinity."

Jack wondered if that was her real name or one she'd adopted in the apocalypse. People did that. Shed their names like snakeskin. Tossed away their old lives in favor of new ones.

"It's my real name, case you were wondering," she said.

A smile broke across Jack's face. The woman had a disarming way about her. He did not feel like he was in any danger. This was a well-organized outfit, whoever they were. You could tell from the way Trinity carried herself. Equal parts charity and wariness.

"So what brings you to our neck of the woods?"

"Looking for someone," he said.

"Who would that be?" she asked.

"My wife."

"Did you lose her?"

"We got separated by the Pulse," he said softly. "I've been looking for her ever since."

Trinity's eyebrows rocked upwards.

"You've been looking for her for all this time?"

"We were living in D.C. when it happened," he said. "But I was on a business trip in California. It's taken me this long to make it back here."

Her brow furrowed. She leaned forward in her chair, set her elbows on her knees.

"It took you five years to make it back here?"

"Yeah," he said. "Well, I couldn't exactly catch a redeye flight back, you know."

"Touché," she said. "What's it like out there?"

Jack was pleased. This was going well; she was invested in his story now, as he'd expected her to be.

"Insane," he said. "I was in San Francisco. Top floor of

this big-ass office building. Took me three days to get out of the building. A month just to get out of the city. People lost their heads."

"Can't say I'm surprised," she said. "Buncha hippies out there."

Jack laughed. It was a funny thing to say, even if she didn't mean for it to be. Five years into this and still he had to listen to partisan bullshit.

"Five years to make it back, though?"

"You wouldn't believe some of the stuff I had to go through to get here," he said.

"Enlighten me," she said.

"The first part of the trip wasn't so bad," he said. "After I got out of San Francisco, I went north. My plan was to come east across the upper plains and through the Midwest. I was on my own, making good progress. I wanted to avoid the southern route. All that desert would have made it hard to find water, which I hear is important."

He said that with a slight smirk, inviting her in on his joke.

"I went north into Oregon and Washington. Ended up in a FEMA refugee camp outside Seattle, but that fell apart in a hurry. Guy took over, made us his slaves. Took me a year to escape. Then I came east through Yellowstone. Broke my leg in about ten places when I fell down a hill. It took me a year to recover from that. Then I stayed to help this family get a homestead up and running. Figured I owed them that for saving my life. Then just making progress east got harder and harder. Lots of bridges washed out or impassable. Some of the time I just had to rest and recharge, make sure I had enough to eat and drink."

"Quite the road trip," the woman said.

"Just glad to be home," Jack said.

"What's your wife's name?"

"Molly."

"Where did you live?"

"Georgetown," he said. He was laying it on thick here. He was impressed by the depth and texture of his deception. He had no idea if she was buying it, but it was still a bravura performance. "She was a math professor."

She was silent a moment as she considered his tale. Just a sorry survivor of their shared predicament. But as the silence yawned into discomfort, Jack felt like he was losing her. He stayed quiet, letting the chips sit on the table for now. The bottom line was that he was getting into the city one way or another. Perhaps Trinity didn't realize that just yet, but that was fine.

"You have a picture of her?"

"I do."

Jack dug in his pack for the old photograph of Molly he'd carried in his wallet. It had been there for years. He didn't know why exactly. It wasn't in his character to be so sentimental. He handed it over to the woman.

"Pretty lady," she said after studying it a moment.

Jack didn't reply.

She handed the photo back to him and it went back into his pack. She did not return his weapon to him, however.

Trinity leaned back in her chair, crossed one leg over the other. She fiddled with a piece of lint or dirt on her pant leg before refocusing her attention on Jack. She leaned forward, set her elbows on her knees, laced her fingers together.

"Now, Jack, is even a single word of that story true?"

Jack smiled mischievously.

It had been worth a shot. The less information he had to divulge about his true mission, the better. But that approach wasn't going to work with Trinity.

"You know, Jack, I wanted to like you," she said, her voice taking a hard edge. "But the first thing you did was come in here and lie to me."

Jack remained quiet. Perhaps it had not been worth the attempt. His rescue of Brett had generated some goodwill, established the most fragile of alliances, and just like that, he had wrecked it.

"I've got half a mind to put a bullet in your head and be done with it."

She said it matter of factly, without any pomp or circumstance, and Jack understood that he had vastly underestimated her. Now he needed to climb out of the hole he had dug for himself.

"Well, I am looking for a woman named Molly."

"Why?"

"We knew each other a long time ago."

"Okay," she said. "So where's home?"

"Not far from Richmond."

He was deliberately vague. There was no need to be any more specific; Trinity did not belabor the point.

"Pretty stable there?"

"Yes," he said. "We work hard but we've been fortunate."

It begged the question of why people continued to

make a go of it in the cities. The urban areas were dank and brutal. The more people per square mile, the higher the chance one of them would kill you for looking at them sideways.

"It's hard here," she said. "But there are rewards too."

"How so?"

"More people means more commerce," she said. "We see a lot of traffic here, especially when the seasons change."

Survivors often migrated north for the summer to escape the brutal heat and humidity south of the Mason-Dixon Line. The flow of traffic reversed in autumn when the air turned crisp and portended snow. Life up north became very difficult once the weather turned. That was why Jack liked central Virginia. The growing season was quite long, but it didn't get so hot that it was intolerable. Plus, he didn't mind the occasional light snowfall. No more than four inches. Anything more than that became a gigantic hassle. It had been a while since the last big storm, at least two winters, maybe three. They were due for one before long.

Trinity had a good point. If you had the fortitude for it, urban areas could be worth the effort. More traffic did mean more goods and bigger selections of virtually everything. Medicines, weapons, tools. If you knew how to use it, you could probably find it. Plus, this was the last big city coming south from the once-crowded northeast metropolises. New York was probably more exciting than it was worth.

"So tell me more about this woman you're looking for."

Jack gnawed on his lower lip, considering how much to share.

Trinity sighed.

"Let's start over," she said. "You're familiar with the Shepherds?"

"A little," he said. He shared with her Danny's confession.

"The only reason I know you're not one of them is that Brett is still alive."

"That bad?"

"Yeah. It's a wonder Brett hasn't gotten himself killed yet. But like I said, he's got his own mind."

"Can you tell me more about them?"

She ran her hands through her hair.

"I've been in the city since it happened," she said. "I worked for the Census Bureau. I was a bit of a prepper, to be honest with you. Had a farm out in Manassas, about thirty miles west of here. But I broke my ankle that afternoon coming down the steps of my office, so all my prepping didn't help me much. A few of my coworkers stayed to look after me. They all were panicked, didn't know what to do. So I just directed them while I recuperated. Before I knew it, people were sort of looking at me as the boss. There were a dozen of us at the start, but over time, our community grew. By the end of that summer, there were four or five hundred. I couldn't well leave them."

She paused for a moment, perhaps reflecting on the journey she'd taken to get this far.

"Finally made it back to the farm about two years later," she said, chuckling. "Everything was gone. All my prep, for nothing. Man plans and God laughs, right?"

"Sometimes it seems like that."

"Anyway, my priorities were security, fresh water, livestock, and agriculture. Everything else we'd make up as we went along. But around that same time, this other group was doing the same. Incredibly violent. They've killed a bunch of my people."

Her voice had grown hard.

"About a year ago, it spilled into open warfare. Believe that? Urban combat, here in Washington, D.C. It's positively medieval. We've captured spies in the past, and they've been dealt with accordingly. I want to be clear here, Jack, is it?"

He nodded.

"Why are you looking for this Molly?"

"She may know how to fix this mess we're in."

"Which mess is that, exactly?"

"The big one. The mess which spawned all the other messes."

"The blackout."

Jack nodded.

Trinity did not visibly react to Jack's bombshell.

"Wow," she said, her voice barely above a whisper.

They sat in silence for a few minutes as Trinity processed the news.

"I know that's hard to believe," Jack said.

She scoffed.

"That's the crazy thing," Trinity replied. "I do believe you. Something has them hot and bothered lately. We have some intel that they'd been hunting for a man and a woman. About two weeks ago, they caught the woman. Not sure what happened to her partner."

Two weeks ago. Molly.

Finally. Actual intel.

"Her partner's dead," Jack said.

Might as well get it all on the table.

"How do you know that?"

"He came looking for me," he said. "But we had a Shepherd operative in my community. He murdered him. I had never heard of the Shepherds before that."

"Interesting."

"Do you know where Molly is?" Jack asked.

"What do you mean she can fix the mess?"

"The world can go back to the way it was," Jack said. "Light switches and ice cubes and computers and SUVs and all that."

"That is quite a claim."

"I know it sounds crazy."

She rolled her eyes dismissively.

"Look, we've been fighting these bastards for two years. Maybe three. I've lost count. They've done so many terrible things. Hurt a lot of people. They control most of the bridges, most of the arable land in the city. They kill with impunity. But we're close to ripping their heart out. And now you show up with this story."

"You have to give me some time," Jack said. "Just a few days to find Molly."

Trinity sat with her right leg crossed over her left. Her hand lay flat against the side of her face as she considered Jack's request. He knew the dilemma she was facing. He was telling a fantastical story. It barely made any sense. And it was too fantastical to even bother with.

Unless it was true.

"If you want to bring these people down for good, then you have to trust me."

“Okay,” she replied. “She’s being held at the Museum of Natural History.”

“Thank you.”

“I’ll give you a week to find her,” she said. “I can’t wait any longer than that.”

“Deal.”

16

Jack spent a chilly but dry night in the warehouse. Trinity arrived shortly after sunrise bearing his pack and weapon.

"I'll escort you to the front line," she said. "After that, you'll be on your own."

Jack nodded.

They made their way to the back of the building, which sat on the edge of the riverbank. Once upon a time, this facility had supplied fuel, equipment, and repairs to the boats that had tied up here.

The weather had turned sour. A brisk wind and low clouds greeted them as he stepped outside. They were very close to the bridge. Jack paused near its edge, looking out across the river, which curved away from him to the southeast. To the east, a wedge-shaped peninsula lay between Virginia and the city proper. It was home to East Potomac Park, which came to a point directly to Jack's east. In the shadow of the next bridge over stood a series of buildings, part of a U.S. Park Police station.

The Department of the Interior had made its home in a building close to the riverbank. Beyond those buildings, farther to the east, lay a bustling tent city, home to hundreds of survivors. It looked cold and miserable. He scanned the camp with his binoculars. A group of kids was shooting baskets on a hoop. The land had been cleared, probably now home to farmland.

Off to his right, flying across another slice of the Potomac, another bridge cut northeast into the city. The bridge, whose name Jack did not know, ended at a marina that had once been home to yachts belonging to D.C.'s rich and famous. None of the yachts was still moored. Two had foundered right here in the channel, their bows still visible in the dirty water. The main building was in rough shape, its windows long since blown out.

They continued north, walking in silence. There wasn't much more to say. Either he would accomplish his mission or he wouldn't. He couldn't have asked her for much more than the chance to do so.

At the intersection of 31st and M Streets, they parted ways. Beyond was an automobile graveyard. Thousands of vehicles wedged together to make it impossible for an advancing vanguard to cross. Clever. Anything could work as an impenetrable perimeter these days if you had the wherewithal to move it.

"Good luck," Trinity said. "I'm rooting for you. The Shepherds, they're bad news."

"You ever wonder they may think the same about us?"

She scoffed.

"They're lunatics," she said. "Anytime we try to make progress, dig ourselves out of this shithole life, they just knock it down."

"Maybe they have a good reason for it."

"Oh, sure, protecting the natural world, yeah, I've heard all their stories. You know what, though?"

"What?"

"It's all bullshit," she said. "Some folks just want to watch the world burn."

She chuckled and gestured to the silent darkness around her.

"As if this wasn't apocalyptic enough for them. I swear to God, if we just went along with them, they would get even crazier, move the goalposts even more. They would decide something batshit, that humanity was an accident, that we were never meant to rule the roost and then pour homemade bleach in our food supply or something."

Jack had to agree with her. For some people, things could never get dark enough.

"True."

Their conversation appeared to be at its end.

"I better get moving," Jack said.

They touched fists. The handshake had never returned to its former glory after the Covid-19 pandemic.

Jack hitched his pack up his shoulders before continuing his journey, leaving Trinity and her army behind. A stiff, icy breeze blew in from the east, chilling him to the bone. It was going to be a very cold day. He tried not to think about the long game here, focusing instead on what he could accomplish today. He was tired, and he still had a long way to go. In many ways, the mission had just started. And he wasn't twenty-five anymore. Back then, he could polish off a twelve-pack, grab a nap and then snap off a ten-mile march with little effort. His regular runs back home helped, of course, but forty-six was forty-six.

The Museum of Natural History lay about a mile due east, west of the Capitol and the U.S. Supreme Court building. The Capitol looked grim and depressing in the morning gray. The dome itself remained intact but many of the windows were missing. Without constant attention and maintenance, it looked tarnished. The green mildew coating it like a second skin was depressingly visible in the sun.

His route would carry him northeast past the White House before a turn south for the last mile to the museum. The sight of these cathedrals to American history made him nostalgic, reminding him of a trip here with Emma not long before she had gotten sick. It was a fun trip, just the two of them while Lucy had worked a double shift. They had left Richmond early, taking the train, spending the day in the city. They had eaten at his favorite joint, a tiny hole-in-the-wall called Snake Burger. It was a simple operation, smashed burgers that were crispy on the outside and hot on the inside. The fries defied physics by staying hot and fresh for the duration of your meal.

There was a certain lurid allure to the physical world now. How weird could things get? How weird would they look? Especially here, in Washington, D.C., the nation's capital. The place where America was supposed to look its best. The place that made the world envious of it, the standard to which all other countries aspired.

Part of him had believed that once upon a time. America wasn't perfect, by any means, but it was a hell of a lot better than most places. Admittedly, that was not a high bar to clear. Based on his travels and work overseas, the depth and breadth of corruption in other countries made America look positively angelic.

But now all the makeup had been stripped away. This Washington, D.C., felt like what it really had been. A place that operated for the rich and the connected and the powerful. Largely on the backs of regular folks who lived in the dark and didn't know how little they knew about the government. And they were supposedly the good guys.

He chuckled.

The good guys.

He kept moving northeast, passing a sign for the Holocaust Museum, which sat farther to his east. He recalled a visit to the museum with Emma on their trip here. They had paused at the small sign marking the museum's main entrance before entering. He wanted her to understand what could happen if you looked the other way.

He considered what lessons a horrific atrocity like the Holocaust might have in a world like theirs. He could not help but consider Molly's complicity in the way their world was. Her actions had brought terrible ruin to countless lives. Jack was one man and he had lost track of the number of people who had died in the years since the Pulse. Lives that would be chugging along if it had not been for the Machine.

These dark thoughts percolated in his head as he reached 14th Street's intersection with Route 29, bracketing the Mount Vernon Square to the north. The museum's main entrance fronted Madison Drive, several blocks south, but he wanted to approach it from the rear.

Gunfire, which had been sporadic since he had

crossed the bridge, had grown in intensity, so he ducked into an alley between two stone-white government buildings so he could better assess the situation. As he took cover behind an old Dumpster, the sound of shouts and gunfire peppered the air. A truck was still backed into the loading dock, its journey complete that May afternoon five years ago. The rollaway door was still open on the maw of the building's interior.

He followed the ramp into the dock, watching each step carefully. The truck's rear hatch was open. Inside the cargo were boxes of ruined computers. The cardboard boxes in which they had shipped had long ago disintegrated. It smelled musty. He moved deeper into the building's loading dock. It was quiet. Water dripped from a ceiling; a permanent puddle had formed in a low spot of concrete.

The gunfire drew closer. He didn't want to get pinned in near a rapidly shifting front line. A door to his left opened up onto a dark corridor, almost pitch black. He primed his ears but heard nothing. The building appeared abandoned.

Another door opened up onto a long concourse. It felt like a standard government office building, ugly and utilitarian. Dim light streamed in through large windows at the far end of the corridor, the building's north wing. Jack made his way down the hallway, finding another staircase at the hallway's terminus. He climbed the stairs to a second-floor landing. A large plate-glass window overlooked Independence Avenue and the Mall beyond.

This window was still intact, which was nothing short of a miracle. From this vantage point, he was treated to one of the strangest sights he had ever seen. Deep trenches had been dug on either side of the Mall, one on the western side, one on the eastern. The middle of the Mall was strewn with bodies, some fresh, most of them badly decomposed, some skeletal. It was as if someone had plucked a scene from a history book of World War I and plopped it right down in the middle of Washington, D.C.

The western trench, which appeared to be controlled by Trinity's army, was bustling with activity. Dozens of men and women were busy scurrying about. Indiscriminate fire across the no-man's-land between the two trenches. Neither side was trying to advance across the Mall. They seemed to be fighting for the sake of fighting. The western line extended across Independence Avenue, barricaded by hundreds of sandbags rising six or eight feet off the ground. A similar perimeter had been built on the eastern side.

He kept a wary eye on the Mall, but there was very little activity for the balance of the afternoon. He was going to have to figure out some way across this strange battlefield; the Museum was behind the Shepherds' lines. He could double back south and try to get behind the lines on their southern flank. But that would take more time, and there was no way to know what other fresh horrors he might encounter. This city was like a haunted house of mirrors. It looked like D.C. at first glance, but it didn't take long to see how truly screwed up everything was.

Whatever the case, he would wait until nightfall to move. He loved the night. He knew how to blend in with it, become part of it. Until then, he needed to catch up on his rest. There was a box window with a platform wide enough for him to stretch out on. He lay down, using his pack as a pillow, and closed his eyes.

HE WOKE UP HOURS LATER, shivering. He felt clearheaded and rested.

It was the middle of the night. Time to make his move on the museum. This time of day was best to launch any stealth mission, especially an infiltration. People were extremely predictable; most of them would be asleep, regardless of which end of the candle they burned. The night owls had been in bed for a while. The early risers were still an hour from the start of their days.

He wound his way back to the loading dock, working in the pitch black from his memory of the building's layout. Back outside, on the loading dock, silvery moonlight shimmered across a dirty puddle in a large pothole. It was bitterly cold.

A full moon hung in the sky on this clear night. A moonless night would have been preferable, but at least the silvery moonlight made it easier to see. He edged his way along the building's wall out to Route 1, which bisected two green areas. The Washington Monument speared the night sky. The trees were barren this time of year. They had grown wild, filling out with extra lumber that wasn't trimmed back.

He kept close to the buildings, taking care to move in silence. At 12th Street, he turned south, continuing along the pedestrian bridge running the spine of the 12th Street Tunnel. Trinity's perimeter defenses lay several blocks to the west. At the end of the bridge, he ducked into a small copse of ancient trees at the corner of Madison and 12th. The branches glinted with ice that had formed in a freezing fog.

The Museum lay just to his east. A line of trees fronted its main entrance. A single sentry patrolled its veranda. He or she was smoking a foul-smelling cigarette. The acrid smoke tanged the cold air and reached Jack's nostrils from his vantage point, some forty yards clear of the stone steps. He chose a spot just southeast of the entrance, near two large barren maples. Their trunks were thick and wide, giving him cover from the sentry, who was paying little attention to his surroundings. It was difficult to blame him. Keeping watch was extremely difficult. Ninety-nine point nine percent of the work was pure, uneventful boredom.

Jack studied the terrain carefully. It was a short jaunt across the front walkway to the steps. He'd have to time it just so to stay out of the watchman's sight. The guard paced the entrance plaza. He sized up the distance to the museum's exterior wall. It would take him fifteen or twenty seconds to cover the distance.

He watched the watchman for a few minutes, hoping to discern a pattern. Eventually, he hit upon one. The guard was tracing a rectangular pattern around the veranda; eight or ten steps east, south, west, north before turning east again. It took him about ten or twelve seconds to complete each leg of the rectangle. Less time than Jack was comfortable with to maintain the element of surprise. He would have to time it just perfectly.

The man was about to restart the circuit; he walked west, his eyes scanning the terrain, as though he could sense something was amiss. A bit of instinct at work, one that he would be well served to heed. But he didn't. He made the turn north, completed that leg, and as he turned east, Jack broke free of his cover.

Jack sprinted as hard as he could, trading stealth for speed. He could allow for a broken branch. The night was full of weird natural sounds. Stealing glances to his east as he ran, he accelerated as the man turned west, giving him a full view of Jack's approach. But Jack made it, slamming into the stone wall before the guard had a chance to spot him. And just like that, the man's life had turned on the most fleeting of moments. He didn't know it yet, but his whole life had been pointing directly at this moment. Jack rested a moment, catching his breath, waiting for the discomfort in his lungs to recede.

The guard made another complete loop while Jack recovered. When he turned back east, Jack made his move. He zipped up the steps, coming in behind the man halfway across the entrance plaza. His head popped up just a moment too late, suddenly alerted to a threat behind him, perhaps ruing his decision to ignore that gut feeling a few moments earlier. Jack jammed the knife into the soft indentation just above the base of his neck, forcing the blade deep into the man's brain; it was messy work, but when done right, it was one of the quietest ways to kill,

And Jack knew how to do it right.

The man's legs buckled, his life extinguished. He had never had a chance. Keeping the knife in place, Jack wrapped his left arm around the man's abdomen and continued across the plaza to its east side. He guided the body down the steps to a dark corner in the shade of the building structure. Jack followed him down to the bottom of the steps to survey his work. He removed the knife from the man's head and cleaned it.

All remained quiet. Nothing stirred. He climbed back up the stairs slowly, hugging the wall. At the doors, he paused. He peered around the corner. The interior foyer shimmered with candlelight. He studied the walls, looking for the silhouettes that might indicate the presence of others. But he saw none. The foyer was empty. He reached for the door handle, opening it slowly. When the gap was just big enough, he slipped inside. The door swung closed quietly behind him.

He was in the museum's main entrance hall. Candles flickered in sconces spaced out around the perimeter of the foyer. Directly ahead lay the brooding shadow of the museum's first attraction. It was a statue of a prehistoric elephant situated on a large stone platform. The shadow of its long trunk flickered against the back wall.

It was quiet and deserted. Jack moved silently to one of the four pillars bracketing this edge of the large hall. Satisfied the coast was clear, he slipped around it and ducked behind a self-service donation booth. To his right lay another corridor, this one leading to a bank of elevators. Ahead of him was the museum's information desk. Beyond lay another portal leading deeper into the museum.

He drew his weapon and crept across the floor of the exhibit hall. He was badly exposed here, but only for a moment. He reached the information desk, ducking low behind the platform featuring the mammoth. He primed his ears, listening for signs of life. In a big drafty place like this, voices would carry a long way. Somewhere in the distance, he thought he could just make out whispers, but that wasn't certain. It could just as easily have been the wind on this cold night. The building would have deteriorated in the years since the Pulse, creating gaps and openings for the elements to find their way in.

He reached around the cubbies of the information desk, tearing through old cobwebs. Inside one was a stack of glossy brochures that had done a reasonable job surviving the elements. He studied one in the dim light of the burning candles. This level of the museum was nothing but large open spaces; there wouldn't be many places to stash a hostage. The museum's work had taken place in the basement, where scientists examined new arrivals, repaired damage, updated biographical information for the museum's exhibits. There were more administration offices on the top floors. Those struck him as the likeliest place to hold a hostage.

He took a moment to consider his next move. There was a stairwell on the far side of the information desk. In the shimmering light of the candle, the sign affixed to the wall read Butterfly Pavilion — Gems and Minerals — 2nd floor. On the third floor was museum administration.

His battle was just beginning, and already he was finding the Shepherds exhausting. It wasn't that he didn't understand their point of view. There was a certain appeal to keeping the world as it was. After all, climate change had been stopped in its tracks. Greenhouse gases were virtually non-existent. No more factories belching their smoke into the atmosphere. No more plastic was being made. No more fossil fuels being burned. No massive server farms consuming massive amounts of energy. No coal mines running. It had all stopped.

But the price they had paid had been so dear.

And that was the problem with extremism. When you lost the forest for the trees. What good was it if half the world's population died? The human toll of the Pulse had been horrific.

It was difficult to wrap one's head around.

None of them had even known how widespread the Pulse had been. Until Solomon had shared his fantastical tale with them, it was difficult to know if it was limited to North America or if it had gone worldwide. Anyone claiming they knew otherwise was full of it. How could you know?

But if Solomon was to be believed, then this had been a worldwide event from the beginning. Ironically, developing nations had likely weathered the storm much better than the world's great powers. If you were already dirt poor, living off the land, not relying on online retailers to drop whatever your little heart desired on your doorstep, then the loss of technology would not have been much skin off your back.

And that was these extremists' guiding principle. Humanity had sacrificed everything for their technological gods, and look where that had gotten them. The true way to live well was for the survivors to move on without their techno-shackles. They were freer without them. And the cost of so many lives just served to drive that point home so much deeper.

HOURS TICKED BY, but Jack still had no lead on Molly's whereabouts. It was mid-morning now, and the building had come to life. People came and went, attending to their duties, chatting, smoking foul-smelling homemade cigarettes. Jack counted dozens of Shepherds, men and women, young and old. Most were armed, their rifles slung haphazardly on their shoulders.

He found cover in abandoned offices and supply closets. The building was big, easy to get lost in. He didn't quite understand the tactical reasons for the Shepherds making a home here, but there was a lot he didn't understand about the group. It was, he supposed, easy to fortify and defend.

Currently, he was hunkered down in a small office near the end of a long corridor. Surplus furniture and file cabinets crowded the room, leaving Jack several hiding places little room to maneuver. The window overlooked a large green space stretching away to the north. It had been converted into farmland. The fields lay barren for now, blanketed with a thin layer of snow.

He was still struggling with the news that Molly had been wrapped up in this. And if she had broken with the group, then her life was in danger, assuming she was still alive at all. The odds were probably no better than even. The only thing keeping her alive was Solomon. Until they closed the loop that his escape had opened, killing her would be premature. The problem was that he had no idea how to keep the loop open. Perhaps this flash drive he had on him was part of the solution.

They could just kill her. That was definitely a possibility. There was no guarantee that had not already happened, based on what he'd gleaned about the Shepherds from Trinity and Brett. But killing her without ensuring they had snipped all the loose threads was foolhardy, and so far, they seemed smarter than that. The smart play would be to find out what Molly knew, who else she'd worked with, what she had done to threaten their way of life.

Which meant they might be torturing her.

The thought made Jack's stomach flip. He could not imagine Molly enduring it. She was made of tough stuff, there was no doubt, but everyone had their breaking point. But torture alone wouldn't be enough to neutralize the threat that she and Solomon had posed. Molly would not know how far Solomon had made it or how much information he'd disclosed. In short, there was no reason to torture her because you could not extract from someone information that she did not know.

Another possibility was using her to harden their defenses of this Machine. They would certainly want to patch any security flaws that she had exposed. He considered that for a moment. Also a possibility. She could buy her life with her work. And it might just work. Especially if they'd learned that Solomon was dead. If they shared that with her, she might assume their mission had failed. And if she was operating under that assumption, she might have concluded there was no point in continuing to fight. In sacrificing her life in furtherance of her cause.

In her mind, they had lost.

Jack became so wrapped up in his thoughts that he did not hear the door open behind him until it was too late. He turned toward the door just in time to see a flash of movement in the corner of his eye, a sharp pain to the temple before the lights went out.

17

Jack came to a few hours later. His head was pounding. He took a deep breath and exhaled slowly. A wave of nausea swept over him and he closed his eyes until it passed. He opened them again and took stock of his location. He was in an uncomfortable desk chair. His ankles were bound to the legs of the chair, his wrists secured behind his back by a pair of zip ties. His right eye was thick and crusty with what felt like blood. About the only good news on tap was that he was not dead.

The room was spartan. A desk, two chairs, and a small bookcase. There was a small picture frame on the corner of the desk. A photo of a young couple was slotted inside it. The door to the office was behind him. He turned his head around; through the blinds covering the small office's plate-glass windows, he could just make out the silhouettes of the two guards positioned just outside. They were big men. But they didn't concern him. If he could free himself from the restraints, he would be able to overpower them.

Zip ties were very secure restraints, but they did have an Achilles heel – friction. His biggest problem was freeing his arms from behind his back. It would be incredibly painful and might even require dislocating his shoulder. He had done it before, and while it was no picnic, it wasn't the worst thing he'd ever experienced. And since he had dislocated it before, repeating the gambit would be a little easier this time. It always was. The years of abuse had left his ball joint as well-seated in its socket as a well-done turkey leg in a Thanksgiving bird.

He hooked his armpit over the seatback and took a deep breath. He drove his body weight into his feet under him and began pulling on his shoulder joint as hard as he could. His eyes watered as he leaned into it, applying increasing pressure. The joint began to give way; the scar tissue that had built up since the last dislocation tore, one fiber at a time. Then, a pop and a sharp excruciating bolt of pain. He gasped, muffling his reaction so the guards wouldn't suddenly pay interest in his activities.

He leaned back in his chair, his breathing shallow and ragged, his heart pumping. Son of a bitch that hurt. He bemoaned the human body's ability to forget previous pain. If he'd remembered how much it hurt, he might not have gone through with it. Sweat slicked his pain-racked body. His mouth was dry. He closed his eyes, worked his way through a series of cleansing breaths. With each passing minute, the pain receded a bit more. If nothing else, it diverted his attention from the throbbing pain in his head.

With that unpleasantness behind him, he moved onto the next step, which promised to be as painful as the dislocation itself. He lifted his bottom from the chair, leaning toward his injured shoulder. The dislocation provided just enough clearance to scoot his bottom through the loop created by his bound wrists. His eyes stung with tears and it took every bit of his internal steel to keep from crying out. But silent he remained; his arms slid freely under his bottom, then under his legs, before coming free in front of him.

The pain was cataclysmic, as though someone had set a blowtorch to his right shoulder. The damaged muscles and ligaments quivered from the trauma. He leaned back in his chair, setting his bound hands in his lap. The easy part was over. Now to see what he was made of.

It had been a long time since he'd subjected himself to this kind of agony. He'd been trained for it. Working in counterintelligence meant he had to take it as well as he could dish it out. But that was a lifetime ago. He could only hope his immunity to pain was still robust enough to get him over the hump. It was okay if he suffered. The point was being able to function in the face of suffering. To get the job done.

He leaned over and carefully untied the laces of his boots, mindful of how much pain that minor exercise triggered. On a scale of one to ten, the ten being the worst, he put it at an eight. It was not a good omen for the work that lay ahead. They were good, thick laces, the kind you found in boots that you worked. He'd been wearing this pair for years.

His body screamed at him to take a break, but he knew better. His body was running on adrenaline now, the hormone that acted as an engine in the face of physical trauma. If he took too many breaks now, the adrenaline would fade and he'd be in even bigger trouble. Adrenaline worked like a mask; it tricked your body that things were better than they were, just to give you enough time to get your work done.

He took a deep breath and carefully removed the lace from the right boot. It was about eighteen inches long completely unfurled. It would be long enough. He took one end between his teeth and pinned the other end under his left boot. Then he began sawing the lace against the plastic of the zip tie. He kept his shoulder as stable as he could as he began chewing away at the restraint. He worked fast, back and forth, never stopping, no matter how much his shoulder throbbed. The repeated sawing motion warmed up the plastic and released a strange chemical smell into the room. Progress. He was getting there.

After ten minutes, he allowed himself a break. He didn't want to stop, but he didn't have much choice. The pain in his shoulder became so unbearable that he felt lightheaded and he thought he would pass out. He leaned back in his chair, caught his breath, thought of happier times.

Once as a young officer, he'd been stationed in Seoul for six months. He took R&R in Bangkok, where he'd met an American woman, a professional soccer player lamenting the approaching end of her career. They had spent one night together. But what a night. It was a juvenile memory; he chastised himself a bit for drawing this memory from the storage banks. He was a grown man and looking back on the sexual conquests of your twenties was never a wise move. But he allowed himself this trip down memory lane. He was having a hell of a bad day. He had earned it.

Okay, break over.

He resumed his work. Sweat poured into his eyes. As the fatigue set in, his form began to wobble, which put additional strain on his shoulder. That triggered ever larger waves of pain shooting through him. Nausea swept through him, and it felt like he might vomit. But his stomach was empty, and there was nothing to bring up.

But he didn't stop this time. He closed his eyes, called on every bit of willpower and toughness he had, every mile he had ever run, every weight he had ever lifted, every sparring session, every beating he had ever taken, to power through the finish line.

Then:

Success!

The connector snapped, freeing his hands. He made quicker work of the zip ties securing his ankles. His shoulder continued to burn, but the work was quicker this time. Ten minutes later, his feet were unbound as well. Now unrestrained, he leaned back in his chair and sighed.

The adrenaline faded quickly, and the shoulder pain started coming ashore like a Category Five hurricane. The pain radiated down his bicep into his forearm and in the other direction, all the way into his chest muscle. It had been years since the initial dislocation, a vicious hit he had taken in lacrosse practice his senior year in high school. It turned out to be a blessing in disguise. This was not the first time he had done this to escape a potentially fatal set of circumstances.

It was time to get the hell out of here. He weighed attempting his escape through the door; it was an option, but it was not ideal. His shoulder was badly injured, and taking on two men was not easy under full power. He looked upward; the building's ventilation system might be a better option. He climbed onto the desk and felt around the edges of the square cover, looking for the screws. It was not going to be easy. This was an old building, abandoned for years, and the screws would be in bad shape. He found the four screws, touching them one at a time like they were Braille characters before beginning.

His sweaty, dirty fingers kept slipping on the screws, so he paused for a moment; he needed something that would strengthen his grip on the screws, the coefficient of friction. He tugged the sleeve of his shirt over his hand and used the fabric to improve his grip.

Slowly, the screw began to turn.

A few minutes later, the first screw was out. He moved on to the next. Each one presented its own challenge, but eventually, all four screws were out. He dropped them into a pile on the desk and then focused his attention on the vent cover. It was rusted and had partially fused with the ceiling. He couldn't bang it loose lest he draw the attention of his guards.

His shoulder was throbbing. At some point, he would need to pop it back into place, but that was another noisemaker he couldn't afford right now. He pried an edge of the vent cover until it finally popped free. Relief flooded through him. Once one edge was loose, he had the leverage he needed to remove the vent cover completely. Now he needed to hoist himself into the ductwork. This was going to suck.

One-armed pull-ups had once been a regular part of Jack's routine, but that was long in the past. Too bad. That certainly would have been a handy skill right now. He wasn't even sure he could lift his injured arm high enough to grab the edge of the vent opening. He was going to have to do it though.

He needed to pop his shoulder back into place. These old buildings were sturdy; he might be able to risk a slam or two into the interior wall without drawing much attention from the men outside. He climbed back down from the table, drifting over to the corner farthest from the door. He listened closely to the conversation outside, waiting for a stitch of laughter or something that would mask his sound. He waited a few moments. Then, boom, a big bellowing laugh. Clenching his teeth, he drove his shoulder hard into the heavy wall. He bit down a scream. His stomach flipped from the pain.

The attempt had been unsuccessful.

He wanted to scream.

Just need a break here. Just a little break.

Then a coughing fit from one of the guards.

He drove his shoulder joint into the wall a second time; this attempt was successful, and the relief from the ball socket back in its place was palpable. It still hurt like hell but at least his body parts were back in their original configuration.

He worked his arm out, testing it to see how far he could push it. He was able to lift it to about a sixty-degree angle. Not all the way, but it would be enough. For the next fifteen minutes, he worked it, loosening it, stretching it, a little self-directed physical therapy. One thing was for certain; assuming he survived this little rodeo, it would give him grief to the end of his days.

He reached up for the lip of the ductwork; driving as much energy to his healthy shoulder, he pulled himself off the desk and into the black maw of the duct tunnels. Just as his injured shoulder threatened to fail, he was done. He lay in the ductwork, sweating, panting, tears in his eyes.

He took a minute to rest, pushed himself up on his hands and knees, and began to crawl. It was slow going; the darkness was complete and made it difficult to maintain a straight heading. He veered from one side of the duct to the other. Cobwebs clung to his face as he plowed along the duct. Dirt and grime and animal droppings caked his hands as he shuffled along.

After about twenty or thirty yards, he reached the vent cover for the next office along the long corridor. Below was the slightest hint of ambient light. More like an absence of total blackness. He peeked down through the slats. The office was like the one he'd just escaped. Then the sound of voices froze him. The room brightened a bit as two figures entered the room from the hallway. He dropped down to a prone position and lay still.

"So who the hell is this guy?" asked a woman.

"We're not sure," said a second voice, this one a man's.

"You think he knows her?"

"We're going to find out," he said. "We checked on him about thirty minutes ago. Still out like a light."

"Hope you didn't kill him," she said. "I want to know what he knows."

"He'll be fine," he said. "He's a big boy."

The pair exited the room, plunging it back into darkness.

Molly.

She was here.

When their footsteps had retreated into the distance, he waited an additional fifteen minutes before getting back to work. The vent cover was secured to the ceiling from the inside of the room. Where before he'd needed patience to work loose the screws, now brute force would be the tool needed to access the room below. He crawled past the vent cover, deeper into the duct system, to give his feet access to the cover.

Jack kicked hard at the cover once, then twice, and then a third time before it came loose. A fourth kick sent the cover down into the office below, clanging hard against the floor. He slid his legs down into the opening left behind. He shimmied down until he was hanging almost by his fingernails. He chanced a peek down. It was about an eight-foot drop. He let go, crashing down onto the desk below.

He waited to see if he had drawn any attention. Silence. He opened the door to this office slowly, peering into the hallway. The corridor was empty. It was extremely dark.

But Molly was close now.

He could feel it.

If he were a betting man, he'd wager she was somewhere in this wing of the building. Efficiency dictated keeping your prisoners close to one another. He moved carefully down the hallway, each step light, staying close to the wall. Some fifty yards distant were the two men guarding his room. They still had not detected his escape.

It wouldn't be long now. At a T intersection, he turned left, out of the sight of the guards.

He needed to find her soon; the longer he spent out here, the better the odds they would catch him again, and he could not allow that to happen. He was reminded how difficult rescue and extraction could be. Two months earlier, he and Lucy had brought down the Haven. But that had been a different kind of mission with a different objective. That had been a straight kill mission. Extraction was far more difficult, and the mission against the Haven had been no picnic. Making things even more challenging was the limited intel at his fingertips. And the intel he did have had come from a potentially unreliable source.

He exited a narrow corridor into a wider foyer containing a bank of elevators. There was a stairwell on the far side of the lifts. He crept slowly past the elevators, past the marble bust of some unrecognizable figure from the country's distant past. He entered the stairwell, gently guiding the door closed behind him. Pitch black. He paused for a few moments, giving his eyes a chance to adjust to whatever ambient light there was. After a few moments, he had to conclude there wasn't. He made his way slowly up the stairs, still taking care to move in absolute silence.

There was a door at the second landing, but another flight of stairs beckoned as well. The voices he thought he'd heard earlier were louder here. As he reached the top floor, the voices faded behind him. He pinpointed the second floor as their location. He filed that bit of knowledge away for later, for the return trip.

He gently turned the handle of the door at the top of

the steps, unlatching it. This put him in a long corridor, lined with small offices stretching away in either direction. The floor was extremely dark but for the dim light of various lanterns and candles burning throughout. There were no exhibits on this level, the business side of the museum. He turned left down the corridor, moving slowly. It was dead silent on this level. If anyone was up here, they weren't saying much. He waited for his eyes to adjust. There was just enough light leaking into the corridor to let him make out the rough outline of furniture, walls, and doorways.

The doors to most of the offices were closed, but a few hung open. As he neared a corner, the sharp sound of a sneeze broke the silence. It was farther down this corridor, running south away from the stairwell. He paused, sneaking a peek around the corner. Another line of offices, maybe a dozen in all.

All dark. Save one.

An office at the end of the hallway was lit, the orange light glowing brightly in a sea of darkness. A lone figure stood guard at the door. Jack's heart raced. Pay dirt. He checked behind him, but the hallway behind him remained clear. The floor remained quiet but for the quiet movements of the guard.

The guard was about forty yards distant. If he could get close to him, he could neutralize him silently, but he would have to be whisper quiet in his approach. Otherwise, the narrow corridor could quickly become a shooting gallery. Jack would be easy pickings. Jack couldn't open fire with his gun, as that would draw unnecessary attention.

He pressed his back to the wall and began sliding

down the corridor, keeping his eyes focused on the guard. The man was sitting in a folding metal chair; a lantern at his feet illuminated him, throwing his shadow on the wall at the end of the hallway. This kept Jack concealed in darkness. If Jack had been lucky, the man would have been asleep, but he appeared fairly alert. There was a book in his lap.

He moved quietly, one step at a time. Closer and closer. Sweat glazed his body. He worked hard to control his breathing and his heart rate. This was much more difficult than taking out the guard outside. That had been child's play. Out there, the cover of the outdoors had hidden his mistakes. Here there was no margin for error at all.

He withdrew his knife; he was good with the weapon, but it had been a long time since he'd hit a target from a distance. And the darkness made it almost impossible. He would need to get uncomfortably close to the man to ensure success.

Half the distance was gone now, but the danger grew with each step closer to the man. A creak of the floor, a pop in his knee, a single noise that might have gone unheard twenty yards ago could mean a quick death now. The darkness was his only remaining friend. As long as he remained invisible, he had a chance. He was closer now, and he slowed his movements. Each sidestep was followed by a full stop. He paused, ensuring he hadn't inadvertently alerted the guard to his presence. Satisfied that he was still in the clear, he took the next step.

The angle of attack would be incredibly awkward, coming up right on the man's right flank. But he had no choice. Two more steps would bring him within striking distance. One. Stop. Two. Stop. He stopped again. The man still had not detected Jack's presence as best as he could tell.

He wasn't as close as he wanted to be, but this would have to do. With his back still against the wall, he tapped the wall twice. The knocks echoed loudly, immediately drawing a stunned gasp from the man.

"Who's there?" he called out in a shaky voice.

He stood up, and that was when Jack struck. As he had with the first sentinel, Jack struck like a cobra, this time driving the knife straight up under the man's jaw. He grunted once and collapsed as his knees gave out. Jack lowered the man to the ground and pushed his body up against the wall between his chair and the back wall.

When that was done, he wiped his knife clean for the second time on this mission. He turned his attention to the lit office. The long corridor to his right remained clear and quiet.

He reached out for the doorknob. It turned easily in his hand; he pushed the door open, and it swung in. Keeping his knife at the ready, he stepped into the room.

18

A lone figure sat on a cot in the corner, her back to the wall. Her knees were bent, pulled into her chest. A candle burned on the barren desk, bathing the room in dim orange light. Jack stood frozen in the doorway for a moment, transported back a time before any of this had happened.

Molly.

She got up from the cot.

They stood in silence, staring at one another. She looked exactly like he remembered, albeit retrofitted with the experience of the years gone by etched on her face. She was a tall woman, about level with his five-foot-nine frame. Her light brown hair, which she had always worn shoulder length, was now tied back in a long ponytail. Just looking at her made his heart race the same way it had so many years ago. Some people just did that to you.

"Hey there," he said.

"Hey yourself," she replied.

She looked back at him with eyes wide open, as

though she could not believe Jack was standing here before her.

"So Solomon found you," she said.

"He did."

"Is he with you?"

"He's dead."

"What?"

"He was murdered," Jack said. "I'm sorry."

"My God."

"We can talk later," he said. "Right now we need to move."

She put on a heavy black coat that was hanging from the hook on the back of the door. Jack gestured for her to follow. Molly fell in behind him as they exited the room out into the corridor. They exited the office, back into the hallway. Molly glanced at the body of the dead guard, but she didn't say anything. The trip back to the stairwell was uneventful. Down the stairs again, in total darkness. The woman was quiet but determined. She stayed close to Jack's hip. Tough. That was how he would describe her. Jack reached the bottom of the steps first.

He opened the door slowly, giving him a narrow sliver of a view into the main hall. It appeared deserted; it wasn't as pitch black as it had been when he first arrived. Dawn was close, the first licks of daylight breaking through the windows.

He glanced over his shoulder at Molly

"We're gonna make a run for it. Stay behind me."

She nodded.

The stairwell lay dead ahead. Jack put his hand on the lever and pushed down gently, trying to keep the sounds of their escape to a minimum. He opened it a sliver. Trouble reached his ears. Hard footsteps pounding their way up the stairs from the level beneath them.

"We can't go this way."

"Dammit," she whispered.

He scanned the hallway stretching to the east. More commotion on that end, but it was difficult to tell how far away it was. The hallway behind them was a dead end.

She led him farther down the corridor. Candles in sconces lit the way. Another fifty yards of hard running brought them to a T-intersection. She gestured toward the left passageway; Jack followed. A bit farther up, a large bay window overlooked the street below. The door behind them had crashed open, spilling a platoon of men into the corridor. They were now closing in on them.

Another group was approaching from the opposite direction. They were trapped.

Jack withdrew the gun from his waistband.

"Cover your face," he said.

He fired a bullet into the bay window, shattering the glass into a million pieces. In the still of the morning, the tinkling sound of glass fracturing was deafening. They took a moment to clear the window frame of glass shards. Then she grabbed the window jamb and pulled herself up into the breach. She slipped through the opening onto the narrow ledge. Jack followed, gasping as he processed the height they were currently negotiating. The ledge was no more than six inches wide, just enough to plant their feet and press their bodies against the concrete wall, ice-cold and slippery in the morning mist.

"We're not gonna last very long up here," she hissed at her as she moved ahead one step at a time, swinging her leg out just far enough to alternate steps along the ledge.

"Just follow me," he said.

The discordant blast of an air horn ripped through the acoustically generous building.

"They got out!" called out a voice. "Next hallway!"

Shit.

The wind was blowing fiercely out here, buffeting them as they negotiated the narrow ledge. Ahead was a fire escape. The pair edged their way along the ledge until they reached the backside of the metal stairwell. Jack reached out for the railing and then swung across the sliver of a gap. He hung precariously from the railing, the wind pushing his body from side to side. His fingers ached as he pulled himself up; with a loud grunt, he cantilevered up and over the railing onto the landing.

Molly was next.

Her gaze was fixed on the sheer drop, some sixty feet to the frozen ground below. Her fear of heights came storming back to him. To be honest, it was a wonder she'd made it this far.

"You can do this," he said.

He did not know if she heard him; the wind caught his words and swept them into the ether. She did not look up at Jack. Her face was frozen with fear.

"Just like any other step," Jack said.

She nodded. Keeping her hand planted on the wall, she reached out toward the railing. Her momentum took her away from the building, and for a moment, he thought she would fall. But she steadied herself, keeping one foot on the ledge and one hand on the fire escape railing.

"Almost there," he said. "Don't look down."

But she continued to look down, which just made it that much worse.

"Okay," he said. "Almost there. Swing your left hand to the railing and hold on tight. I'll make sure you don't fall."

Her hand came free and swung across the gap to the railing. As she did so, her foot slipped and her grip began to weaken.

"Jack!" she shrieked.

He clamped her arm against the railing with one forearm and then reached down for her free arm, dangling at her side.

"Reach up for my other hand! I got you!"

Slowly, she dialed her arm skyward, a little bit at a time, until he was able to grasp her wrist. He was much bigger than her, but she wasn't a petite woman, and it wasn't clear this rescue would succeed. Despite the chill, sweat poured into his eyes and his body rapidly warmed from the exertion. His heart was racing so fast the individual beats were barely distinguishable. To make matters worse, the wind had picked up; her body swayed from side to side. From the corner of his eye, he could see her left hand struggling to maintain purchase on the railing.

Ensuring he had a strong grip on her, he gently backed away from the railing, pulling her up as he did so. Their eyes met between the railing. Her green eyes were wide with shock and fright.

"A few more seconds, and you can grab the top of the railing."

She nodded once, firmly.

He pulled hard again, cantilevering Molly's body up another five feet and then inward toward the landing. She cleared the railing and fell against Jack's chest. Her forward momentum took them both to the cold ground.

"Up!" he barked. "We gotta run!"

They staggered to their feet and began a rapid descent down the stairs. Wild gunfire exploded above them, clinking against the metal fire escape. This pushed them to accelerate. At the second-floor landing, Jack spotted movement coming from the north. A squad of Shepherds was racing to intercept them. But at their current pace, they would likely make it to the ground before their pursuers caught up to them.

"This way! He came this way!"

They made it to the ground in one piece. The Shepherds were still about fifty yards distant, picking their way through the museum's entrance plaza. The ground was icy and slick, forcing them to slow down.

Jack's legs were burning with fatigue, and of course, his shoulder was nothing but pure misery. The situation had just spiraled out of control so quickly. But that's how it went sometimes. You made a decision based on the intelligence you had before you, and you hoped for the best. If he had to do it again, he wouldn't change anything. He would always try to escape. It was who he was. And if they got caught, well, he wouldn't be in any worse shape than he already was.

It had happened to him before. Once. He was stationed in Beirut, tasked with gathering intelligence on a Hizbollah terror cell. He'd set up a meeting with an informant who supposedly had information on the location of one of the cell's leaders. They planned to meet at a café in Aley, a small hamlet in the foothills just east of the capital. The informant did not show up on time, and Jack had become nervous, and then he had not shown up at all, filling Jack's stomach with nervous butterflies. They had nabbed him as he left the café, throwing him in the back of a Red Crescent ambulance.

He was dead.

As he bounced around the back of the ambulance, he understood that he was about to die. An undercover intelligence officer, made by Hezbollah. This would likely be the highlight of their year. Terrorists loved to kill American intelligence operatives, even if they were just on loan to the agency and not an actual CIA field officer. He had to hope they killed him quickly or that they were so stupid that they gave him an opening to escape. Because the remaining alternatives were far worse.

They had taken him to a safehouse up in a little town called Hasbaya, down in the southern part of the tiny nation near the Lebanese-Israeli border. And Jack Goodwin was alive today because of sheer dumb luck. It was a small concrete structure, a single level, three rooms. One of the rooms had been converted into a cell. A Hezbollah bigwig had unexpectedly made an appearance at the safehouse, bringing with him women, food, and liquor. These were all no-nos in the Islamic faith, but these men were terrorists first and Muslims last, so Jack wasn't terribly surprised.

That night, his guard, drunk and full, had not been careful while delivering Jack his meal, earning him a broken neck. Jack fled. He traveled by night, sleeping during the day, until he made it to a CIA safehouse in

Beirut. They whisked him out of Lebanon, to Ramstein Air Force Base in Germany for a debriefing.

So being held captive was nothing new for Jack Goodwin.

Jack and Molly fled.

19

They sprinted south, side by side, staying close to the edge of 12th Street. A light rain was swirling, misting them as they ran. In the old days, this would have been the worst kind of weather. Bone-chilling rain and bitingly cold but too warm to snow. Nowadays, however, snow was the worst. Snow was deadly.

A short tunnel ran under Route 50, carrying them beneath the National Mall. As they approached its entrance, Jack spotted a pair of sentries at its maw. He fired on them; his shots missed but pushed the guards clear of the entrance and to the safety of the bollards lining the street. They withdrew their weapons, but the conditions made their work slow, and Jack and Molly slipped into the darkness of the tunnel before the guards could get a bead on them. Gunfire rang out behind them. A bullet chipped at the wall of the tunnel to Jack's left.

They needed to get farther south, out of Shepherd territory. They splashed through the cold standing water covering the roadway and up the ramp to street level. A group of four Shepherds on mountain bikes had joined the chase and was now closing in behind them. The road had been cleared here in the intervening years, giving the bike scouts room to maneuver.

Molly, fit as ever, kept pace with him as they ran. They curled east onto the sidewalk, pulling obstacles down behind them as they ran. Here an old trashcan. There an abandoned baby carriage. Anything to buy them a little time. The sidewalk was clear for another quarter mile but ahead were two cars that had flipped over long ago, still resting where they had landed on the day of the Pulse. Both were rusted and scarred with burn damage. The skeletal remains of the driver still buckled in the upside-down vehicle.

"They're gaining," Molly spat between lungfuls of air.

Jack thought they would just make it. It was going to be close. They slid under the Eisenhower Freeway overpass that slung overhead. The river was now about a hundred yards away. They curled east toward Banneker Park, home to a large fountain, long since dry.

Jack stole a glance behind him; the Shepherds were just out of their line of sight. He scanned the riverbank, hoping he had made the right gamble. There! An old boathouse on the far side of the fountain, just a few yards from the river's edge. It might contain what Jack was looking for.

"Boathouse," he whispered to Molly.

They covered the ground in less than a minute, escaping under the cover of the building just as the Shepherds cleared the fountain. The leader held up a fist, and the group skidded to a halt in between the large stone structure and the water.

The boathouse was dark and stitched with thick spiderwebs fluttering in the breeze. There were two kayaks on the left side and two canoes on the right. The kayaks were two-man vessels. Just what they needed. Falling back into their old rhythms, each knowing what the other was thinking, they set to work releasing a kayak from its wall moorings. Jack peeked inside to ensure the oars were there. They were.

"Ready?"

She nodded firmly.

They burst from the cover of the boathouse, making a beeline for the water. The riverbank was wet and muddy, grabbing at their boots as though conspiring with the Shepherds to slow them down. They set the kayak down at the riverbank and pushed it into the water, scrambling aboard as it pushed away from the shore. Each grabbed a paddle and began driving the blades through the water for all they were worth. The river was cloaked with a light layer of fog.

The sleek fiberglass of the boat cut through the gentle waves like a knife. The current was running south, which was fine with Jack. He didn't care which way the water carried them, as long as it was out of range of the Shepherds' weapons.

Right on cue, the air cracked with the report of gunfire.

Jack and Molly ducked as low as they could without sacrificing speed. The terror of being so exposed was real and visceral. Jack stole a glance at the shoreline. Their pursuers had stopped firing from the shoreline for the moment; they had retreated to the boathouse themselves.

Seconds later, the Shepherds were in the water as

well. One in the one-man kayak and the remaining five in the two canoes. Jack drew his weapon as Molly drove the paddle blades through the water. The three Shepherds, large men, in the front-moving canoe quickly closed in on Jack and Molly. The sound of gunfire pierced the air; but the river was moving fast that morning, and it was tough for anyone to get a bead on them, even good marksmen. Jack let the oars go for a moment to return fire; he was loath to slow their progress, but return fire would help keep them at bay. He hoped.

The current picked up as they moved into deeper waters. To the left sat the cold ruins, the ghost of a once-popular spot he and Molly had frequented years ago – Hank's Oyster Bar, right at the river just south of Maine Avenue and its intersection with Seventh Street. Even in the frenzy of the escape, as the air snapped with the whiz of bullets, memories of a bucket of icy Budweisers and plates of raw oysters flashed through his mind.

Another check behind him delivered bad news. The lead Shepherd canoe was drawing ever closer. Close enough that Jack could make out the features on the three Shepherds' features. The one at the front was a thick, burly man with a graying beard. His eyes were set deep in his head. He looked like a man who was comfortable on the water, even in conditions as shitty as this.

Jack needed to get rid of him.

It would cost them speed and a bit of their lead, but it would be worth it.

"Keep it as straight as you can," he called out to Molly over the sound of the waves crashing over the bow of the kayak. He drew his gun and rotated his body one hundred and eighty degrees. It was painful on his aging back and hips, but he just needed to hold the position for a few moments. Bracing his elbow on the stern of the vessel, he waited for just the right moment that the boat settled on a straight line through the water.

"Just keep it steady for a second, Mol!"

"I'm trying!"

He cast a quick glance back toward her. Her entire body was coiled and taut, struggling to keep the boat on a consistent heading. He looked back at the approaching canoe; Beard Guy was now brandishing his own weapon while struggling to keep their boat steady.

Jack pushed out all extraneous thoughts, anything that wasn't related to firing the purest shot that he could. The kayak went up a small wave before crashing down onto the surface of the water again. For a brief, blessed second, the vessel was stable.

He fired.

His mirror did the same.

The bullet caught Beard straight in the chest knocking him into the belly of his canoe. The wash of a large wave veiled Jack's view as he fired; he could just make out the man falling backward. He did hear the twangy sound of a bullet piercing the hull of their canoe. Immediately, the stern of the kayak dipped low in the river and begin taking on water.

"Molly, we're hit," he shouted.

"Shit!"

They would have to abandon ship. He fired off the rest of his rounds wildly. One found its target, the second man in Beard's canoe. The bullet struck him in the shoulder, jarring loose his weapons; it clattered on the side of the canoe before slipping into the water. In a desperate attempt to save his weapon, the man lunged toward it, throwing off the canoe's center of gravity. It rolled one way, and then another, before losing its center. It capsized a few seconds later, pitching the dead man and his two surviving comrades into the cold waters of the Potomac.

As Jack and Molly struggled to keep their kayak afloat, the current pulled the two men downriver past them. They quickly disappeared into the fog and the waves.

"We have to bail out," Jack said.

"No shit!" Molly snapped back at him, wriggling free of the tight seat she occupied.

There was no time or space for dramatics. Once they were out of their seats, both of them slipped over the side into the icy waters of the Potomac.

20

Jack gasped as he hit the water and his head slid under the waves. The water temperature was in the low forties this time of year, not much different than a bathtub filled with ice. His clothes began absorbing water and adding instant weight; it was an invisible enemy, seeking to pull him down into the depths. He kicked as hard as he could for the surface. When he broke clear, he gulped in a lungful of icy air, swinging his head around to look for Molly. She had surfaced a few yards away, but it didn't look like she'd spotted him.

"Molly!" he shouted.

Her head perked up and swung around toward him. She waved frantically. The current was pulling them south, funneling them to the center of the river. They needed to get out of the water quickly. The low water temperatures would quickly overwhelm them; he gave them five minutes before the hypothermia finished them off.

He took a few seconds to triangulate their location. The river curved southeast before unfurling south again. There was a large park to the east. Potomac Park, if he recalled the name correctly. They were closer to that shoreline.

"Molly!" he called out, gesturing hard to the east.

She flashed a thumbs up. She swam up alongside him.

"Stay close to me," she said. She had been a swimmer in college, and she still bore the lithe body of one.

They began kicking for shore, Jack swimming as hard as he could, but feeling like they were making no progress. As his clothes became increasingly saturated, the river felt like a magnet that simply would not let them go.

His lungs burned and his extremities were numb and heavier than lead, like weights dragging him to the bottom of the river. As the river swirled around him, his head went under again, and he was just able to seal off his lungs as the water enveloped him. The extreme cold was a living thing, a predator seeking to extinguish his life.

He did not know where Molly was. Then he felt her hand on his, pulling him upward again. He breached the surface once more, gasping and sucking on sweet air, the fine mist of the rough river spraying his face. He dug deeper for the last bit of energy he had, settling back into something resembling a freestyle stroke. Molly was just off his right flank, swimming hard.

He poked his head up to look for the shore. They were close now, so close. A few more strokes. Then his feet brushed the riverbed; he crawled a few more feet, to where he could stand up in the four-foot deep water. He looked back for Molly, but he did not see her. He desperately scanned the surface of the water, but she was nowhere to be found.

Then a single bare hand popped above the waves. She was so close to the shore, but her body had burned through its reserve tanks. He dove back out toward her, grabbing her hand and forearm and tugging her hard toward him. It was like trying to move a steel safe, dead weight as she was.

The wet clothes made it easier to get a grip on her and he dragged her the last few yards, back to a point that he could stand up and get her head above water. She was conscious, but just barely so. Her eyes had rolled into the back of her head. He dropped to a knee and slung her over his right shoulder. She was heavier than he expected, and his legs buckled under the stress. But he righted himself after a couple of staggering steps, and he sloshed his way to the riverbank. At the water's edge, his legs gave out entirely, and the pair crashed to the ground. He pushed himself up to his knees, tucked his hands under her arms, and dragged her clear of the small waves lapping at the shore.

On the relative safety of the muddy bank, he pulled her close and wrapped his arms around her, hoping the pair's body heat would help stop any further drops in their core temperature. This was only a brief fix, the briefest respite. They needed to get indoors and out of these icy wet clothes. His body shivered uncontrollably, and he could barely focus on his surroundings. Molly was shivering as well. His trick to warm them both up by using their combined body heat did not seem to be working. He needed to get them to shelter.

"Molly?" he said loudly.

Her eyes fluttered open, and she grunted softly.

"I'm gonna get us some shelter."

She nodded.

He checked her pulse; it was rapid, but it was strong. Her lips and fingernails were blue; his nails didn't look much better. That was to be expected, as the body pulled blood and oxygen to save its vital systems.

Now that he was certain Molly was alive, even if just barely so, he took a moment to regain his bearings. They had come ashore near the Lyndon Johnson Memorial Bridge on the east bank of the river. There was no sign of their pursuers or their boats. Just beyond the riverbank was a narrow line of trees running the spine of this narrow sliver of land in between the river and a boundary channel. Overhead flew the George Washington Memorial Parkway.

Through the trees, he could just make out a small cluster of homes. They were a good piece away from the city proper and hopefully unoccupied. He would have to be careful, of course; you never knew these days.

He tapped Molly gently on the cheek. She opened her eyes.

"Can you walk?"

"I think so," she said softly.

That was a good sign. He climbed to his feet slowly, his entire body virtually numb. It felt as though he'd been jammed into an ice machine. When he was upright, he reached down with both hands; Molly grabbed them, relying on Jack to get to her feet. She was weak and unsteady. They were about the same height, but she had far less body fat than he did, and the effects of the cold would be slower to affect him. It wouldn't buy him much time, maybe a few minutes, but just enough to make a difference.

They began their trek, his arm around her back and looped under her right arm. She wrapped that arm around the front of his chest, and together they walked, in the slowest display of the three-legged race ever recorded. The numbness was almost welcome; he did not want to think how cold he would feel otherwise. But they were in grave danger now. When you stopped feeling cold, the end was not far behind. There was no path through the trees, and so they had to carefully navigate the narrow gaps, the low-hanging branches tearing at their faces, grabbing their wet clothes as though to prevent them from moving.

They came through the tree line, coming up against another channel of the river that broke off from the main tributary. Ahead was a narrow bridge spanning the channel, which led over to the mainland and the cluster of homes. He was tired, so tired, but they had a bit farther to go. Molly was upright but dead on her feet. He needed to get her warmed up.

"That bridge," he said to her. Her chin was drooping down at her chest, so he lifted it with two fingers.

This seemed to energize her; the strain on his supporting arm immediately dissipated.

"I can make it."

He slowly slid his arm free as their pace picked up. Jack took the point at the bridge, a narrow metal structure that wasn't fixing to be much fun on an icy morning like this one. He gingerly put one foot out onto the bridge and then a hand on the railing. It was slippery but sturdy. Molly was close behind him.

The wind cut hard across the bridge, blowing in from the northeast, biting into his exposed skin like the teeth of a wolverine. It took away what little breath he had. Behind him, Molly groaned, the utter discomfort and misery settling in on them. They completed the bridge crossing; finally, a task that hadn't devolved into an elemental fight for survival.

The largest of the houses sat in the foreground. The rain had picked up in the last few minutes, adding to the urgency of his search for dry and warm environs. Ominously, snow had started to mix in with the rain; a serious winter storm could be brewing here. They needed to get inside.

He didn't think they would be much better off in a drafty old building. They wouldn't get any wetter, but they would be in a large drafty building with no way to warm up. He guided Molly to the building's entrance, which mercifully was covered by a stone awning.

"Wait here," he said.

Hypothermia was setting in; his vision was blurry and starting to double. He just needed to hold it together a little longer. There were three houses at this end of the lane, situated in a semi-circle, following the cut of the river. Each had its own boardwalk and pier. Jack and Molly staggered to the edge of one property, along a stone patio bordering the riverbank. A long-abandoned fire pit sat in the center, ringed by a mishmash of beach chairs and Adirondacks. To the west was a wooded area. A path diverged from the banks and up into the trees.

Jack checked the center of the fire pit; there were some old logs in the bottom, blackened and mushy. It had been some time since the pit had last been used. The house itself sat at the top of the point, the yard graded down toward the river. A wrought-iron fence cordoned off part of the yard.

Everything was quiet and dark. Nothing stirred in the house. He drew closer to the yard, extremely exposed here. If someone was inside looking out toward the water, they would spot him instantly. But it was a risk he had to take. They had to get out of the elements and near a heat source.

They passed under the heavy branches of a mighty old pine tree. The gate was just a few steps away. Still no movement inside. It had the feel of a place left behind, a place abandoned. With Molly no more responsive than a sack of groceries, he didn't have much time left. Her organs could start failing soon. So could his.

He lifted the latch, which was stiff with disuse. That was a good sign. With a bit more oomph, he released the latch and pushed the gate open. The side door to the house was parallel to the gate. He twisted the knob; it turned easily in his hand. The door led them into a sunroom. Several of the windows were broken, but at least they were out of the rain.

A long wooden picnic table bisected the sunroom. To the left was the door to the main house. It, too, was unlocked, suggesting a hasty retreat from the house. He carried Molly inside. The house featured an open concept design. The kitchen, eat-in area, and small sitting area were combined into one large space. He carried Molly to a couch facing a large fireplace. She was not unconscious, but she wasn't exactly alert, either. He rummaged through the downstairs, finding a few blankets tucked on the shelf of a bedroom off the main living area. They were old and tattered, but they were largely intact. He dreaded the next step to come.

"Molly!" he called out loudly.

She opened her eyes and looked Jack squarely in the face.

"We need to get you out of these wet clothes," he said.

She laughed dreamily.

"Aren't you gonna buy me dinner first, sailor?"

He ignored the quip, a callback to times where there was no hesitation in their removal of one another's clothing, but those times were long in the past. He started with her sweatshirt, which was about as cooperative as hardening concrete. He finally got it off, followed by her t-shirt and sports bra. He then worked to remove her Potomac-soaked jeans, which were even more recalcitrant than the sweatshirt. Finally, they came free as well. Then he wrapped her with the blanket like a burrito. Her skin was frighteningly frigid to the touch; he spent a few minutes massaging her forearms and legs, trying to get blood flowing to her extremities.

There was a stack of wood next to the brick hearth, his first break in days. There was even a fireplace lighter. Jack's heart soared at the lucky break. With Molly tended to for the moment, he set to work building a fire. After ensuring the flue was open, he set to work arranging the logs in the appropriate matrix. They were damp from exposure so it was going to take some time and patience to get the fire going.

He found some old newspapers in the kitchen;

including one from the day of the blackout, still encased in its yellow plastic sleeve, presumably the last date any newspapers had been published. They were old and brittle; the headlines were pedestrian and normal. The G8 meeting in London. A breakthrough on a universal Covid vaccine; the pandemic had been largely contained by the day of the Pulse, but booster shots were scheduled to begin that fall. The boosters had never come to be, and Covid hotspots erupted from time to time in the post-Pulse world. Jack himself had been vaccinated about two years before the Pulse. He hadn't wanted to get the shot, but Lucy would not hear it. Several of her coworkers had died of Covid, and she had become ill with it herself.

He grabbed the newspapers and shoved them into the base of the woodpile. Success did not come easily. He was treated to a good hour of small fires flickering to life and then sputtering away. He grew colder with each passing moment. Molly trembled on the couch, even ensconced in the blanket. His thoughts grew fuzzy, and he pushed away all thoughts but focus on the fire. Finally, the wood caught, slowly growing, from a small corona to a heavy blaze roaring in the hearth. As the fire crackled to life, he stripped off his own icy clothes and lay them flat to dry.

Relieved, he sat there and let the heat wash over him; he could not remember the last time something had felt so good. He climbed to his feet and lifted Molly off the couch, setting her down on the ground next to the hearth. Although she was more asleep than awake, she sighed as the fire's warmth swept over her.

By his estimate, the fire would last five or six hours before burning out. He would need to find more fuel if this proved to be an extended stay. The dip in the

Potomac had been quite the shock to their systems; it might take a couple of days to fully recover, especially if the weather did not turn in their favor soon.

As the sitting room filled with warmth and light, he checked on Molly. She was sleeping now, her respiration and pulse normal. He left her there while he went to explore the rest of the house. He committed the home's layout to memory as he swept from room to room. He started in the long galley kitchen, which connected to an eat-in area bearing a long glass dining table. Some nautical-themed art hung on the walls.

Beyond was a game room featuring a full bar and a pool table. There was a built-in bookcase here, lined with old paperbacks and hardcovers spanning the decades. It reminded him of Lucy's bookshelves back at the old farmhouse. He'd never been much of a reader before the Pulse, but he found himself increasingly drawn to books. Books contained the knowledge they needed to survive. Books were precious. He focused on books about management and leadership, about self-sufficiency and survivalism. Although he was familiar with many of the concepts, it never hurt to keep learning. Every now and again, a work of fiction. He particularly had enjoyed fantasy novels, in part because they were stories set in worlds that had never had electricity in the first place.

He continued his loop of the house, passing through the front foyer and the front door. On the east side of the house were three bedrooms, all quite large. The beds were unmade, the sheets spackled with animal droppings. A coffee mug sat on the bureau. He picked it up. Inside were the petrified remains of an ancient cup of coffee. The coffee had hardened into something resembling volcanic rock.

The bureau in the master bedroom revealed a treasure trove of clothing. A pair of corduroy pants and a heavy sweatshirt for him. A pair of sweatpants and a thick cardigan for Molly. He pulled the dry clothes on; they felt transcendent after the dip in the river. He set the clothes aside for Molly to change into when she woke up. Then he explored the kitchen for any leftover perishables, especially canned goods, but found none. The place had long since been cleared out.

He was exhausted. He circled back to the sitting room and folded himself into an oversized armchair for a little shuteye. The chair faced the bay windows overlooking the yard, down to the river below. He glanced over at Molly, now sleeping deeply. Her chest rose and fell rhythmically. Her left arm twitched three times and then fell still again. As he drifted off himself, he noted absently that it had started to snow.

21

Molly was already up when Jack started awake early in the afternoon. Jack had fallen asleep sitting up, his head angled strangely, leaving his neck stiff as he swam back to consciousness. It took him a moment to remember where he was. The fire was still roaring, its snap and crackle incredibly soothing after the chaos of their escape.

He sighed loudly and stretched. His body was sore and stiff. That damned middle age catching up to him. He pushed himself off the couch and did a quick self-assessment. All systems normal. Just old.

"You alright?" asked Molly, standing at the window, her back to him.

He watched her for a few moments, remembering what once had been, regretting what could never be. Had she truly been part of unleashing this insanity that surrounded them?

"I'll live."

He joined her at the window, watching the snow drift

down. It was coming down heavily. At least two inches were on the ground. A check of the sky betrayed bad tidings. The clouds were thick and low in all directions and it did not look to be slowing down anytime soon. That dirty gray of winter. It had been a long time since the last big winter storm back home. At least a year, maybe two. They were due for a big snowfall. Just their luck.

"Pretty," she said.

"Pain in our ass is more like it."

"You always had a way with words."

As he watched the snow drift down, he began making a to-do list. No matter how difficult their lives were, bad weather always added an unwelcome degree of difficulty. They would need fuel to keep the fire going. They would need food. Not right away, but soon. With a fresh snowfall, water would not be an issue. Snow was whiter and purer these days thanks to the zero-emissions goal the world had reached.

A silence dropped between them once more. He glanced at the profile of her face, her neck, and he recalled happier times between them. Times long behind them. He could not think of anything to say at the moment; she had a strange ability to render him silent.

"I'm gonna get us some food," he said.

"Okay," she replied softly. She didn't appear to be in any rush to begin whatever process of reconciliation that lay ahead of them. At least she didn't seem to be mad at him anymore. God, she had been so angry. And deservedly so.

He went down to the pier. There were a couple of old fishing rods still in the rod rack mounted near the end of the pier. The fishing line was old but still intact. Jack scoured the dirt and the mud underneath the snow and found a few nightcrawlers, enough to put him in business. He pierced them with the hook and dropped a line in. The fish were running strong, and he pulled in enough for dinner. Fishing had remained one of his true passions. The lake at Promise was an excellent source of food for the community; keeping it stocked had been one of their early priorities. Eventually, it had become self-sustaining as the schools took hold.

He returned to the cottage with a dozen fish. There was an old cooler on the sun porch. He cleaned it out as best as he could and then packed it with snow before storing the fish away. The fish would keep out here for a day. Tomorrow he would fish again. By the day after that, they would be on the road again. He peeled off his coat

"I'm gonna gather up some wood," he said. "And then you and I are gonna have a long talk."

It wasn't much, but it would do. He cleaned and filleted the fish by candlelight, and they roasted it over the fire. The blaze he'd built upon their arrival was still going strong, enhanced by the most pleasant surprise of the day. A cord of wood had been left unmolested in a dark corner of the sunroom, which sported a large fireplace. This would serve their needs for several days.

They sat at the dining table by the dying light of the day. The snow was coming down steadily now; close to three inches were now on the ground. The skies showed no signs of clearing anytime soon. It had the feel of a massive snowmaker now, just pulses of moisture in the atmosphere colliding with the extremely cold air. A winter jackpot.

"Together again," he said, holding up a cupped hand in a mock toast.

"Yep," she said, returning the gesture.

Neither of them spoke for a moment; the silence filled the room, pushing out like an expanding balloon threatening to crack. He sensed her awkwardness, an understanding on her part that she knew he knew.

"So what do you want to know?"

He chuckled softly. As he sat there, looking at her as she looked back at him, a deep wellspring of sadness bubbled up. Knowing now that she had been involved with the Pulse left him adrift, being swept along a raging river with nothing to grab onto.

"I need to know everything," he said.

"Ask me no questions, I'll tell you no lies."

"Dammit, Molly!" he bellowed, banging his hand on the table, hard enough that she flinched.

"Sorry," she said. She leaned forward in her seat and set her laced fingers together on the table. Her head was down, her chin at her chest.

"Can you tell me what happened with Solomon?" she asked.

She looked up at him.

"I'm sorry," he said. "He came in talking about being able to turn the lights back on. Word got out. Someone inside our community murdered him. He almost killed Lucy too."

"Oh my God. Is she okay?"

"Yes," Jack said. "Her shoulder was badly damaged,

but she'll live. The thing was, she's pregnant. We don't know if the blood loss affected the pregnancy."

Molly looked back down at the table. She traced an invisible circle with her finger.

"I was so very sorry to hear about your niece."

Molly had only met Emma once, shortly after Emma had been born. They had broken up before Emma had taken her first steps. Strange to think how two people that had been so monumental in his life had never even known one another.

"Thank you."

They sat in silence for a moment.

"Do you know why he did it?"

"He said he was with a group called the Shepherds."

Molly buried her face in her hands and sighed deeply.

"I guess you're familiar with them."

"The think tank," she said. "They became the Shepherds."

"Well, I guess they didn't have any second thoughts about the Machine."

She looked up from her hands, a weird little smile on her face.

"No," she said. "They most certainly did not."

"I'm sorry about Solomon," Jack said. "I know you were close."

"So is it true?"

"Is what true?" she said.

"What Solomon said," he replied. "That you did this."

As if she would not know what he was referring to, he gestured broadly around them.

Tears filled her eyes.

She shook her head, her eyes welling up. She sat silently, staring off into space.

"Molly, I've done a lot of things I'm not proud of."

She held a fist to her lips, searching for the words.

"Yes," she said with an air of finality. "I helped build the Machine."

Jack struggled to maintain his composure. Somehow, hearing it directly from her lips was a punch in the gut. It was difficult to process. This brilliant and gentle woman had been partially responsible for perhaps the greatest atrocity in human history. Certainly, he did not know the extent of her involvement, but sitting here, watching her wrestle with a soul on fire meant that she had been knee-deep in it.

But he did not say anything. Because he was the last person in the world who could afford to judge anyone, let alone Molly.

"You have to understand," she continued. "We were screwed. Just totally screwed. The models I built showed massive famine, agricultural collapse, water shortages, coastal cities inundated, war. And it wasn't decades away. It was a decade away. At the very most."

"But they were just models," he said. "Right? Models can be wrong."

She nodded. She plucked a stray morsel of fish from her plate and popped it in her mouth

"This is good."

He smiled.

"Thanks."

"Yes," she said, returning to the topic. "Models can be wrong. But this one wasn't."

"How do you know?"

"We run tests on them," she said. "It's called hindcasting. You run the model from the present day backward, and then you compare the model results to what actually happened to see if the model's predictions had been accurate. We had some powerful AI working for us too. The technology had jumped ahead by leaps and bounds."

"And I take it the results were not great."

She scoffed.

"To say the least."

"And the solution was to trigger an apocalypse?"

Jack was rippling with anger. Their so-called cure could not have been worth it. Millions, perhaps billions, had perished in the last five years.

"It wasn't my idea."

"But you didn't stop them."

Her lips tightened and her eyes closed.

"I didn't think they would go through with it."

"What was your role?"

"I programmed the Machine."

"Jesus, Molly."

"I know," she said. "At first, it was more of an academic exercise. We knew that we were doing this to the planet. Our energy use was pushing us to the brink. All the factories and cars and laptops and server farms were having a much bigger impact than people realized. So as a joke one night, someone, I think it was Chandler Lovell, said, 'what if we just turned everything off.' We'd been drinking a bit. People were so depressed. I mean, we used to throw around all kinds of crazy ideas. So this was just another brick in the wall of crazy.

"Anyway, the next morning, Iris Erickson — she was

the head of the think tank — called me and asked if it was possible. If it was possible to build a device that could shut down the world's energy grid. I had no idea if it was possible, but I was intrigued by the puzzle of it."

Jack could picture that. You put a challenge in front of Molly, and she would solve it. It was who she was.

"So I got to work," she said. "It became this kind of game, to figure out how to do it. Nothing like it had ever been tried before."

"And you succeeded."

She took a short, sharp breath and let it out slowly.

"Yes, eventually. It was all I worked on for five years."

"Jesus, why did you keep working on it?"

His question was met with silence. She looked up at the ceiling, as though she had never seriously considered it.

"We'll get back to that. So how does it work?"

"Without boring the shit of you, there were three parts to the world's power grid," she said, holding up three fingers. "Generation, transmission, and distribution. Generation means converting it from fossil fuels, nuclear reactors, or solar and wind, for example. Transmission means transporting it from the power plants into communities, and distribution, of course, means delivering it into businesses or people's houses. And the world wasn't on one electrical grid. It was a large series of interconnected grids."

"So where did you come in?"

"I wrote an algorithm."

"What kind of algorithm?"

"To create a kind of pulse," she went on. "A pulse that

interrupted the world's ability to generate power, to prevent the initial conversion from the source."

"And what generates this pulse? After you wrote the algorithm for it?"

"We had an engineering team that worked on it."

"All these people really conspired to do this? I find that hard to believe."

She laughed softly.

"So the truth is, no one thought it would work. I certainly didn't. Until it did. Anyway, when the electricity is delivered to the end user, the power alternates between positive and negative voltage. The oscillations of the alternating current come in at various frequencies. This is called the line frequency. In most of the world, it's sixty hertz. In Asia and the Americas, it's fifty. I discovered this left the grid quite vulnerable to an exterior attack. If you screw with the oscillations, the whole thing comes apart. A single pulse can damage or destroy the equipment, but that can be fixed. A perpetual pulse prevents the grid from ever being on the right frequency. The trick was to write the program to interrupt the grid at all frequencies, so it could never find the right one."

"What about batteries? Why did those fail?"

"Those were easier because they operate on a fixed frequency. Basically, if it generated power, I figured out how to stop it. Permanently."

"How big is this Machine?"

"Not very big. About the size of a freezer."

"A freezer?"

"You know, like someone might have in their garage?"

"A freezer," Jack repeated softly.

It seemed absurd. Suddenly the Machine became

very real in his mind. Just knowing its dimensions made it seem like something he could touch. Something he could destroy.

"Where is it?"

"On the roof of the Library of Congress."

He chuckled at that. Something the size of a freezer, sitting atop their cathedral to learning and knowledge, had lain waste to their civilization.

"Can we destroy it?" Jack asked. "Would that turn the Pulse off?"

"I wish," she said. "We built a fail-safe into it. The group wanted the Pulse to be irreversible. The uranium core will melt down if it's not deactivated."

"So it can be deactivated."

"Yes."

"How?"

"I built a kill switch."

"A what?"

"The Machine is designed to operate in perpetuity," she said. "It has a uranium core, meaning it will continue to generate the pulse for centuries, if not longer. When I realized they were serious about doing this, I wrote a kill program for the Machine."

"Why didn't you ever use it?"

"I never got a chance," she said. "I had to run. Solomon and I were on the run for years. We never slept in the same place twice. But they never stopped looking for us. They wanted the kill switch."

"So if we got to the Machine, what do we do?"

"Well, in theory, the kill switch will safely power down the Machine."

"Where is this kill switch now?"

"I put it on a flash drive and hid it in Solomon's pack."

Jack's heart nearly stopped.

He got up from the table and fished through the inside pocket of his winter coat. It was still there. He tucked it into the palm of his hand and turned back toward Molly. He held the baggie by the zipped end and let it unfurl before her. Molly reached out for the bag; she gently clamped the flash drive between two fingers, as though she could not believe it was there.

"You found it."

"I'm sorry I didn't know what it was earlier," he said. "Solomon died before he had a chance to tell me he had it."

She burst into tears; at the same time, a smile ran across her face.

"If we can get to the Machine, we may be able to stop it."

"Okay," Jack said, standing up. "That's what we're gonna do. We are going to shut that Machine down and end this goddamned nightmare."

22

Snow fell for the rest of the day. Molly had fallen asleep again, still exhausted from their escape from the Shepherds; as she napped, Jack went outside to set snare traps for the few woodland creatures that would be out and about. He placed them at twenty-yard intervals in the trees surrounding the property. The snow was light and dry and piled up quickly on the frigid ground. As he worked, he considered the ramifications of what Molly had told him.

It was hard to believe. A possible off-ramp from the highway of crap they'd been riding for five years. It wouldn't solve *all* their problems, not right away, but a glimmer of hope now existed when before there had been none. At the very least, they could begin using battery-based technology once again. Flashlights, ham radios, gas-powered vehicles. His heart fluttered at the possibilities, at a potential future that had been unimaginable just a few days ago.

After setting his sixth snare, he returned to the

sunroom. With the sun cloaked behind thick, wintry clouds, the day's dim light was fading quickly. He crossed the yard and stepped back inside the sunroom. It was even darker in here, so he lit a candle.

He set the candle on the tabletop and took a seat. He removed the flash drive from his pocket and turned it over in his hands. This small device, no bigger than his thumb, held in it the potential to change the course of history. He thought about the danger it had been in since Molly had brought it to life, about the journey Solomon had taken to deliver it to him. How he had died before he'd had a chance to tell him what it was for. How lucky they had been to simply stash Solomon's backpack in the clinic office. If Jack had been a little bit later coming up on the clinic, if he had turned the other direction, he may never have spotted Danny in time. He could have killed Lucy as he turned the clinic upside down looking for it.

He had to keep this drive safe. At all costs.

It got cold quickly, so he went back indoors. Molly was sitting in front of the fire, her knees drawn up to her chest, her chin resting on her arms. She did not react to his approach.

He wondered what it was about her that had left him so enraptured. What combination of traits had deactivated his longstanding desire to just generally be left alone. He had enjoyed female companionship, but he had never wanted what people his age normally wanted. Marriage, kids, family. It had never been like that for him. He was broken in some fundamental way. Perhaps he had seen too much of the world's darkness to feel good about bringing into it two-point-two children and a dog and a fence.

And when he had met Molly, he wondered if he too would now want the things he had long eschewed. For a while, he had almost believed that he did. He had believed that he had believed he did. She had wanted them. When she told him what she wanted, because Molly was a woman who put it all out there, who did not hide the ball, because she knew what she wanted, he had flinched.

He had flinched because things did not hold together. Everything wound down. Everything broke. All his married friends were miserable. His parents had been miserable. If he married Molly, the same thing would happen to them. Marriage was a system like any other system, and it would break down. And no matter how much work you put into it, it would always be deteriorating. When he told her that he wasn't sure he ever want to get married, she had done the prudent thing, because she was also a prudent woman. She didn't want to get married for the sake of getting married. She wanted to marry him, and if he didn't reciprocate, well, thank you very much, she would be on her way.

He had been right about one thing, however. He was broken.

"I'm sorry," he said.

His voice was loud and echoed off the walls of the long-empty house.

"For what?"

She didn't turn to face him. She continued to stare at the fire.

He considered his words. He didn't know if he'd get another chance like this one. Soon, they would be busy with the dangerous mission ahead. That was what no one told you when you were growing up. That often, there were no second chances. No opportunity to set right what you had so badly screwed up. And you often didn't learn that lesson until it was too late.

"I'm sorry I couldn't be what you needed."

"Forget it."

Her words stung. So dismissive. Filled with contempt. But here was the thing. He deserved every bit of her contempt and scorn. He had wasted her time when she had specifically asked him not to do so. The incident was still burned on his brain with clarity and detail.

It had been their second date, at an Italian restaurant named Costa's, known for its intimate seating and delicious food and large portions. They put the leftovers in these fancy small boxes, tied with a bit of twine. As they had shared a plate of antipasti and a bottle of wine, a Pinot the server had recommended, she had taken his hand in her own, setting down her glass of wine.

"Listen to me," she said.

He was still enraptured with her and did what she asked. Her hand was warm and soft in his.

"This has the feeling it could go somewhere," she said. "You know what I mean?"

He did know. He could feel it too.

"Yes."

"So I want to give you an out now," she said. "If this isn't your thing, if going somewhere with me isn't your thing, you just say the word. I won't hold it against you. I know some people just aren't into it. Maybe they will be down the road, maybe not. But I don't want to wake up two years from now and find out that it hadn't been your thing from the beginning and you had just said it was because you didn't want to hurt my feelings or because you liked the sex or whatever."

It was as if the room had gone pitch black but for a hard spotlight shining down on him and him alone in that little restaurant. She had had him pegged from the start, and maybe she had always known the truth about him, and maybe just a little part of her was hoping that her gut was wrong this time.

Because he had told her it was his thing.

And that second date had turned into a third and then a fourth and then they were living together, and then exactly as she had predicted, two years later, he had told her he couldn't do it anymore and he had moved out, shattering her. He had tried, Lord knew he had tried, but he just couldn't. Because it meant giving himself over to someone else in a way that he was not capable of doing. Later, he would wonder if this trait had helped make him such an efficient con man.

It was a bad trait to have. He didn't know what had made him the way he was.

He waited until she had finished a big project at work. She had been working twelve, fourteen hours a day on a new algorithm to better control America's drone fleet. She had come home to find him sitting on the front stoop, his duffel bag on the walk at his feet. He had considered leaving a note and departing before she got home but that seemed unimaginably cruel. Not that this was any better.

It was more symbolic than anything. She had come up the sidewalk, coming around the hedgerow guarding their walkway, Jack concealed from her view until she was virtually on top of him. She stopped suddenly, clapping a hand to her mouth. There were no tears. She just stood there, sizing him up, hating herself for having known all along that this day, this moment was inevitable.

"Didn't I tell you?" she asked. "Didn't I say you could just walk away?"

"You did."

She chuckled then, looking up at the sky, as though she could not believe her stupidity, her naïveté. He had done what she fully expected him to do. Somehow this made him feel even worse, and that was saying something. But he couldn't stay. Where others saw the beginning of a new and better life with another person, he saw walls closing in on him. Opportunities began to disappear. Lives that could have been lived were being snuffed out with each passing day.

And kids?

Forget it.

Once you had kids, that was it. That was the final chain on the door. There was no getting out after that. Not without causing major damage. Whether he would have wanted to get out was a question he did not ponder until later, but just the prospect of it was enough to send him for the hills. By the time he had realized that his life would have been far better with her in it, it was far too late. For too long, he had expected some level of perfection in his life, both personal and professional; later, he realized that this search for perfection had given him an easy out every time. Even with Molly, who had meant more to him than anything. And yet he had done it anyway.

God almighty, he was such a coward.

They had stood there for a few minutes, staring at each other, looking for something to say, understanding that everything that needed to be said had been said. It was over. As the sun set behind her on that chilly fall afternoon, she brushed past him and went inside like it was a regular day. He got up and watched her through the window for a bit. The house was clean; he had seen to that himself while she was at work. She threw her coat and laptop bag on the kitchen counter and then sat down on the couch in front of the television.

He watched a bit longer as the images on the screen threw shadows on the wall behind the couch and then he had left. It was a weird evening. He ate a burger and drank two beers at a pub not far from the house he had shared with Molly. He spent the next week in a hotel before finding a small one-bedroom apartment he spent a year in.

"I told you that you could leave," she said.

She said it quietly, as though speaking to herself now. A reminder that perhaps she had known all along what he would do.

"Get some sleep," she said. "I'll take the first watch."

SLEEP DID NOT COME EASILY for Jack. He tossed and turned on the sofa. Part of it was a belief that Molly would nod off at some point. Overnight duty was a lot tougher than people realized. The terrible mundane work of watching and waiting for something that likely wouldn't happen. It wore on you, drained you of what little energy that you had to begin with.

But she seemed alert and focused. She patrolled the house nonstop, her gentle footfalls somehow soothing to him. The storm started winding down sometime after midnight, leaving behind a moonlit sky atop an icy landscape blanched with snow.

The blaze in the fireplace flickered brightly, a bit more than Jack was comfortable with, but it was a risk worth taking. With the blinds and curtains pulled tight, it was difficult to see it from the outside of the house.

Molly drifted by him; before he realized what he was doing, he had reached out and squeezed her arm as she brushed past him in the chair. Immediately, he felt awkward, like he had broken some status quo between them. He did not know how she would react, so he pushed himself out of his chair quickly. They were face to face now, just inches apart.

"I'll take over," he said. "You get some sleep."

He thought he could smell her perfume, and he didn't know if he was actually smelling it because it was incredibly unlikely that she wore the same perfume she had more than ten years ago or that she would even have access to it in their new world. Smell could be a powerful trigger of old memories, so strong that even the memory of a scent had dredged up images of days gone by; perhaps he was just wishing he could be back in that old time, long gone now, eating Chinese food in a tiny apartment, just enjoying being together, in the quiet and the dark, the traffic whooshing by outside.

"I wish I had been better," he whispered to her.

"Me too," she replied.

Now her hand was on his hip, and their eyes were focused on each other now. Everything else fell away. It was hard to say if she kissed him first or if he kissed her, but it quickly became irrelevant as his hands combed through her hair and her arms slid around his waist and pulled him close. Their entwined bodies tumbled toward the couch, their clothes coming off in an avalanche. He did not know if what they were doing was wise, but it certainly felt good, and good was an emotion that was often in extremely short supply these days.

Now they were on the couch, him pushing up against her and then inside her while she pulled him close to her, and it was new and familiar at the same time. It was over quickly for both of them, a short burst of joy, as though they both knew they were toying with fate and time. He understood that this was the last time for them, a bow on the whole thing, forever and ever, amen.

They dressed quickly, not saying anything, not needing to say anything. He would always love her. She would always love him. But there would always be something missing between them. It was like having a car without a transmission; from the outside, it looked like a running vehicle, but without that critical piece of equipment, you weren't getting anywhere.

"Get some sleep," he said. "It'll be light in a few hours."

She nodded. Already, their tryst was fading rapidly into the background. Just a pleasant distraction from the challenging work that lay ahead of them.

"Yeah," she said. "You good?"

"Wide awake."

"You have changed," she said, winking at him. It was a little jab at his tendency to fall asleep minutes after they'd had sex.

She stretched out on the sofa, pulling up an old blanket over her. She was asleep in less than a minute. He did a loop of the house again, finding everything copacetic. He returned to the oversized chair and sat down. Time ticked by as it always did. Near dawn, the fire began to die down a bit, so he worked it a little with a poker from the rack of tools next to the hearth. When he was done, he plopped down on the floor, his legs crossed at the ankles, his arms curled around his shins.

Somewhere outside, he heard a noise.

23

He reached for the gun. He had left it on the coffee table bisecting the room, in between him and the sofa upon which Molly now slept. The gun comforted him, as it often had in times of danger. He rose slowly to his feet, staying low, on full alert.

There were many noises down here by the river; he needed to identify this one immediately. Wildlife, cracking ice, tree limbs snapping under the weight of snow. But this one had fallen outside the parameters of comfort he allowed for. He didn't understand how these parameters were formed, only that it resulted from years of learning — sometimes painfully - which ones you could safely ignore and which ones you couldn't.

This one he couldn't.

This one was manmade. Someone was outside. There was no way to know if they were dealing with ordinary bandits or if the Shepherds were out there. If he were a betting man, he'd lay good money that the Shepherds had found them. And at night, the curl of smoke would have been visible in the moonlight.

Send out enough inquiries, and you might get some useful intel. A man and a woman on the run, new to the area, would have stood out as newcomers. People were always on alert, mainly for safety but also for information. It always paid to keep your eyes open. You never knew when someone would pay for a little scrap of information. Useless to you but gold to someone else.

He scurried over to the couch and shook Molly by the arm, gently but firmly. She opened her eyes instantly. Thankfully, she'd always been a light sleeper; the slightest disturbance drew her out of sleep, no matter how tired she was.

"We've got company," he whispered.

She slid off the couch, joining him on the floor. He tried not to think too far ahead. His first priority was neutralizing the threat. Once the immediate danger had passed, he could think about the next steps. He and Molly traded a glance. He pressed a finger to his lips. She nodded her understanding. Her eyes were wide open. He did not know if she was scared. He did not know how the years had changed her; if she was hard now, or if she was the same.

He visualized the downstairs layout, visualized the home's best entry points. The front door was to their left, down a short hallway, opening onto a small foyer. The most direct route of escape was the back door, but that was likely also the most dangerous path.

He scrambled across the room to the eat-in area.

Large windows overlooking the yard gave him a bit of a view down to the river. He kept his head low, just under the window line. The snow turned out to be a blessing. The snowpack amplified what little light shone down from the crescent moon.

A shadow shimmered along the line of the window. Jack waited to confirm that there was only one bandit on this side of the house. But he was confident this wasn't the only attacker he'd need to deal with; rarely did people attempt this kind of attack solo.

The figure closed in on the screen door connecting the yard to the sunroom. Jack moved in tandem with him, planning to meet him at the porch. The door was unlocked, as the locks were inoperable from years of disuse and abandonment.

He glanced back toward Molly, watching him like a hawk. He held up a fist, directing her to stay put. She nodded. The prowler was now at the door; he pulled it open slowly, slowly. It creaked on old rusty hinges. The door froze as the intruder waited to see if he had drawn any interest from his target. Jack opened the door connecting the living room to the sunroom, stepping in just as his would-attacker joined him. The man gasped in surprise; Jack delivered a sharp fist to the man's throat. He grunted in pain, temporarily disabled by the attack on his windpipe. Jack moved in closer, wrapping his arm around the man's neck and pulling him close. The man's arms windmilled as his oxygen supply was suddenly cut off.

Jack tightened his grip on the man's throat. He shifted his armbar just so, giving him a bit of a ledge to work with. Then he quickly snapped the man's head across his forearm. The man's neck broke. His body drooped limply, as though a puppet's strings had been cut. Jack eased him to the ground. His heart was racing, but he felt strong.

He peered back into the house, finding Molly's eyes searching for him. He gestured for her to join him. She checked her surroundings quickly before scampering across the room to the door. She glanced down at the dead body, but only in passing.

"There are others," he said.

"I heard whispering on the other side of the house," she said.

"Follow me," he said.

This was not a random attack. There were a thousand ways to skin a cat. Why risk a nighttime raid on an unknown target? That meant the Shepherds had found them. Fine. Good. Jack looked forward to ridding the world of a few more of these assholes.

They crouched low and crab-walked past the dining room table, past the kitchen island, and to the threshold before the game room. The room was silent, dark, brooding. The only light came from behind them, from the still-burning fireplace. They ducked behind the staircase, giving them a line of sight toward the front door. As they crouched, the knob to the front door began to jiggle. Jack eased Molly away from the door; then, satisfied she was safe, he took two steps toward the wall by the door. The door opened toward Jack, keeping him shielded from the second Shepherd.

As the man stepped into the foyer, Jack stepped up and pressed the gun to his head.

"Drop it."

The man froze.

But he did not drop his weapon.

"I'm gonna count to three," Jack said.

"Three.

Nothing

"Two."

Nothing.

A sharp squeal behind him.

"Jack!"

Shit.

Molly.

The second Shepherd took advantage of the distraction to knock Jack's weapon clear. The gun clattered to the floor and discharged. The tongue of flame briefly illuminated the foyer. A window shattered, sending in a whoosh of cold air from the outside. The man swung the barrel of his weapon wildly, catching Jack in the face. As his head whipped around, a third Shepherd started pulling Molly back toward the game room.

The man with the gun rotated it around, looking to fire on Jack; the brief delay gave Jack a chance to recover. He drove his shoulder into the man's midsection, taking them both to the ground. As they went down, he reached out for Molly's captor, grabbing his leg as he tried to slide by. The man stumbled, and they went down in a heap. All four were now on the ground in what looked like a deadly game of Twister.

Molly wriggled free of her captor, but as she stepped clear, a hand clenched around her ankle a second time. She kicked back hard, twice, catching him in the nose on the second. As she got to her feet, her feet tangled with Jack's and the second Shepherd's, and she went down again. Jack was pinned under the man, who struggled to get leverage over Jack's weapon. They were all too close together to risk firing it. He could just as easily end up shooting himself or Molly.

That didn't mean he couldn't use it as a weapon, however. As the man tried to rotate it into a firing position, Jack grabbed one end of it and smacked it against the man's head. He loosened his grip on the stock; Jack hit him again, and his clamp loosened even more. Jack wrapped an arm around the man's waist and flipped him over; now Jack was on top. He drove the butt of the gun directly into the man's temple. A noticeable crack as the man's skull fractured. He went still.

He pushed himself clear of the man, turning his attention to Molly. They were on the steps, moving backward. The man's arm looped around Molly's neck. His gun was pressed against her temple. Jack retrieved the dead man's gun, but in the dark gloom of the house, there was no chance of taking a clear shot.

They moved up one step at a time. Jack followed, his gun up.

"Anyone else here?" Jack asked.

"Shut up or she dies."

"You're not getting out of this," Jack said. It wasn't a boast. It wasn't braggadocio. "Might as well let her go. If you hurt her, you die. Let her go, and you live. It's that simple."

They were at the landing now. The staircase turned left here for its final ascent to the second floor. As he stepped back for the next stair, Molly drove her elbow into the man's midsection. Jack rushed at him, tackling him. They crashed to the steps. The man grunted in pain as his back slammed down against the edge of the stairs.

Jack reared back and drove a right cross to the man's

face. It immediately took the last bit of fight out of him. Jack picked him up and slammed him against the wall. He was about Jack's height but quite a bit leaner in build. The man flung his head forward, catching Jack on the nose. Jack lost his grip on the man, who stepped forward to launch his counterattack. Then Molly stepped in, her hands clenched together in a double fist, and swung her arms hard against the side of the man's head. Her fists clubbed against the man's temple, spinning him around like a top. Jack recovered and drove the man back into the wall. He grabbed him by the collar and slammed him back against the wall. This time, the man did not retaliate.

"Get downstairs," Jack snapped.

They moved back down the steps. Jack kept the gun trained on him. He desperately wanted to shoot him, but they needed to press him for intel. If he was a Shepherd, they needed to know what else was lurking out there.

Jack and Molly led the man back to the sitting room. He pushed him into the oversized chair. In the bright orange of the fire, the man's face looked blank.

"Anyone else out there?"

The man didn't reply.

"Look, my friend, you do not want to play this game with me. I'll ask once more. Is there anyone else?"

The man remained silent.

"Do you really want to die for these clowns?"

This seemed to draw the man's attention.

"No," he replied.

"Well, that's obviously not true," Jack said. "Either you start talking or your face goes into that fire."

Jack grabbed the man's chin and turned it toward the blaze. The man's eyes widened with fright.

"How did you find us?"

"We put out some feelers," his eyes fixed on the roaring blaze. "A be on the lookout for a man and woman on the move. People will do anything for a little food. One of the neighbors spotted you."

"Where are your buddies?"

"I told you there isn't anyone else."

They were getting nowhere. It was time to escalate things. He grabbed the man by the collar and yanked him off the chair, dragging him toward the fireplace. Fire was the great negotiator. The man's arms windmilled as Jack drew him closer to the hearth.

"God, please, no, I swear to God, I don't know!"

They were almost there.

Then a shot rang out, and the man's body went limp. Molly screamed, dropping to the floor. Jack dove across the table, taking cover behind the couch. A second shot rang out.

"Get down!" she screamed.

The man had lied, of course. There was at least one more Shepherd out there.

They had to end this now.

He gestured for Molly to join him by the couch. Again, he called up the home's layout in his mind. There was a utility closet in between them and the back door. He crawled toward it, Molly close behind him, and opened the door. Inside was an old gas water heater. He reached behind the heater, tearing away thick cobwebs until he found what he was looking for.

The gas line.

He wrapped his fingers around the metal tubing, hoping this would work.

He yanked the line loose from its fitting. Immediately, he was rewarded with the hiss of escaping gas. They had to move, now, as the gas filled the house, searching for a catalyst.

"Run," he said.

They were up on their feet now, sprinting for the back door. Two more Shepherds were approaching through the foyer. Spotting Jack and Molly, they broke into a run, shouting instructions to each other. They only had a few seconds left. Jack grabbed Molly by the hand, pulled her through the door to the sunroom. They barreled through the door and into the elements. He curled around the gate, bringing them out into the open. The snow was howling now, blowing hard into their faces.

A loud whoosh filled the air. Jack glanced over his shoulder as they neared the riverbank, spotting the two men in silhouette in the instant the gas ignited, the flash of light filling the house before explosion. Jack pulled Molly down into the snow, hopeful they were clear of the blast zone.

The house went up like a Roman candle. A huge flash of light filled the night sky, followed instantly by the ear-splitting booms of the highly flammable gas exploding. Waves of heat radiated against Jack and Molly's faces. They were about sixty yards clear of the house, but it was still terribly close to the epicenter. He felt a chunk of debris whiz by his face. Molly grunted in fear. Then he felt a sharp hot pain in his leg. He gasped in surprise.

Shit.

He must have caught a piece of shrapnel; it would

have to wait until they were safe. Instinctively, he reached inside his jacket pocket to check on the status of the flash drive. It was still intact, safely ensconced inside the plastic baggie. It was warm with his body heat. Snug as a bug in a rug. It was safe. The flash drive was the only thing that mattered. He ignored the growing pain in his leg.

"We need to get out of here," Jack said, ignoring the pain in his leg. His voice was firm and he hoped it concealed his anxiety. Even in a depopulated region, the explosion would attract a lot of attention quickly, especially if there were other Shepherd patrols in the area. At the very least, it would intensify the search for them.

They were at least twenty miles from the Machine. It would take hours to cover the terrain in these conditions. They were not dressed for the weather. Jack was in a sweatshirt and jeans. Molly wore snow pants and a heavy sweater. The temperature was in the upper twenties. Clouds had started filling the sky again; more snow could be on the way. At this point, death from exposure was as likely as from the Shepherds. Probably more likely. The cold would eat at them, chew away at them, nonstop. Mother Nature was merciless.

The force of the explosion had scattered debris across a wide field, giving the fire less surface area to feed on. The remains of the house were still burning, but the blaze was dying out quickly. In the distance, Jack could hear conversations, shouts, and yells.

He gestured for Molly to follow him. They carved a path along the river bank toward a copse of trees to the north. It was a stretch of old pines, reaching up into the dismal sky like skeletal fingers. The cold air was redolent with the tang of pine. The trees were bunched closely together, making it difficult to find a direct route. The going was slow and tortuous.

He pressed a hand to his quad muscle, burning with pain; the glove came back tacky with blood.

It was going to be a long night.

24

Dawn broke with a film of gray gloom. Flurries were falling again. It was difficult to tell whether these flakes were the death throes of the previous storm or merely an intermission of one still in play. Jack could only hope that the weather didn't worsen too much. He was utterly exhausted; every few steps, he would drift off, only to start back awake after a second. Only the prime directive to survive was pushing him along. Molly wasn't in much better shape.

They were on Route 28, which had intersected with the forest they had traversed during the night. The highway was covered with deep snow; the only way to even identify it as a road were the signs marking the way. The city lay about fifteen miles to the north.

The pain in Jack's leg had grown steadily worse as the day had brightened. Blood had seeped through his pants, but the cold had helped it congeal. Better than dripping down his leg, he supposed. At some point, the injury would need to be addressed. How that would happen remained a bit of a mystery.

Molly's stomach rumbled loudly. He ignored it, as there wasn't anything they could do about it. He wasn't hungry himself. Given the leg injury, that probably wasn't a great sign regarding its severity. On the plus side, the snow was enough to keep them hydrated. They would freeze to death long before they died of hunger or thirst.

Ahead was a black sport utility vehicle, one of its doors hanging open. Molly drifted ahead to examine it; he tried calling out for her to be careful, but it seemed like more of an effort than it was worth. He was limping heavily now, and she was deep into her search of the truck before he even reached the bumper.

"Anything?" he asked.

"Still looking," she said. She was in the middle row, leaned over the seat back and rifling through the cargo area.

"Still looking," he repeated, laughing. "Still looking!"

This was a fool's errand. Vehicles had long been stripped of anything useful. This truck's only utility would be as shelter if they found themselves on the road as night fell. If things got bad, it could double as his final resting place. They wouldn't survive another night in the elements. He did not share this sentiment with Molly.

Jack's stores of energy were near zero. He did not want to admit it, but everyone had their limit. He began wondering what deactivating the Machine would even accomplish. It wouldn't be like flipping a switch, after all. The lights wouldn't simply come back on. The power grid had suffered catastrophic damage, damage that might take years to repair, assuming they could repair it at all.

And human nature being what it was, the return of the power would trigger an entirely new arms race. Control of the power would mean control of the world. And after five years of this feral existence, it was naïve to believe that anyone would act altruistically in such a world.

Was it worth dying out here for? Was it? They had done pretty well on their own. They had made a life. They would keep making a life. Was it an easy life? No. Not in the slightest. But it was theirs. One they saw to with their hard work, with their blood, sweat, and tears. If others couldn't hack it, well, that was the way it went. Nothing was promised to anyone. Not another day on this Earth was guaranteed.

Perhaps it was best to turn back.

He could go home.

He could bid Molly farewell.

That was how this ended.

There was no future for them.

Nothing would change the fact that she had helped make this world. Whatever her noble initial motivations had been, whatever steps she had taken to undo—it did not matter. The damage was done. As much as he wished he could go back in time, he could not. It filled him with such deep sadness that it took his breath away. Molly deserved to pay a price for what she had done. She deserved to face justice. Her victims were entitled to that. And it was unlikely they would ever get it.

The day suddenly dimmed before him.

His legs felt rubbery. It suddenly required more effort than he had to lift his foot from the snowpack and plant it ahead, the crunch-whoosh, crunch-whoosh of walking through deep snow. He needed to sit down. Just sit down and think for a moment. He leaned back against the driver's door of the SUV and slid down to the snowy road.

"Jack?"

Molly's voice sounded small and far away.

It felt good to sit down after a long day on your feet, you know. That sudden burst of relief from getting off your feet after a long day. He was down on his bottom now; strangely, the snow did not feel cold, although somewhere deep down, he knew it should have.

Vaguely, he noticed the pain in his leg.

He smiled.

Oh, right. His leg was cut to hell.

He had almost forgotten about it.

Where was Molly?

Was she still cold? Because he was not cold anymore. A voice was screaming at him, but it was locked up tight, a prisoner in his own mind. It was insistent and urgent, this voice, but he did not know what, precisely, the voice had up its butt. He wasn't cold anymore. He was getting used to it now; he could walk for miles. He felt great. Just as soon as he rested here for a bit. Five minutes, maybe ten minutes, and he would be as right as rain.

"Jack!"

Again that voice. It sounded even smaller and farther away than before. It was a familiar voice, one he should have known. Like the name of that song in your head that you couldn't quite pin down even though you'd heard it thousands of times.

"Wake up, Jack, don't you go to sleep on me."

Sleep?

Why would he go to sleep? He was just resting here for a bit; then they would be on the road again. They were going to turn for home. Back to Promise. That was where he belonged. He was going to be an uncle again. He loved being an uncle. He had loved Emma. But then she was taken away from them. Now they had Norah, and he loved her like she was his own. And this new baby, this new life growing inside Lucy, he would love that child as well. He would teach him all the things a child of this world would need to know to stay alive, to thrive, to have a life that was worth living, beyond simply existing.

Where were they?

He looked around. It was hard to keep his eyes open. He was tired, sure, but his eyelids felt like concrete. It shouldn't have been this hard to keep his eyes open. The black SUV sat at the crest of a hill. The road ran down into a shallow valley, which was peppered with small ranch houses and Cape Cods along the highway.

They seemed very far away, like a child's toys.

They had a long way to go.

Molly was standing over him, her hands on his wrists, trying to pull him to his feet. He laughed at that; he towered over her, had her by a good hundred pounds, she wasn't moving him an inch. He yanked his arms away from her, laughing at this silly woman trying to pull him off the ground.

He looked down at his hands. He peeled off his gloves, although Molly tried to stop him from doing so. He did not know why she was trying to stop him. His fingertips and the nailbeds bore a bluish tint. That probably wasn't great news, although for the life of him he could not remember why. There sure was a lot of snow. Hell of a storm. He wondered how Promise had fared. Mid-Atlantic storms could be tricky little beasts. The rain-snow line for these storms usually ran from southwest to northeast; a final demarcation often depended on how far south an Arctic air mass had pushed. D.C. might see a foot of snow while folks fifty miles to the south would be treated to a messy mix of sleet and rain that didn't amount to a lot. That always disappointed the kids.

But back to his hands. Were they supposed to be this color? He was having a hard time remembering what color his skin was. Something wasn't right. That voice in his head was still screaming like a hostage trapped in a basement, desperate to get out, desperate for help. It was like that sometimes. You would notice a mole on your neck and then you would wonder if that mole had always been there; then you would look at it constantly and you couldn't remember if it had been there all your life or if it had suddenly appeared the previous Tuesday.

But the more he considered it, the more he was certain that his hands should not be blue, that those houses seemed much farther away than seemed reasonable, and that this snow should have felt a hell of a lot colder than it did and finally that voice broke free of its cell, screaming:

WAKE UP WAKE UP WAKE UP....

And then everything went dark.

IT WAS dark when he woke up.

He didn't move at first. He just took a few minutes to get his bearings, to get his wits about him. A fire crackled warmly to his left. The blaze roared mightily in a deep, severe-looking hearth. He was lying on a hard floor, and his back felt stiff. The fact that he was lying under blankets in front of a fire suggested he was safe, at least for the moment.

What the hell had happened?

He dialed back through his memory banks. The last thing he clearly remembered was the flash of the river house exploding as the Shepherds had closed in on him. After that, things got very fuzzy, very quickly. They had fled for their lives with the clothes on their back and not much else. God, it had been so damn cold. He thought they could make it on the strength of their belief in the mission. But the cold didn't care. Cold nibbled away at you like a hungry rat, starting with the extremities but never getting its fill, nibbling until it had hollowed you out. Snippets of his arctic-fueled fantasies came back to him. The hypothermia had done a number on him. As he grew more alert, he became aware of the tingling sensations in his fingers.

Their quest had been doomed from the moment the house had exploded. You couldn't just expect to get far through a snow-covered wasteland without the right supplies and equipment, the temperatures dipping into the twenties. Even if they hadn't had much choice. The choices had been to die now or die later. And the blizzard had very nearly finished the job the Shepherds had not.

He became aware of murmurs in another room. He sat up slowly, feeling weak but refreshed. As he peeled off the covers, he noted that he was wearing dry pajama bottoms and a hooded sweatshirt. He touched his quad; he could feel the rough texture of a bandage. His snow- and ice-crusted clothes lay in a pile by the fire. He sat there for a moment, enjoying the almost alien feel of warmth. He stood up gingerly. His feet felt tingly; he shook them, trying to flush life back into them. It would take time for them to feel normal again, assuming they did so at all.

After exiting the bedroom, he padded down a small hallway out toward the main living area. He curled around a couch dividing the family room from the kitchen. Molly was chatting with a woman. They did not appear to notice his approach. The woman was about his age. Her hair was silvery, cropped short. She was tall and lean, but she slouched a bit, as though she had spent years hiding her height. She wore a heavy flannel shirt and jeans. The woman noted his approach with a nod of her head and stopped speaking.

"Good to see you up," she said.

Molly turned toward him, a look of relief evident on her face, a hand pressed to her chest.

"How are you feeling?" asked the woman.

"Good," he said. "Thanks."

Introductions followed. The silver-haired woman was Hannah. She lived on this secluded farm in southern Fairfax County. She had been a schoolteacher before the Pulse. For more than five years, she had eked out an existence on this little farm. Chickens and pigs. A decently sized vegetable patch. She traded with a few other farms, but not frequently.

"I take it you're the one who fixed me up," he said.

She nodded.

"Thanks."

"You're very welcome," Hannah said. "Gotta be honest. It was touch and go that first night."

"How long have we been here?"

"Three days."

"Wow."

"You'd become septic," she continued. "I really didn't think you were gonna pull through. But I had some antibiotics that took care of it."

A wave of guilt washed over him. Antibiotics were precious. More valuable than gold. And God knew how much they had used to save his ass. He was indebted to them forever.

"I don't know what to say," he said. "I'm not sure I can ever repay you."

Hannah laughed.

"Not according to your friend here."

His brow furrowed in confusion. He glanced over at Molly, who returned his gaze with a somewhat guilty look on her face, as though she had been caught with her hand in the till.

"I don't understand," he said.

He was still worn out, beaten, and he wasn't catching up with the discussion as quickly as he would have liked.

"I told her about the Machine," Molly said.

He chuckled softly. He wasn't upset. He wasn't even all that surprised. Molly had bought his life with the promise of a better future. The IOU to end all IOUs. Sharing the operational details of their mission wasn't ideal, but, he supposed, there wasn't much harm. If this woman had meant them harm, she easily could have killed them.

"Is she telling the truth?"

"She seems to think so," Jack said, glancing over at Molly. "She's the smartest person I've ever met. So if she says it's possible, then I would believe her. But it won't be a quick fix. It'll take months to get even a little bit of the grid back online. Maybe years."

"But batteries would start working again immediately."

"Yes. Theoretically."

"Follow me," she said.

Hannah led Jack and Molly to a back bedroom, dimly lit by two rows of candles on a bureau. Another lantern burned on the end table. A woman was sitting up in the bed. There was a book in her lap, but she appeared to be sleeping.

They made their way back to the kitchen.

"Her name is Janine," Hannah said. "We've been married thirteen years. It hasn't been easy."

Jack understood. As it turned out, scraping away the veneer of civilization had opened them to homophobic attacks from certain sectors of their new world.

"She was on oxygen," Hannah said. "Bad case of Covid. Ten days in intensive care. Her lungs never fully recovered. She had just gone on oxygen when the blackout hit. She didn't need much. Just a little to take the edge off. But slowly it's gotten worse."

Then Jack understood. A battery-operated oxygen concentrator would be a lifesaver for someone in Janine's position.

"I don't know what I'd do without her," Hannah said. "You think you can pull this off?"

"I don't want to get your hopes up," Jack said. He wanted to pull everyone back into reality. They were a long way from the Machine, and even if they were able to infiltrate the compound, there was no way to know if Molly's flash drive would work.

"All we want is a chance," Hannah said. "For five years, maybe six years, I don't even know anymore, we've been hoping for something to happen. And now here you are. Like a miracle dropped from the heavens."

"As long as you accept the fact it's a long shot."

Hannah laughed.

"Long odds are better than zero odds."

Jack could not argue with that.

25

After another good night's sleep on the floor, Jack woke up feeling as good as he'd felt in weeks. It was early and Molly was still snoozing. He let her sleep, dressed quietly, and went out into the living room. Hannah was just coming back inside, having seen to the animals.

"Good morning," she said.

"Morning," he said.

"You still planning on pushing out today?" she asked.

"Yeah."

"I couldn't sleep last night," she said. "I kept thinking about this Machine."

"I know," he replied. "It's hard to believe. But Molly is insistent."

They were quiet for a few minutes while Hannah saw to the coffee. The small house filled quickly with the aroma of the beans' earthy smokiness. She handed him a cup. He sipped it slowly, savoring it, not wanting to finish it too quickly. It was delicious. He did not want to know how much it cost.

"It's an extravagance," Hannah said, wrapping her fingers around her mug. "But we have to enjoy life when we can, right?"

Jack nodded. He held up his mug in a toast. She returned the gesture.

"So, Jack," she said. "I could ask how you're all wrapped up in this."

They had not told Hannah exactly *how* they knew so much about the Machine; it seemed unlikely their hosts would be so gracious if they learned one of their houseguests was responsible for this catastrophe.

"You could."

"And you'd tell me the truth."

It wasn't a question as much as a statement of fact.

"You think so?"

"Yes."

He would have told her the truth. At the very least, he could be honest with this generous woman who had saved his life. Given the uncertainty of the mission that lay ahead, truth might be the only thing he could give her.

"I'm not going to ask," she said softly. "Because I don't think I want to know the answer."

He didn't reply.

"I want you to succeed," she said. "What can I do to help?"

"We need to get to the Library of Congress," he said. "But that part of the city is heavily guarded by this group called—"

"The Shepherds," she said. "Yes, I've heard of them. Never had to deal with them in person."

"Well, I need to figure out a way to get us to the building."

"Wait here," she said.

Jack sipped his coffee while she disappeared into the back. It was a simple kitchen, well organized. On the counter was a stack of potatoes and onions, staples of the late winter diet. There were also a handful of eggs nestled into a blue hand towel. Hannah returned a few minutes later with a black marker and maps of the city and the Metrorail, the region's subway system. Jack lay the map flat on the kitchen counter. He pointed out the Shepherd territory.

"They control it from here to here," he said, tracing his finger around an imaginary perimeter. "And the Library is the most heavily guarded. It's the crown jewel."

Hannah studied the maps carefully.

"What about the Metro tunnels?" she asked. "This station here is just a block from the Library. I doubt they keep a close watch on the tunnels. They're mostly flooded."

"I thought about that," Jack said. "But the water is too cold to survive in."

"What if you had wetsuits?"

Jack froze. He looked up at Hannah, whose eyes were still focused on the map.

"I think that would do it."

She looked up at him.

"Well," she said. "It's your lucky day."

~

In addition to the wetsuits that now adorned their bodies, Hannah outfitted Jack and Molly with snowshoes, cross-country skis, winter clothes, including parkas and snow pants pilfered from nearby houses that had been abandoned after the blackout. Generously, she also provided them enough food to last for three days. She wanted to give them more, but it was all she could spare. After breakfast, they exchanged farewells.

"This is very generous," Molly said.

"It's an investment," Hannah said. "One I hope pays off."

"No promises," Jack said.

"No promises," Hannah said. "How will we know?"

Jack had never let himself get that far. To imagine success at the end of this quest. To picture a future in which they had done what they had set out to do. Sometimes that could be valuable, visualizing the outcome you were hoping for. But not right now. It seemed too big, too fantastical. Better to tackle one step at a time.

"You'll know."

They pushed out after breakfast, slow at first on the skis but quickly picking up speed as they became accustomed to the sticks. There was hardly anyone out and about. The storm had been fierce, leaving at least a foot of snow on the ground. If you had been in the storm's path, you better have had your crap together ahead of time. And with no weather forecasts to count on, that meant always having your shit together, especially in wintertime. No, people would be hunkering down right now, staying warm, stretching out their rations.

They followed Hannah's directions to the Vienna Metro station. It was the westernmost terminus of the

Orange Line. They skied along Route 34 for a few miles before turning north onto Lassiter Highway. They passed a once-bustling commercial district, now buried in snow. Fast-food chains, gas stations, daycare centers, the full spectrum of services an urban population had once needed. Near the subway station were a few condo towers set off the main road, undoubtedly once-hot real estate for their proximity to the trains. In the morning light, Jack spotted the flutter of a few curtains, people watching them ski by. The utilitarian subway complex lay ahead. One train sat about a hundred yards shy of the track's endpoint, dying either just before reaching this station or just after departing it. Either way, it had not moved an inch in half a decade.

They unbuckled their skis and carried them to the entrance of the desolate station. The doors were broken, and graffiti stamped the exterior walls of the building. Jack was alert for squatters here, people who had made the stations their home. Jack armed himself with his Glock. They traipsed down a long corridor, down the dead escalators. Wind howled through the open windows and doors, filling the building with a ghostly whistle.

The tracks were at the end of the platform. It was about a thirteen-mile trek from Vienna to Metro Center. Absent too many delays, they could make it to the city center by early afternoon. Decades earlier, the track had been carved into the median of Interstate 66, providing the commuters some relief from the terribly snarled traffic that had earned this area a reputation as one of the worst commutes in the country.

On either side of them, an ocean of dead vehicles stretching east and west. The track wasn't wide enough for them to ski side by side, so he put Molly on the point and brought up the rear. He preferred being able to keep his eyes on her. They both had experience skiing, and they quickly fell into a rhythm. They passed through the Dunn Loring and West Falls Church stations without incident. Just east of East Falls Church, the track dipped underground, and here they encountered their first obstacle. A train had stalled here, blocking the track.

The trains had been designed to run in either direction. Each train's end car was equipped with a control center for the train operator. He could still hear the unintelligible drawl over the speakers, announcing the train's arrival at each station, service to such-and-such station at the end of the line.

Jack used his gun to blow out the windshield. The report of the gun was loud and echoed for miles across this winter wasteland. Jack climbed in first, pushing their gear through, before helping Molly clamber in after him.

They picked their way through the six-car train before exiting on the far side. It was dark but for the luminescence of their glow sticks and necklaces. They put off just enough light to illuminate their path. Once a kid's toy, now an incredibly useful tool. They found the back of the train and hopped down to the track. The skis would be useless now, as the rest of their journey would be underground until they reached the Federal Triangle station.

On the far side of the train, the track descended toward the tunnel. Even from here, Jack could see the water lapping at its edges. Snow had blown inside the tunnels, giving the interior walls a glistening white sheen. It was almost festive. The tunnel was silent but for the soothing sound of the rippling water, the current driven by the breeze that whistled through the Metro tunnels. They stood at the water's edge. The track descended gradually into the darkness.

Most of their supplies would be abandoned here. The ones going with them went into sealed plastic bags. They tied off the ends of the bags with rope and tied the other end to their wrists. They pulled on the diving shoes that Hannah had provided. Jack's shoes fit snugly and weren't terribly comfortable, but they would protect well against the water's chill. They hung glow sticks around their necks so they could track their progress in the water. Lastly, they pulled diving masks over their faces.

"How are those stitches holding up?" Molly asked.

"Not bad," Jack said, absently pressing a hand to his quad. Time would tell if they would hold.

"You ready?" he asked.

She nodded.

The warmth of Hannah and Janine's home seemed far away. But their brief time together had recharged Jack. Seeing the experience of folks outside of Promise had affected him in a way he hadn't expected.

He thought about home for the first time in days. About Lucy and Norah and his future niece or nephew. He very much wanted to get back to Promise, but he did not know if that was in the cards. He put the odds of their success at no better than one in five. The Shepherds would know they were coming. The Machine would be heavily guarded.

But they still had to try. He had given himself over to this quest now. It was too important to abandon. There was an old saying. *Better to die on your feet than to live on your knees.* Jack believed that. He had believed it when they had fought the Haven, a foe more powerful than Promise, and he believed it now, battling an enemy that remained largely inscrutable to him.

They took their first steps into the tunnel; even with the wetsuits, the cold hit them hard. Molly gasped as the water reached their waists.

"Holy God this is cold," she said between gasps of air.

"Relax," Jack said. "The wet suit is protecting you."

She nodded.

"Just breathe," he said. "You don't want to hyper-ventilate."

A few seconds later, the water had deepened enough that his feet had drifted off the ground. The water was cold, so cold; the darkness hardened around them as they drifted deeper into the tunnel. The light of the glow sticks was barely enough to see by.

"Stay close to the walls," he said. "They'll guide us."

He kicked over to the wall, placing his hand along the tiled surface. Slowly, they began piercing into the tunnel system. An hour went by, then two. They passed the Ball-ston Metro station; above his head lay the blackened ruins of the Ballston Mall, destroyed in a fire in the days after the Pulse. His sister Lucy had started that fire.

With each passing step, the darkness in the tunnel deepened. The light from the glow sticks, fading for the last hour, had disappeared entirely. It felt like they were floating in deep space. Molly's breathing grew shallower as they continued. It was hard to tell how much farther they had to go before the next station.

His ears and face were almost numb with cold. After what seemed like an eternity, ahead there was a slight softening of the absolute void – the Virginia Square-George Mason University station. Clarendon and the Courthouse followed; it was like a slow-motion trip through his past. Soon the tunnel began a slight downward grade, dipping below the Potomac River.

As they continued drifting along, he didn't notice how high the water had gotten until his head brushed the ceiling of the tunnel. There was barely enough room to keep his nose above the waterline. He reached out for Molly's arm.

"It's gonna be tight," he said. "There's only about an inch of air above the water."

"We're gonna drown," she said.

"No," he said. "Just stay calm. The tunnel openings keep air flowing through the entire tube."

They continued paddling through the tunnel; Jack's head bumped against the ceiling a few times. At one point, the water sloshed high enough that both their heads went underwater. He panicked for a moment, wondering if he'd miscalculated. If the other end of the tunnel was blocked, perhaps there would be no air pocket. Molly's hand, already holding his, gripped even more tightly, until he could barely feel his fingers, which were already numb from the cold.

The water receded slightly, and they found air once more. As his head broke the surface, he could hear Molly hacking and wheezing on the icy water she had choked on. She grunted in misery.

This painful and stealthy approach to the city reminded him of his service gone by. He'd spent most of his career in various stages of discomfort. It had gotten where he didn't know what it was like to not be suffering.

As clichéd as it sounded, surveying his life as they approached the end of this trek seemed appropriate. There was so much he wished he could undo. From his days in the military, when he would do anything they had asked him to do. America was no angel, of this he had no illusion, but things were worse in many parts of the world, and the world's stability had depended on men and women like Jack Goodwin, individuals possessed of a certain moral flexibility, in that gray area that America relied on to maintain its role atop the mountain.

And he had been good at it. Very good. He had helped keep America safe. Commitment to the rule of law was something that sounded good. But when you needed intel on a suicide bomber or a missing briefcase holding enriched uranium, you did what was necessary to get the job done. When you had a guy in a safe house in some tiny Pakistani village and his intel turned up results, who cared how you got it.

They continued along, both of them numb with cold and exhausted. Somewhere along the line, Jack noticed the water level had started to drop. It got lower with each passing minute until eventually, their feet were bumping along the ground. The echoes grew louder as they approached the next station. The throaty sound of water rushing downward filled the air. He suspected they were near a larger station, one with multiple levels draining off some of the overflow.

When his feet planted on the ground, he stumbled forward, falling to his hands and knees as gravity pushed back the water's buoyancy. Molly staggered by him, reaching for the side of the platform to keep herself upright.

"Where are we?" she asked in a whisper.

He looked around; the station was cavernous and even Molly's soft words echoed off the walls. In the distance, he could hear gunfire.

"I think we're here," he said.

26

Metro Center had been the centerpiece of the Metrorail, the D.C. metro area's sprawling subway system. Its fingers reached out to the Maryland and Virginia suburbs, but here four different lines merged – Blue, Orange, Red, and Silver. Once upon a time, you could travel anywhere in the metropolitan area from this bustling hub. It was a large station, two subterranean levels laid out in a cross shape at the intersection of G Street and 12th Street.

Jack pulled himself up onto the platform; then he took Molly by the hand and boosted her up next to him. His legs were a bit rubbery, but they would stabilize with time. They were on the lower level of the facility. There was definite evidence of recent activity here. Lanterns mounted onto sconces burned, filling the station with dim light. Jack and Molly lingered by the platform for a minute as he surveyed the terrain. At the far end of the wide corridor was an escalator leading to the top. On that level was the street access.

There was a single sentry posted at the top of the staircase. What a terrible duty to pull that must have been. Down in the mustiness and mildew, eyes open for a threat that may never arrive. He glanced at Molly, pressing a finger to his lips. She nodded.

They clung close to the wall, staying in the shadows. Trash and debris swirled in the cold air blowing through the station. They made it undetected to the back side of the escalator. The guard coughed twice but did not appear to notice anything amiss. He squeezed Molly on the shoulder, directing her to stay put.

Jack eased his way around the side of the escalator, putting him less than five feet away from the guard. When the man turned away, Jack slipped up behind him and drove the knife into the base of his neck. The man crumpled to the ground. Jack dragged him back into the shadows and left his body against the escalator. He gestured back toward Molly; she followed.

Now with his gun drawn, Jack made his way up the long staircase one step at a time. Daylight filtered down into the underground stairwells. It was a gloomy day, chilly, flurries dancing in the air, hinting that the powerful winter storm had a few more haymakers to throw. Jack paused at the last landing before the final push to street level, listening for any signs of activity. Hearing none, they continued to the top of the subway entrance, coming out onto 12th Street.

The White House lay three blocks to the west. They were inside Shepherd territory now; every step would be fraught with danger. The winter storm, for all the misery it had inflicted, had been a bit of a blessing, keeping people off the streets.

"The Library is about two miles to the southeast from here," he said. "You're sure that's where the Machine is?"

"Yes," Molly replied.

"Why there?"

"Nice flat roof. And a bit of a middle finger to the world for not taking climate change seriously enough. There was also something a bit poetic about using a library. To remind people that we were in this because we had turned our backs on education. On learning."

She paused.

"When we started to demonize education, that's when I knew we were in trouble. I don't know why it had to be this either-or thing. Of course we need the trades. The world desperately needs electricians and plumbers and custodians and garbage truck drivers. But somewhere along the way, we made higher learning some kind of enemy and romanticized jobs where you went home covered in soot or whatever. That we looked down on those who didn't go to college or whatever. Not saying there weren't people like that. But when people made it seem like that some random car mechanic's opinion about the climate mattered as much as Solomon's, and that we needed to decide for ourselves, that was when we lost."

She laughed.

"I mean. Solomon didn't know how to install a light switch. He never looked down on anyone who could. But then society decided to look down on the very disciplines that got us to where we were. As though the internet and vaccines and space travel just fell out of the sky fully formed. That it didn't take years of trial and error, mostly error, before you got to where you wanted to go."

"But no one even knew about the Machine," he said. "Why did it matter where it was?"

She nodded, a far-off look in her eyes.

"Yeah. Kind of an inside joke, I guess."

A second question, one that had been banging around since Solomon had told him his tale, burst to the forefront of his mind.

"Were you there?" he asked softly. "When they turned it on?"

He was pretty sure he knew the answer, but he wanted to hear it from her lips.

Their eyes met as they stood under the overhang of the subway station. She held his gaze for a few seconds before cutting her eyes to the snow-covered ground.

"Yes."

She said it in a whisper, barely loud enough for him to hear.

So there it was.

"I didn't want to be," she said. "But I had no choice."

Molly. The love of his life. The woman who had done to him what no other could had helped unleash the apocalypse. He chuckled softly. Boy, he sure knew how to pick'em.

"Something funny?" she asked.

"No."

They stood there a moment longer; he searched for something to say, something that might comfort her. But there was nothing to say. There was no undoing what Molly had done. Even if she now regretted it, even if she now was actively working to make amends. Her fingerprints were all over this cataclysm. He would not judge her, because he had been no Boy Scout himself, but he could not absolve her of her sin. It was something she would have to live with, a burden she alone would bear for the rest of her days.

"We need to get moving," he said.

THEY CUT south along 12th Street before angling southeast along Pennsylvania Avenue. To their right, about a block east, stood the statue of Benjamin Franklin, which Jack found strangely appropriate.

Electricity was good while it lasted, Ben! You wouldn't believe what we did with it!

They moved cautiously and in tandem, ducking under the cover of each abandoned storefront, keeping north of the National Mall perimeter. Trinity had told him that this area of D.C. was largely uncontrolled. The Shepherds were a powerful adversary, but their numbers were limited, and they could only secure but so much of the city.

This gave them the freedom they needed to approach the Library from the north, which would undoubtedly be heavily guarded. Jack guessed that it served as the Shepherds' primary headquarters. Protecting the Machine would be paramount, especially given the ramifications of its destruction.

At the intersection at Tenth Street, the National Mall came into view. He paused at the corner and removed his binoculars. As Pennsylvania's southeast heading drew them closer to the Mall, he detected additional signs of Shepherd activity. The security would only tighten as they got closer to their target. Getting inside the Library, much less to the top of the roof, was going to be a tricky proposition. This would call for a much different plan of attack than his and Lucy's recent assault on the Haven. That plan – go in and blow shit up, which had worked swimmingly – had been child's play compared to the mission that now lay before them. He shuddered to think of the destruction that might follow their failure to safely deactivate the Machine. Hell, if the Shepherds felt that the failure was imminent, they might choose to blow the Machine themselves, the consequences be damned.

Their plan would have to be flawless.

In the days after the Pulse, Lucy had posed as a prisoner as a ruse to gain access to Norah, who had been captured by Simon Conway, the future leader of the Haven. But that wouldn't work here; they were already known to the Shepherds. They could not risk being taken into custody; he'd already managed one escape; they weren't likely to let him get away a second time. He also had to acknowledge the possibility that this was a one-way trip. He was fairly certain that a good plan would get them to the Machine. But any plan to deactivate the Machine and safely get away might require a level of perfection that was impossible to achieve.

Meaning they could die.

But that was okay. Death would be an acceptable price to pay for the safe deactivation of the Machine. They would have done their part. All things being equal, though, he would like to make it home and see Norah and Lucy's baby. And he wasn't going out without a fight.

The Library of Congress occupied three buildings on Capitol Hill, each named after a former President. The James Madison Memorial Building sat on Independence

Avenue between 1st and 2nd Streets; the John Adams Building lay steps away on 2nd. The third building, the big kahuna, was the Thomas Jefferson Building, which fronted 1st Street, between Independence Avenue and East Capitol. On the roof of this third building sat humanity's ruin and possible salvation.

To the south, Trinity's army had begun to mass. So it was happening. Jack had to remind himself that theirs was not the only story unfolding here in the former capital, the once great city that had served as a beacon for the world. These people that had helped him find Molly?

They'd had their own reasons for bringing the fight to the Shepherds. They had their own people to look after. They needed access to clean water and growing fields. The Shepherds were demanding too dear a price for them to continue as mere pawns in the game that Jack and Molly were playing. And after all, there was something to be said for a good diversion. Perhaps it would give them the opening they needed.

Something continued to haunt Jack. Even if they succeeded in deactivating the Machine; it wouldn't solve all their problems. Sure, it might restart Hannah's oxygen tank, and that was a great thing. But that was a small sample size. Whether it would be enough to trigger significant change remained to be seen.

But they still had to try.

And much as Trinity could help them, he and Molly could help Trinity.

It was time to get to work.

They were still moving along the northern edge of the Mall, careful to stay in the no-man's-land. Louisiana Avenue branched off to the northeast; there was additional movement in the Senate Park, a triangle-shaped wedge of land that broke away from the main Mall complex. Louisiana dumped them onto Columbus Circle, a roundabout fronting the southern edge of Union Station, the city's large and once-bustling Amtrak train hub.

"Hang on," he said to Molly. "I want to see something."

"You want to go sightseeing?"

"You'll want to see this, too."

They picked their way around the automobile graveyard. The cars and trucks sat bumper to bumper and were buried in snow. Their tires were flat, and their chassis had started to rust. He followed the line of the building, around to its north side, where the tracks terminated at the depot. The main structure was crumbling; the side had completely caved in.

Then he saw what he had come looking for.

The last train. Broken and strewn about the train yard. Large chunks of twisted and charred metal poking through the deep snow. The train had come apart at the end, passenger cars tossed about like a child's toys. He traipsed through the snow, stopping to look at each car, ripped apart, broken. He peeked inside one that had cracked open like an egg. It still housed skeletal remains, these poor people entombed for all time. Lucy had told him about the crash, of course, but until he saw it with his own eyes, it had been difficult to comprehend what she had been through.

"What are we doing here?" Molly asked, breaking him from his trance.

"Lucy was on this train."

"What?"

Jack nodded.

"She was on this train," he said. "She told me about it, and I thought I understood what she had gone through. But I didn't. Not really. Not until I saw this."

Molly continued navigating the cold, rusted, snow-blanketed wreckage.

"My God. How did she survive?"

Jack blinked away tears.

"I don't know."

But survive she had. She had crawled out of the smoking burning carcass of this train, and she had rescued Norah, and together they had walked through hell to get home. She'd had no help. Just her wits about her. Just the stuff inside her that made Lucy Goodwin who she was. Thinking about his sister's valiance, her heroism in keeping that kid safe when she did not have to, filled him with pride. There would have been no shame for what someone did that day.

"You did this," he said to Molly. "This train crashed because of you."

He turned to look at her; she did not return his gaze. He wanted to scream, he wanted to shout, he wanted to grab her by the shoulders and yell at her until she could explain to his satisfaction why she had done it.

Then the fight went right out of him; she wasn't worth it. She would be a tool now, an instrument to help him see this mission to the end.

Now it was his turn to make things better. His alone.

Someday, he would be dead and gone, and all that would matter would be what he had done to make this world a little bit better. There was so much to fix, but this could be his gift. His legacy. He picked his way through some of the wreckage, placing his hand on the side of one of the train cars.

He looked back at Molly.

"This ends today."

27

Twilight came early. The days were short now, most usable daylight gone before dinner. The gray skies had grown progressively darker, and a light snow had begun to fall again. the landscape was as bleak as he could remember. The acrid tang of woodsmoke filled the air.

They lingered at the crash site for a bit longer, watching the sun set and taking the time to fill their stomachs with the last of their food. No point in saving it. There was no guarantee they would be alive by the time the sun rose the next day. It was good. Some flatbread and hard cheese from Hannah's farm. Made with care, made with love, by good people.

When they were done, they hoisted their packs back on and headed southeast, passing the rear of the Library complex to the north before turning south. They kept a block-wide buffer between themselves and the Library's perimeter. This gave them a decent vantage point to conduct surveillance. Taking cover in a cluster of trees to the east, Jack surveilled the complex with the binoculars. The news was not good.

Guards were posted at each corner of the building and at each entrance that he could see. It was safe to assume they knew the raid on the river house had failed and that the targets had escaped. As a result, they had hardened their defenses. Farther west, a small contingent of fighters was engaged in a gun battle with the Shepherds.

"Where's the Machine?" he whispered to Molly, pulling the field glasses away from his face.

She pointed to the northwest corner of the rooftop.

"In that corner."

"How did you even get it up there?"

She chuckled.

"We pretended to be an HVAC repair crew."

"And they just let you up there?" Jack asked in disbelief.

"They didn't check our credentials that closely," she said. "We had boxes of equipment. Uniforms, ID badges. Some of the staff even helped us carry the boxes to the roof."

Jack shook his head. The fate of their civilization had turned on a few bureaucrats not doing their homework. If someone had taken five minutes to pick up a phone, make a call, this might all have been averted.

"Amazing."

The ruse might work again, if done right. This time they'd put the Shepherds on the receiving end of it. The Jefferson complex was a big, sprawling building. They just needed to get inside. Once they got in, they could quickly get lost in its labyrinthine corridors and stacks. It could give them the head start they would need to deactivate the Machine.

"Too bad we don't have pizza delivery drivers anymore," he joked to Molly.

"What?" she asked, confused.

"Nothing. Bad joke."

"So what do we do?" she asked. "This isn't my area of expertise."

"You sell yourself short," he said. "We're not going to shoot our way in. There's too many of them. We don't have time to figure out how to sneak in. Not with Trinity's army coming in soon. We have to deactivate the Machine before they try to take the building. Otherwise, your buddy Iris might blow the Machine as a last resort. Anything to preserve this new world."

"I don't think she would do that. The devastation would be unimaginable."

"But she might."

Molly held his gaze.

"Yes, she might," Molly conceded.

"I think she will," Jack said. You say that she's a true believer. She thinks of herself as a holy warrior. Devoted to the cause. In fact, I think it's very likely that she blows it."

Molly did not reply, but she did not need to. Jack could see exactly what she was thinking sketched out across her face. Molly did not want to believe she had cast her lot in with these kinds of people, even though that was exactly what she had done. She wanted to believe she was not as bad as the others, that she had gotten here for the right reasons, and in fact, was taking steps to undo what she had done. But you didn't always get a second chance. There were things people did that were irredeemable.

It was sad, but it was the truth.

Molly was damned by her own choices. Perhaps she knew that already, deep down. And with each passing moment, it was bubbling to the surface where she would have to acknowledge it. And that wasn't an easy thing. She would have to acknowledge her sin. Most people never got that far. They painted over it with lies and rationalizations and drink and drugs. They imploded long before they ever got to where they needed to be.

As Molly struggled with her truth, an idea took hold in Jack's mind.

"Wait here," he said.

"Wait, where are you going?" she asked.

Jack returned forty-five minutes later, having successfully located what he was looking for. Fortunately, the particular item had been ubiquitous in those heady last few years of civilization, and he'd had no problem finding one. He had gone south along 2nd Street, finding an abandoned office building. The doors had been shattered. Standing water, mixed in with ice, engulfed the lower level. He had splashed through the darkness to a reception desk. It hadn't taken very long. Inside the top drawer had been three of them.

"Where were you?"

"I've got a plan."

He reached into his pocket and removed the item he had acquired. He handed it to her; she looked down on it with a look of confusion written on her face.

"It's a flash drive," she said.

She turned the small device over in her hands.

"Yes."

"But what do we need it for?"

"It's a decoy," he said. "You're going to tell them it's the one they're looking for."

"It won't fool them very long, if it does at all."

"I don't need it to fool them very long. Just long enough."

She looked down at the device a bit longer as the details of Jack's plan fell into place for her. She was an incredibly bright woman, and she would figure it out quickly.

"You want me to give myself up."

"Yes."

She took a deep breath and let it out slowly.

"And you're giving them back the flash drive," Jack said.

"What about you?"

"I'm your prisoner," he said.

On that note, he handed her his weapon.

"They're not going to believe that you're my prisoner."

"Not under normal circumstances," Jack replied. "But remember, I was badly injured."

She nodded.

"Then what?"

"Wait for my signal. When we're inside."

"What's the signal?"

"You'll know."

"How do I know you won't abandon me?"

"Because like it or not, you have to be the one to do it," Jack replied. "I don't know what I'm doing."

"Why am I coming back?" she asked. "What do I tell

them when they ask me why I returned voluntarily? They'll be suspicious."

"You tell them that you still believe," he said.

"Believe what?"

"That you're one of them."

"But I'm not," she said. "Not anymore."

Jack smiled sadly.

"That's the thing," he said. "You are."

JACK EMERGED from the tree line with his hands on his head; Molly trailed behind him with his gun aimed squarely at his back. She had not responded to his final assessment of her. That she was still one of them. It must have hurt to hear it. It sure as hell hurt Jack to say it. But it was the truth. They would want her back in the fold. They would want to know that she had not betrayed them. And what better way to prove that than to deliver what they coveted above all else. The sole threat to their way of life.

His heart pounded as they approached the sweeping staircase servicing the Jefferson Building's southern entrance. It tapered at the top, leading to a stone plaza before the doors of the magnificent structure. The snow had picked up, adding a new layer on top of the already significant snowpack. It would take days, if not weeks, to dig out of a storm of this magnitude. It only underscored the urgency of Jack's quest. It wasn't like the old days, when you could pass a snowstorm in front of the fireplace, your phone in hand, your belly warm with hot chocolate. No, now, every winter storm had the potential to kill you. It was a tough old world out there now. Countless people were at risk in the eye of the storm.

Their approach drew the attention of the sentry posted at the door. He raised his weapon and aimed it down at them. He was young, not much older than Norah. He'd likely been a boy when the Pulse had hit; this had been his fate.

"Hey, hold up!"

Jack laced his fingers together and slowly placed his hands on his head. This was the riskiest moment of their gamble. A guard with an itchy trigger finger might decide to shoot and ask questions later. They needed someone equivocal, who wouldn't know what to do with the bizarre situation unfolding before him, who would look up the chain of command for someone to tell him what to do.

"Guard!" Molly called out. Her voice was shaky and unsure. "Don't shoot us!"

"Not another step!" he called out. His weapon trembled in his hand.

Such was the lot of the lowly underling. Ninety-nine percent of their service was spent cloaked in mind-numbing tedium; the other one percent could be their doom. The good news was that he was hesitating. He didn't seem to want to shoot them. Especially if it threatened to bring hassle down on him later.

"It's Molly," she called out. "I need to talk to Iris!"

"Who's Iris?"

"You know goddamn well who Iris is!" she barked back. She was finding her sea legs now, as Jack suspected she might.

"She's not here," replied the guard.

"You find her," Molly shouted. "You find her and tell her that I'm back with the flash drive."

This seemed to catch the young sentinel's attention. Jack was getting anxious. If this took much longer, they risked drawing the attention of the other guards stationed around the perimeter of the complex.

"What flash drive?"

"You know what I'm talking about, don't you?"

He licked his lips nervously.

"Yeah, I think so."

This didn't surprise Jack. News of the Shepherds' desperate search for Molly and her flash drive would have spread quickly through the ranks.

"I need to talk to my commander," he said.

"Good idea."

He stood frozen, as though he didn't know what to do next, or at least, how to talk to his commander. Jack cut his eyes to the left; another sentry who'd noticed the bizarre scene was approaching now. The clock was ticking down quickly.

"Follow me," he said gruffly, his hemming and hawing finally complete.

He turned and led them back up the stairs; he did not seem to be waiting for his colleague. They were almost there. Jack couldn't believe it; Molly had pulled it off. He was planning his next move. The guard's weapon was up, the muzzle poking Jack in the ribcage.

They entered the library single file, passing under the massive stone archway. The words Library of Congress were carved into the stone. The guard went first, moving backward, facing Jack and Molly. Jack went next; Molly brought up the rear. All three of them were now inside the Great Hall. It was cold and dark. Lanterns flickered, filling the room with glowing orange light. The walls bore ornate carvings and murals.

The staircases to the upper floors lay just ahead. It was time to move. He glanced at Molly and nodded. She turned her weapon on the guard, catching him unaware.

"What the hell are you doing?" he asked, his voice catching.

"The roof access," Jack snapped. "Where is it?"

The man stood dumbly silent. His gaze swung from Jack to Molly and then back again. When he didn't respond, Jack gestured for Molly to hand him the weapon. She passed it over.

"She might not shoot you," he said. "But I will."

The man's eyes widened with fear.

"Where is the roof access?"

The guard tipped his head toward a staircase at the edge of the Great Hall. As he did so, a flurry of commotion erupted at the building's main access. In the distance, an explosion boomed across the landscape. Gunfire erupted.

Trinity's army had begun its attack.

Dammit, Jack thought. He hoped to have a bit more time before they launched their assault on the Shepherds. Well, what was done was done. The timeline had been pushed up. They were running out of time.

The Library's main door clattered open. Two more sentinels came rushing in, weapons drawn. They opened fire immediately. Jack slung the rifle over his shoulder while simultaneously leaping at Molly and pulling her to the ground to avoid the gunfire. The guard was not quick enough. A stitch of bullets caught his flank and he crashed to the ground. Jack rolled into a prone firing position and returned his own burst. His rounds did not find their targets, but they were enough to push the shooters back outside.

They jumped to their feet and bolted toward the staircase the guard had pointed out. As they reached the doorway, another burst of gunfire raked the room, cracking and splintering the library's gorgeous flooring. The gunplay was certain to attract additional attention and would only make their mission more difficult.

They ducked through the door onto the landing, taking cover from the Shepherds now coming in the front door. The stairwell was dimly lit with lanterns. Jack prepared to take his first step, but his heart sank as he heard additional footsteps descending from above.

"Jack," Molly said, grabbing his arm. Her breathing was shallow and her voice was trembling.

Ignoring her, he peered back through the port window set in the door. Additional Shepherds had arrived, a dozen or more now in the Great Hall. All were armed; several had broken away from the main pack and were approaching the door to the stairwell. The footsteps from above grew louder.

They were trapped.

28

After Jack and Molly surrendered, a pair of Shepherds escorted them to a room on the second floor, past the Gutenberg Bible exhibit. A small sign mounted outside the door indicated it was the Librarian's Ceremonial Office. On the way, they passed the Gutenberg Bible display hall. The Bible sat in a large ornate display case. Jack recalled reading about it years earlier; the Gutenberg was generally considered the first book to be mass printed in Europe using movable metal type.

It was a momentous occasion, a paradigm shift for civilization, making the printed word available for the masses for the first time. Jack had lived through another paradigm shift, one far different than the advent of the printing press. One that had sent humanity back into darkness rather than bringing them out of it.

Two Shepherds stayed with them while they waited. A third went to retrieve restraints for the prisoners. Jack studied them, looking for a weakness he could exploit in an escape attempt, but he found none worth the risk. They were alert and cautious. They seemed to grasp that Jack posed a legitimate threat, and that kept them on their toes. Outside, the sounds of battle intensified, the thick ancient walls of the library muffled them.

They had sent someone to find something to bind their wrists with, but the person had not returned. That was the only bit of good news they had right now. Jack didn't intend to let them tie him up again. Whatever they were going to do, they'd have to do it before the cuffs came out.

After an hour, the door to the room opened. A woman entered, two more Shepherds trailing behind her. She took a seat in a third chair across from Jack and Molly. She wore black glasses. Her eyes were set deep in a face lined with wrinkles. She was tall and lean. She wore a heavy parka, stained with blood.

"Molly," said the woman.

"Iris," she replied.

So this was Iris. The leader of the Shepherds. The mother of the project. The strange thing was how utterly normal she looked. How utterly normal she was, according to Molly. A single mom. She had loved to read and garden. She owned a small cabin in Maine that she had visited every chance she got.

And she had helped turn Western civilization to ash.

"I didn't think we would see you again."

"I'm stubborn," Jack interjected. It was something to say, to insert himself into the conversation.

Iris glanced over at Jack, as though noticing him for the first time. They stared at one another a bit, each taking the measure of the other. This was what a true believer looked like. Throughout his life, Jack had learned how dangerous people like her could be. This was what it looked like when someone decided how something should be for everyone else.

"I don't want to hear from you," she said. "Unless I ask."

She turned her attention back to Molly.

"So why are you here?"

Molly cleared her throat.

"You were right."

"What was I so right about?"

"The Machine. Everything."

"Hmm. You were out there a long time. A very long time. Why are you just coming to this understanding just now?"

"I didn't ask for him to rescue me, you know," she said, nodding toward Jack.

Well, this was an interesting approach. And now that he thought about it, he had no idea if she was telling Iris the truth or not. A chill rippled through Jack. Had he and Molly even discussed this at all? Had she expressed remorse for what she had done? Had she even felt remorse for what she had done? Maybe spending time locked up had made her realize that she did not want to undo what she had done.

"Where is it?"

Molly glanced over at Jack. Jack's heart was racing; he did not know what she was about to do. Suddenly, this woman he had loved for so long, that he had thought he truly had known, looked like a stranger off the street. Someone he did not know at all. It was chilling. Whatever happened here, it wouldn't change what had already happened. She had cast her lot in with these people, and there was no undoing it.

Molly took a short breath and let it out slowly, as though she had made a decision on a subject that she had long been debating. She reached inside her jacket and removed the decoy flash drive. Somewhere outside, another explosion rocked the morning. The assault on the Library was heating up.

"Here it is."

"Molly, no!" Jack said.

She handed the flash drive over to Iris. Jack scoffed, anxious to show a little disgust with what Molly had done, hoping that would sell it a little. Iris cut her eyes to Jack as she accepted the offering from Molly. She held it in the palm of her hand, turning it over once, before closing her fist around it.

"I'm glad you understand, Molly," Iris said. "This is how it has to be. This is the way."

She glanced over at Jack.

"Sorry to disappoint you," she said. "I know you've gone to a lot of effort. But the old world was no good. We were hurtling toward catastrophe. How much longer before another pandemic blew up in our faces? Something deadlier than Covid? Something they couldn't make a vaccine for in a year. It was coming. It was definitely coming."

Jack was barely listening, already working on the next move. The ruse had worked, at least for the time being, and the genuine flash drive was still safely tucked away.

"Mm-hmm," he said, studying the small room. Simply busting out of here would be risky. Iris' two guards had their weapons drawn, and so there was no way to take both of them out before one got a shot off. The desk was clear; there was nothing that he could use as a weapon.

"Search him," Iris said to her guards.

Jack's stomach fluttered. The game was just about up; the decoy drive had gotten them inside the building but no farther. It was probably a fool's errand to think it would accomplish much more. Oh well, it had been worth it.

The first Shepherd squeezed in behind Iris.

"Stand up," the man said.

He was a big man, of course, as men like this always were. He wore a heavy parka and dirty torn jeans. His long gray hair was tied back in a messy ponytail. Jack blew out a noisy sigh. He hadn't wanted to do it this way, but he wasn't going to have much choice. The man was a few steps away from him; his weapon hung loosely from his shoulder, courtesy of an old strap. He hitched his shoulder to better secure the weapon. As he pulled his hand back to smooth out the strap, he left his hip open for a moment.

Jack stepped towards him and fired a jab into the man's body. The blow caught him right in the sternum, doubling him over. The man's rifle became dislodged, the strap sliding down his arm. A sudden gasp filled the room. Profanity and yelps. As Jack reached for the weapon, the dull boom of another explosion echoed through the library. The concussive blast rocked the building; the sounds of walls shattering and crumbling followed closely behind. More shouts and screams outside. The gunfire was closer than ever now.

Jack pulled Molly by the arm as the scrum intensified.

Iris threw herself at Jack, beating at his chest and face. She grabbed a handful of hair and yanked hard; the intense pain made Jack's eyes water. He dug into her shoulder blade and peeled her off like a leech. Now Jack and Molly were free, shimmying toward the exit. Jack barreled into the second Shepherd still by the door. He'd been struggling to swing his weapon up into a firing position; off-balance, he toppled to the ground as Jack rolled over him. Jack grabbed the weapon, an old M-16 rifle, tucking it under his arm as they made their escape.

They were back at the Gutenberg Bible display. They raced past it, back toward the open staircase in the middle of the exhibition hall. He ushered Molly ahead of him, urging her up the stairs. Iris and the two Shepherds gave chase. As they climbed the steps, Jack hazarded a look down to the ground floor. A group of Shepherds was involved in a shootout; they had taken positions behind kiosks and display cases.

Trinity's army would soon overrun the building, and there was no telling what might happen then. They reached the third floor as their pursuers began the climb from the second. Jack squeezed off a burst from the M-16, catching one of the Shepherds in the leg. The man went down, but Iris and the other returned fire, pushing Jack away from the railing. The tongues of flame from the gun barrels were bright in the darkened corridors.

More Shepherds had joined them, giving Iris additional firepower in the exchange. Jack had to back off. They turned and continued down the midway toward another doorway marked with a sign reading Roof Access. Another stairwell. It felt like his whole life had been spent racing up stairwells. Just two months earlier, he'd been on the rooftop at the Haven, trying to neutralize a threat to Promise. But now he had a much different mission to complete, one that carried with it far-reaching implications.

If they could do it, they could change so much. They could fix so much.

Jack's legs were burning by the time they reached the top of the stairs. He paused to catch his breath for a moment. But only a moment, because they would soon have company. Then he drove his arm into the door's release bar. It clattered open. The wind hit them hard. The snow had picked up again and was blowing sideways.

Jack pushed his way onto the rooftop, Molly trailing behind him. The building's multi-level rooftop was huge, covering a swath as big as a football field.

"Where is it?" he shouted over the howl of the swirling winds.

"Follow me," Molly shouted back.

She followed a line along the edge of the elevated rooftop, bringing them near the edge of the building. As Molly turned north, Jack paused and look down at ground level. A sizable group of attackers had taken positions in the trees across from the library's main entrance. They were firing toward the building. The building's defenders had the high ground, and, for the time being, were holding the line. Black smoke swirled from a lower floor, but Jack couldn't pinpoint its exact source.

Things were getting hairy quickly. They did not have much time.

The door to the roof banged open behind them. Jack ducked around a corner as shots rang out. One round caught the edge of the elevated roofline, splintering the stone. Jack followed Molly along a narrow edge separating the platform from the roof's very edge.

"There!" she cried out, raising her arm and pointing an accusatory finger. "It's just up ahead."

Jack reached in his pocket for the plastic baggie containing the flash drive. His gloves were bulky and made it difficult to work, so he ditched them, trading warmth for precision handling. He reached inside and withdrew the remarkable device. The bag fluttered away into the snowy headwinds, its purpose finished.

Up ahead, Jack finally saw it.

It was not very big, about the size of a standalone freezer. Rectangular in shape, it was about waist-high, six feet wide, three feet deep. It was black. His initial look led him to think it was a single entity, but as he got closer, he saw that it had been assembled from several smaller pieces. It was emitting a strange glow, almost purple, almost as if it was breathing.

The Machine.

29

He stood before the Machine, somewhat taken aback. He had not expected it to have such an impact on him, but now that he was in such close proximity to it, it was difficult to not feel overwhelmed by it.

Before he could study it any further, a flash of movement caught his eye. He turned just in time to spot a Shepherd coming around a corner to his east, having been shielded by the elevated cupola. The Shepherd's gun was drawn; Jack grabbed Molly as the man opened fire, pulling her back behind the cover of the west side of the cupola. A single round whizzed by as they took cover.

He thought they'd gotten clear in time, but a pained grunt from Molly told him otherwise. Her hand was pressed against her abdomen. When she pulled it away, her winter glove was tacky with blood.

Jack peered back around the corner; the Shepherd gunman was close now. Behind him trailed Iris, brandishing her own weapon. Jack lowered Molly to the ground and shoved the flash drive in his pocket.

No, he thought, gently tilting her face up toward his own. She was conscious but clearly in a lot of pain. He had no idea how badly she was injured, but if he didn't take care of Iris and her henchman, it wouldn't matter for very much longer. He peered back around the corner and squeezed off a burst. The first Shepherd caught the fusillade and went down face first into the snow. Iris dropped to the ground with him, but she came up firing.

Jack ducked behind the corner, waiting for her to get a little closer, but when he turned back to fire again, the M16 jammed. Iris dropped down to the ground. He retreated behind the corner again and tossed the weapon to the side. There was no time to attempt a diagnostic on the rifle. He pulled Molly to her feet, and they staggered back away from the Machine, into the labyrinth of corridors.

"Wait here," he said to Molly.

She nodded, her face in a grimace of pain.

He grabbed the edge of the upper level of the roof and pulled himself to the top. He dropped low into a prone position, lest he present an easy target for whoever was up here. A quick scan of the roof revealed four Shepherds prowling the various narrow corridors separating the cupolas. Iris had disappeared into the gloom of the falling snow

The Shepherds continued to patrol the rooftop, hunting for their prey. Eventually, they found one another, coalescing into a pack of four – Iris and three nameless gunmen. They escorted her to the edge of the building, where Iris took a long look at the secondary threat now facing her organization. From the sounds of it, the battle's intensity had faded, like a bag of microwave popcorn slowing down. The gunfire was not as frequent. Trinity's plan to take the building in a surprise assault had, for the moment, failed.

Jack shimmied back down to Molly's level to check on her. The bleeding had slowed a bit, but it had not stopped entirely. Her breathing was rapid and shallow. He checked her pulse. It was extremely rapid and somewhat faint.

"Jack."

Her voice was soft but firm.

"I can't stay awake much longer," she said. "I'm not going to make it. You need to upload the drive."

"No," he whispered back, just as firmly. "You need to do this. I have no clue what I'm doing."

"I'll try, but I don't know, Jack."

"Up. On your feet, soldier."

He knelt next to her, slid an arm under hers, and gently lifted her to her feet. If this was indeed the end for Molly, she was going to use the time she had remaining for a little redemption. That was how it would have to be. Slowly, one step at a time, they began moving again, like drunken revelers at the end of a long bender. Her legs were weak, and without his support, it was unlikely she could hold herself up.

"Listen, if I don't make it, you need to know what to do."

He did not argue with her. There was no time, and if her self-assessment of her condition was correct, she did not have much time left anyway.

"On the side of the machine is a small USB port," she said. "It's under a small plastic cover."

"Got it."

"Snap it off," she said, wincing with pain. "And you'll see the port."

"Okay," he said, his eye on the blood continuing to seep through her gloved fingers.

"Then plug it in," she said. She coughed. A little blood bubbled at the corner of her lips.

"Is that it?"

"That's it," she said. "I wrote the deactivation program to self-execute because I knew I wouldn't get much time to deactivate it, if I ever even got the chance."

Jack nodded.

The wind had picked up, and snow was blowing in sideways. As visibility faded to almost nothing, it took him a moment to get his bearings again. The good news was that it would be harder for the Shepherds to spot them. The bad news was that it was almost impossible for anyone to see anything.

The snow stung his face. His hands were all but frozen; he focused all his attention on ensuring the flash drive was secure in his fist. He glanced over at Molly, but she was all but out on her feet. He would have to retrace their steps back to the Machine.

He set her down on the ground once more; a quick but careful jaunt to the roofline confirmed that he was still on the side of the roof where the Machine made its home. By risking a peek down, he could just make out the Library's main staircase. He returned to Molly, lifting her to her feet again. Jesus, this was exhausting. If he survived this, he was gonna sleep for a week.

Big if.

Unlikely.

But damned if he wasn't gonna try.

He curled his left arm around her waist to keep her upright. Slowly they picked their way along the roof's edge. The wind howled and swirled, filling the air with a ghostly moan. In the gloom, Jack could just make out the outline of the Machine; he had already committed its dimensions to memory. Not every day you came face to face with a Doomsday device.

"Just up ahead," he said to Molly, hoping to encourage her back to semi-consciousness.

As they came to the final intersection with the pass-throughs separating the cupolas, another flash of movement. He froze, pushing Molly back down to the snow again. He was running out of chances. He ducked low, and when the attacker came around the corner, he grabbed at his weapon. The Shepherd gasped in surprise, having not seen Jack in the driving snow.

Jack wrenched his gun free and then gave the man a shove over the edge. There was no scream, the man barely able to process what had happened before he hit the staircase below with an audible thump. Jack spun around and saw another silhouette rushing at him from between the cupolas.

He lowered himself into a crouch; as the man lifted his gun to fire, Jack sidestepped him and sent him over the edge as well. The path to the Machine was clear. He hurried to it, going over Molly's instructions once more. He knelt next to the corner of the Machine, brushing away the snow clinging to it. The Machine gave off no heat at all but was free of any snow cover.

There was so much about this thing he would never know, never understand. That such a thing could even exist bothered him in a way that nothing else ever had. Ironic that Molly and her confederates had used the zenith of human technology in an attempt to undo the damage that their technology had caused.

And the irony had been lost on them.

In their desperate attempt to make things better, they had made things so much worse. They had taken it upon themselves to decide for humanity what was best. But it had not been their decision to make. Look what it had wrought. Unimaginable suffering. Unimaginable loss. Unimaginable devastation. They had traded one cataclysm for another.

He glanced back at Molly again.

She had done this.

He wasn't sure he could ever come to grips with it.

Enough philosophizing, my man.

He checked that the coast was clear once more and set to work. He ran his palms against the side of the Machine, looking for the seam that Molly had told him about. He found it near the bottom left corner. He wedged his finger into the tiny gap. He panicked a moment, unsure that it would come loose. Then it did. Popped right off like a TV remote's battery cap.

He dusted the snow off the USB port.

"Found it!" he called back to Molly.

He glanced back at where she was sitting, but he did not see her. She was gone. No time to look for her. As he moved to plug the flash drive in, he felt an enormous hit from behind. The flash drive fell to the ground as his face smashed into the side of the Machine. Panic raced through him again - not for his own well-being, but for the integrity of the device. He bucked hard as he felt the crook of an elbow slide in under his throat.

He delivered an elbow to the midsection of his attacker. The grip on his throat loosened, and he instinctively took a deep breath. He bucked hard, and the attacker completely lost his grip on him. He stood up, spotted the flash drive, and dove for it before his opponent could. His hand closed around it just as he felt another hand scraping for it, clawing at his face.

He turned and found himself looking directly into Iris' face.

"Don't do it," she said. "You'll kill us all!"

"This has to end!" he yelled over the driving snow.

"No!"

Iris reached into her coat and lifted a knife high over Jack's head. As she prepared to bring it down, a single shot rang out.

30

Iris doubled over, apparently the target of the mysterious bullet. She staggered toward Jack, the knife still in her hand, but her movements were much more uneven. She charged one last time. Jack readied himself for a final defensive stand

"Jack, now, the flash drive!" called out a familiar voice, weak, spent.

It was Molly. She came staggering out of the pass-through between the two closest cupolas, a gun trembling in her hand. Molly dropped the gun and rushed at Iris, burning whatever fire still blazed in her furnace. She drove into Iris' flank and the two wounded women pirouetted toward the roof's edge. Before Jack could move, Molly carried Iris right over the side and they fell out of sight.

"Molly!"

Jack rushed to the edge and dropped to his knees, but it was far too late. The women had already hit the ground, their bodies tangled and broken. He looked down at them for a moment, shocked by how it had all unfolded, and then reminding himself there was more to do. He rushed back to the exposed USB port. He held the drive out, paused for a moment, unsure what he was about to unleash on the world.

He plugged it in.

At first, nothing happened. Everything had fallen silent, even the wind. The snow fell quietly. The sounds of battle had faded to nothing. Jack knelt by the Machine, unsure of what he was supposed to do, or if he was even supposed to do anything.

Then the Machine began to glow.

Slowly at first, so imperceptibly that he thought he was imagining it. But then the color began to intensify, and there was no denying that something was happening, even if he did not know what that something was.

It was a purplish-blue glow, not unlike a series of LED strip lights. He watched for a moment, entranced. He glanced around the cityscape beyond, part of him wondering if the windows in the various office buildings would suddenly blaze with light. Of course, he knew on a rational level that wouldn't happen; even if they interrupted the Pulse, broke its hold over the world's power grids, they would need to restart the grids somehow. But that was a battle for another day.

Today was for Molly's algorithm. If it didn't work, then nothing else mattered.

The Machine was now glowing brightly, cycling through various colors, red, orange, yellow, green, blue, indigo, violet. The colors of the spectrum. He placed his hand on the side of the Machine, but he felt nothing. No hum, no vibration, not even any warmth to indicate that it was heating up. But it continued to glow, ticking through the color spectrum, and growing brighter with each cycle.

Within a few minutes, the colors grew so bright that they had become uncomfortable to look at. Jack decided it was time to take his leave. He retreated along the edge of the roof, turning at the cupola nearest the door to the roof access. The lights from the Machine grew increasingly bright, engulfing the rooftop in a kaleidoscope of colors, almost blinding, making it hard to see. It was like closing your eyes as tightly as you could, forcing the explosion of bizarre colors against the black void of your eyelids. Jack ducked through the doorway, pulling the door closed behind him, relieved to be free of the Machine's garish light show. He descended the steps as quickly as he could in the dark, careful not to turn an ankle.

But the light was everywhere now, pouring into the stairwell. Fear filled him, real fear, not for himself, but for what he might have done. Molly was gone now, and all he had was her belief and assurance that this had been how to fix what she had broken. He was running blindly now, unable to see anything but large shapes as the Machine continued to pulsate. He made it to the ground floor. Around him, the remaining Shepherds had devolved into complete panic, crouched down on the ground, their faces buried in their arms to shield their eyes from the sun-like light of the Machine. They appeared unsure whether they should flee or hold the line. The colors ticked by in rapid-fire succession now, so quickly it was not much more than a blur.

He raced for the exit, hoping to put as much real

estate between himself and that cursed Machine as he could. As he burst through the door, onto the front entrance and the wide sweeping stairs of the Library, the lights stopped.

He froze.

His vision was blurry; he passed his hand in front of his face, hoping to confirm the Machine hadn't partially blinded him. He blinked a few times, and after a few minutes, his hand came into clear focus. His eyes began to return to normal now that the visual assault on his pupils had ended.

It was over.

He glanced up at the rooftop, toward the section that had housed the Machine. Everything looked normal. There appeared to be no smoke, no fire, no indication of any explosion. He could not see the Machine from this vantage point, but the building remained intact.

Was that it?

Was it over?

He became aware of shouts and yells around him; he remembered he was literally on the front lines of the battle between the Shepherds and Trinity's soldiers. He bolted down the steps, running for the safety of the treeline to the east of the Library.

An idea occurred to him.

He jogged through the trees, coming up on Second Street SE and the line of dead cars choking the avenue. He searched the cars one at a time, his mind focused on a specific item. But he came up empty. Each of the vehicles had long been scavenged for supplies, for anything valuable.

He continued down Second Street, stopping at each

of the former storefronts making up this little commercial strip. The first was a little lunch place called Pete's Diner. It had once been a popular lunch spot for the city workers. Now it sat empty and cold. In their current world, it might serve as shelter from the elements. He stepped inside. The door was cracked but still intact. The stenciling on the plate-glass windows had long since faded to a dirty yellow.

He checked his surroundings. The area had cleared out completely. The Machine's psychedelic light show had sent everyone scurrying for the hills. Thirty minutes ago, the air crackled with the sounds of automatic weapons and sharp commands. Now it had fallen silent, and he felt like the only person in the city. He slowly made his way inside the diner. Chairs and tables were strewn about, but there was nothing else here. He checked near the register for what he was looking for, rifling through the drawers.

Nothing.

Patience.

You'll find it.

He continued to the back of the diner. A place like this would have had a little office for the owner, a place where he could keep the books, place orders, hire and fire people. There, at the back, he found it. He stepped inside. It was like a time capsule. A desk covered with papers and books and files. Most had suffered water damage, but it looked about the same as it would have on the day of the blackout. It was almost pitch black in here; just a bit of ambient light from the outside guided Jack's way.

He dug through the desk, finally finding what he was looking for in the last drawer on the bottom.

A pack of double-A batteries.

The package was not sealed, but it would have to do. Batteries had a fairly long shelf life as long as their casings weren't compromised, and these looked to be in fairly decent shape. He removed four from the packaging; as he did so, an old radio on the edge of the desk caught his eye. He flipped it over, looking for the battery case. He removed the cover but was disheartened to see four batteries that had corroded inside.

He carefully removed each of the ruined batteries and then used the corner of his shirt to clean out the gunk and goop that had collected in the battery slots. After ensuring the battery leads were clean, he snapped in four new batteries and snapped the cover back on.

He flipped the radio back over.

His hand hovered near the switch.

"Don't get your hopes up," he whispered.

He took a deep breath and let it out slowly. There were numerous reasons that this experiment would fail. The batteries might be no good; the radio itself might have been ruined by the elements. It didn't necessarily mean that Molly's flash drive hadn't worked.

But he needed it to work.

His hand continued to hover over the power switch. He thought about what it would mean if it worked. What it would mean for him, for his sister, for his unborn niece or nephew. For Norah. For all of the people back in Promise. There would be so much work ahead to bring the world out of their unwanted and unexpected Stone Age. Whatever status quo they had built would vanish in a puff of electrical smoke. There would be fierce competition for power.

He thought about what it would mean if it *didn't* work. If he had gone to all this trouble, all this suffering, only to see it fail. That would mean their situation, as it were, was permanent. He didn't know if people actually believed that it was *permanent* permanent. Maybe they harbored fantasies that somewhere, someone was still working on it. But now Jack knew there was no one else. It was him or nothing. And if this didn't work, that would be it, forever and ever amen.

He decided that he would be okay with that too.

Because he had done what he could. He had given all he could. He could live with that.

He switched the radio on.

Silence.

The radio's power lamp remained dark.

Nothing.

His stomach curdled.

He thought it would work. He really did. He wanted it to work.

Dammit.

"Shit!" he yelled, his voice echoing in the empty diner.

He shoved a pile of files onto the floor. He kicked the desk; the radio tipped over onto its side. That was when he noticed something. The volume dial. It was turned all the way down. He took a deep, shaky breath, carefully picking the radio back up.

He cradled it gently in his arm, his fingers trembling over the dial. He turned it.

The sound of radio static filled the room.

AFTERWORD

Two years ago, I wrote the first words in the American Midnight trilogy:

More than anything, Lucy Goodwin wanted to get home.

Those words have new meaning for me as we turn the tide on the Covid-19 pandemic. Although the Delta variant of the virus has extended the pandemic longer than any of us wanted, I hope that the worst is behind us, largely thanks to the miraculous vaccines that science has brought us. As those of you who've been with me since the beginning know, I wrote most of this series as Covid began its silent spread in late 2019, as it barreled through humanity throughout 2020, and finally, as we brought it to heel in 2021.

I received the first dose of the Pfizer vaccine on January 26, 2021 (my day job was classified as high-risk for Covid exposure), and my second dose on February 17, 2021. I experienced a few side effects, but mostly I have felt relief, knowing that my family and I are now protected from this insidious viral threat. That said, access to these vaccines remains limited in many parts of the globe, and getting shots in the arms of as many human beings as possible must be a priority in the coming months and years.

But we are almost home.

Home will look different when we get there. The pandemic has fundamentally changed all of us, even those who made it through without the virus seriously sickening or killing friends or loved ones. A dear friend of mine nearly lost both his parents early in the pandemic. Two men I know, both my age, were both hospitalized and lucky to survive. Two women I know have struggled with long Covid.

We saw the best and worst of humanity. Some of the things I envisioned in my pandemic novel THE IMMUNE came to pass. The most troubling development was the rejection of science by large swaths of the American population, even as the pandemic worsened in the fall and winter, and it's only gotten worse with time. There were reports of people refusing to believe that Covid existed *even as those people were dying of Covid.* I'm not sure what to do with that other than to highlight the importance of science education in our school curriculum. Imagine where we would be if the vaccines had not been so successful. We would be looking at one of the worst catastrophes in human history. We may have been facing some degree of societal collapse.

I hope we have learned something from this terrible experience. Millions are dead (it's weird to write that – it feels like something you read only in the novels like the ones I write). Tens of millions more will have long-term health problems. The psychological effects of the lockdowns and isolation are only now beginning to be understood. I worked very hard to protect my loved ones and myself from this terrible disease, and the price I paid for it was not insignificant. The pandemic has exposed long-existing fault lines carved by racial inequity and income disparity.

But one thing is very clear. When faced with a threat like the one posed by Covid-19, we must work together. Or we will die alone. We must trust science, even when it's slow and looks messy from the outside, because slow and messy is how scientists figure things out. We must look out for each other because we need each other. And we must make sure that everyone can get the vaccine.

Because none of us are safe until all of us are safe.

Thank you for coming on this ride with me. And get the vaccine.

David Kazzie

September 2021

ACKNOWLEDGMENTS

To all my advance readers, thank you for your feedback, support and encouragement.

All errors are mine alone.

ABOUT THE AUTHOR

David's first novel, *The Jackpot*, was a No.1 bestselling legal thriller. He is also the author of *The Immune*, *The Living*, *Anomaly*, *The Nothing Men*, *Shadows*, and *Nightfall*.

His short animated films about law and publishing have amassed more than 2.5 million hits on YouTube and were featured on CNN, in *The Washington Post*, *The Huffington Post*, and *The Wall Street Journal*.

Visit him at his website or follow him on Facebook (David Kazzie, Author).